UNSCRIPTED

NICOLE KRONZER

UNSCR

AMULET BOOKS • NEW YORK

Cataloging-in-Publication Data has been applied for and may be obtained from the Library of Congress.

ISBN 978-1-4197-4084-8

Text copyright © 2020 Nicole Kronzer
Book design by Steph Stilwell

Printed and bound in U.S.A.
10 9 8 7 6 5 4 3 2 1

Amulet Books are available at special discounts when purchased in quantity for premiums and promotions as well as fundraising or educational use. Special editions can also be created to specification. For details, contact specialsales@abramsbooks.com or the address below.

Amulet Books® is a registered trademark of Harry N. Abrams, Inc.

ABRAMS The Art of Books
195 Broadway, New York, NY 10007
abramsbooks.com

FOR DANNY, ELIZA
AND ELEANOR

CHAPTER ONE

I stared at the dashboard clock: only two more hours.

Twisting my frizzy curls into a bun, I tucked the seatbelt under my armpit and pressed my forehead against the Subaru's window. Now that we were in southern Wyoming, the view was miles of flat grasslands punctuated by bedraggled fence posts that reminded me of old, weathered cowboys.

I imagined the cowboy fence posts in conversation.

"What's up, Earl?"

"What's *up*? As in *vertical*? Just me, Clyde. And barely at that!"

I smirked. Some jokes were best left where they started: in my head.

Small gray mounds suddenly peeked above the horizon.

I frowned. Were those mounds *mountains*?

Mountains meant Colorado. Colorado meant—

I glanced to my right at my brother, Will—he of the shaggy black hair, and, since crossing into Wyoming, the brand-new boyfriend. While he and Jonas swore up and down when we left Minnesota that they were "just friends," Jonas was now curled up under Will's right arm, his eyes closed.

"Hey, Will," I whispered, watching him smooth Jonas's dark brown curls back from his light brown forehead. "There's only two more hours until we get to camp. Will you run one-liners with me?"

He closed his eyes and sighed. "Nhhh-nnnnn. Jonas is sleeping."

Sure he was.

"Will," I whispered again.

His eyes stayed closed.

I exhaled slowly through my nose and peeked out the window.

The mountains loomed larger.

I felt sick.

You've really done it this time, Zelda. You and your huge mouth and your huger ideas. Improv camp? And not just any improv camp, but THE improv camp?

A road sign promising a rest stop in ten miles whipped past our car at six million miles per hour.

This trip was going too fast. We were going to be there, and I wasn't going to be prepared.

"Will." I nudged him again.

He opened one eye.

"I'm not ready."

He closed it again. "Yes, you are. You sent in your script."

"I know."

"And your space work and character work are good."

"But—"

"They're *good*, Zelda, and you know it."

"Okay, maybe, but that stuff's just about being truthful in the moment and connecting with your fellow players to tell a story. I can *do* that—"

"You're *good* at that."

"Thank you, but, one-liners, Will. I freeze up. Will you please help me?"

Jonas snuggled deeper into Will's arm. A sleepy smile crossed Will's face. "Go to sleep, Z. There's only two hours left. You're either ready or you aren't. And you're ready."

I gritted my teeth.

How was I supposed to get on the top team when I had a brother more interested in his boyfriend of seven hours than in his panicking sister of seventeen years?

I dug into my backpack at my feet and pulled out my favorite book on improv comedy: *The Scene Must Win* by Jane Lloyd. Jane had died more than a decade ago, and I was sad I would never get a chance to actually meet her. But I willed her to give me guidance from the beyond and flipped open to a chapter at random.

"As a performer," Jane offered, "avoid asking questions of your fellow player. Instead, make statements and assumptions."

Make statements.

Right. I could do that.

I leaned in closer to Will. "With two hours," I said, my voice low, "you could go to an elementary school carnival and win all the goldfish."

Eyes still closed, he shook his head. "Zelda. *Please.*"

"With two hours," I said, ignoring him, "you could make a show-stopping Victoria Sponge on *The Great British Baking Show.*"

He fought to press down a smile.

I leaned in even closer. "With two hours," I stage-whispered, "you could take Jonas on a first date that isn't getting nachos at a gas station while your parents and sister are spying from the king-size candy bar aisle ten feet away."

Now his eyes flew open. "You were *where?*"

"With two hours," I said, raising one eyebrow, "you could create a Spotify playlist for your brand-new boyfriend that *isn't* titled 'Doorway to my Soul.' Puke, by the way."

Will's arm tensed around Jonas. "Oh, I'm killing you later," he promised, glaring at me.

I shrugged. "When you loan your sister your phone, that's an open invitation for snooping. You must know that."

"That's Zelda's way of saying that we're all just so happy for you," Mom whispered, winking at me in the rearview mirror from the driver's seat.

Will blushed furiously.

"With two hours," I said, cracking my knuckles, "you could do any of these things, or more! But do you know what would be really great?"

Will sighed. "I think you're about to tell me."

I threw an arm around his shoulder. "To-spend-those-two-hours-practicing-one-liners-with-your-sister-who-desperately-needs-to-in-order-to-get-on-the-top-team-at-improv-camp!" I punched him in the thigh. "Let's play World's Worst."

Ta da! Statement!

"World's Worst?" Jonas's eyes flew open.

Asleep, my ass.

"I'll play World's Worst with you, Zelda," he offered.

Will unwrapped his arm from around Jonas with a flash of regret in his eyes. He sighed. "Z, this is our first time at this camp. Don't count on making *any* of the top teams, much less *the* top team. Just relax. Have fun. Don't care so much."

I twitched. "Don't *care* so much? Jane Lloyd started this camp!" I thumped *The Scene Must Win* against his shoulder. "Every year representatives from Second City and iO and UCB come to the final show. Which only the best performers get to be in. If I'm going to be on *Saturday Night Live* by the time I'm twenty-five, this is my best chance to get a foot in the door. Did you not read anything they sent us? Don't you remember me talking about this, like, nonstop?"

Dad groaned, adjusted his Twins baseball cap, and wiped sleep out of his eyes. "*I* do, Zelda-belle."

"Thank you, Dad." I reached up to the passenger seat and squeezed his arm. "I'm glad someone believes in my dream."

Will scoffed. "Come on, Zelda. Jonas and I love improv, too. I'm just tired—"

"World's Worst sibling? Should we start there?" I asked.

"Hi." Will smirked. "My name is Zelda."

I rolled my eyes. I'd walked right into that one.

"How about World's Worst ambulance driver?" Jonas offered. "Or garbage collector?" He dug into his bag. "Tell you what—I'll make a list."

I grinned at my brother. "I really like your boyfriend."

Will shook his head at me. "Enjoy this now. Until he learns not to let you manipulate him."

I scoffed. "I'm not manipulating him. I'm just a really good convincer."

Will snorted.

I dropped the book on my lap and folded my arms. "This is going to be amazing," I assured him (and myself). "Mom and Dad will be hiking for two weeks, and you and Jonas and I are going to hone our improv skills in the mountains of Colorado. And isn't it going to be even better if we make the top team?"

"For the love of god, Zelda..." Will shook his head but the corner of his mouth curved into a small smile. "You're really lucky I kind of like you and stuff."

"I know," I said, bumping his shoulder with mine.

My phone buzzed, and I flipped it over.

AR: Hey. Question for you.

My heart beat a little faster. Alex was the latest improv guy I had a minor crush on who I was pretty sure did not think of me in that way. Like, as a girl-person he could have feelings for.

ZBC: Fire away.

The ellipses danced on my screen as his typed his response. I waited. A question for me. It was probably just about the rehearsal schedule... But it could be something else.

AR: Jenn's starting rehearsal again on the 25th?

I grimaced. Or not. But then again, maybe absence would make the heart grow fonder...

ZBC: Yup... I'm with Jonas and Will on our way to improv camp in CO! Back in 2 weeks!

The ellipses again. Responding right away to my text... good sign...

AR: Oh, that's right! Have fun, dude!

Dude.

What is that saying? Always a bridesmaid, never a bride? For me it was more like always a friend, never a girlfriend. And at least up until now, Will had been in a similar boat. But suddenly I was the only one in the family who wasn't in a boat built for two.

Mom always says you can let yourself drown in self-pity, or you can choose to swim away.

So fine.

I flipped my phone over, closed my eyes to regroup, and front-crawled toward the shore: *Boyfriend-schmoyfriend, Zelda. You're going places: Jane Lloyd's improv camp. Second City. Then* Saturday Night Live.

CHAPTER TWO

The car had barely come to a stop in the parking area when I threw open the door and jumped out, skidding a little on the gravel because I was too busy looking up at the breathtaking mountains. "Breathtaking" is a doubly accurate description, actually. *Breathtaking*, because up close, the Rocky Mountains are aggressively beautiful—rocks and trees jut into the sky at impossible angles. But breath*taking* as well because it's really hard to breathe.

Seriously.

"We're at 9,200 feet above sea level," Dad told us, pointing at small print on the Rocky Mountain Theatre Arts Summer Camp sign in front of the Main Lodge. "That's nearly two miles!"

"No wonder it feels like there's a vise on my lungs," Will complained, pulling his backpack out of the car.

"You'll feel a lot more acclimated in a few days," a deep voice called out.

I loaded up a joke about needing to be carried around until then, but when I turned to fire it off at the owner of the deep voice, I choked.

It was Thor.

Thor minus the hammer, plus flip-flops.

A six-foot-tall, tanned, blond Scandinavian god stood before us clad in dark jeans and a baby blue long-sleeve T-shirt pushed up at his elbows.

"Ben," he said, shook hands with my parents, then Will, then Jonas, then me. At least he probably shook hands with me. I was a little busy trying to remember how talking worked. Mouth open? Then words?

"Welcome to RMTA," he said. "I'm one of the coaches."

Coaches? He didn't look that much older than Will and Jonas and me.

"You look so young!" Dad exclaimed, adjusting his baseball cap back on his head to get a closer look.

Even though I had just been thinking the same thing, I stared hard at Dad until he met my eyes. Seeing my reprimand, he shrugged. "What? He does. How old *are* you?"

Thor/Ben smiled. "I'm twenty."

"Are the other coaches this young?" he pressed.

"We're all in our early to midtwenties," he said, folding his arms.

"But you're the earliest of early twenties," Dad countered. "They put you in charge of people only a couple years younger than you?"

I tugged on Dad's elbow to get him to lay off, but Ben took it in stride.

"It's experience in the professional world they look for," he said smoothly. "I'm an actor in LA. I've done some film and TV and have been teaching and performing at UCB for two years."

"Upright Citizens Brigade," I translated for my father, "It's an improv theatre."

"I know what UCB is," Dad said, swatting my hand away. "I listen to you when you talk."

Ben raised his eyebrows at me. "You know your stuff."

Unable to respond with human verbal language, I smirked and shrugged at Ben and tried to catch Will's eye to exchange the Uh-Are-You-Seeing-How-Cute-This-Cute-Guy-Is? look. But Will was pulling his suitcase out of the trunk. I took out my phone to text him, because *seriously*, but Ben interrupted me, lifting my phone between two fingers.

"No cell service up here." I melted a little as he slid my phone into a pocket of my backpack. Then I glanced at Will again. Was he *seeing* this?

But now Will was hauling Jonas's suitcase out of the trunk. Jonas protested and tried to take it from him, but Will insisted. There was a lot of smiling. And hand touching. And gagging.

Wait—that last part was just me.

Mom must have noticed their "fight," too. "Uh, Ben, just one little development since these guys applied . . ."

"Sure," he said easily, unfolding a packet of papers he retrieved from his back jeans pocket. "Who is this concerning?"

"William Bailey-Cho," she began.

"*Mom!*" Will abandoned the suitcases and sprinted toward her.

"And Jonas Eikenberry," she said, ignoring him.

"Yes?" Ben asked, ticking off their names.

"They're—"

"*Mom,*" Will pleaded, nearly bowling her over. "*Please.*"

10

"We're together." There was Jonas, holding the suitcases. His quiet voice was proud. There was finality to it.

"So ... different cabins then?" Ben asked, skimming his lists.

Will was too busy basking in the glow of this admission from Jonas to counter Mom and Dad's insistence of "*yes*."

"You got it." Ben made a notation on his sheet and turned to me. "And you are?"

"Nobody who needs to be separated from the boyfriend I suddenly made in Wyoming," I blurted.

Ben's lips twitched.

I blushed.

"That makes things easier then," he said, meeting my eye. "What's your name?"

"Zelda." I swallowed, trying to get saliva flowing in my mouth again. "Zelda Bailey-Cho." I nodded at Will. "Will's my brother."

Ben paused. He looked at Will, who was now leaning with Jonas against the car, pointing at some nature thing, then at Dad, then at Mom, then back to me.

"We're like a Korean/Scottish Brady Bunch." I smiled.

He grinned. "Okay. Parents, this is where you say goodbye. It's an all-improv zone from here on. The cabins are down that path." He pointed away from the Main Lodge. "Eventually, you'll move into a cabin with your team, but for tonight, Will, you're in Bill Murray, Jonas, you're in Dan Aykroyd, and Zelda, you're in Gilda Radner."

Dad laughed. "The cabins are named after comedians?"

Warmly, Ben said, "Yes, comedians-slash-improvisers." He shook my parents' hands again and approached another pile of people climbing out of their van.

"I love you," Mom said, snapping me out of staring at Ben. She hugged me tightly. "Have fun. Learn a lot. I hope you meet great people." She dropped her voice. "And keep an eye on Will and Jonas."

I looped an arm around her neck. "Try and stop me."

Then Dad wrapped his arms around me. "Good luck," he said into my hair. "And be careful."

I pulled back. "Be careful of what? Bears?"

"Different kind of animal, Zelda-belle. There are a million boys here! Plus, there's no cell service, and Mom and I have never been away from you this long before. So please. Be *careful*."

"Dad," I chuckled, "boys see me as their funny friend Zelda who can keep track of when rehearsal is. But they don't *like* like me."

He coughed. "The fact that you think that makes me worry even more." He looked over my shoulder. I followed his gaze and spotted a line of uniformed Boy Scouts hiking down the road and cutting into a path in the woods.

"Improv camp *and* Boy Scout camp?" he grumbled. "This keeps getting worse and worse."

"Dad," I said, whacking his shoulder. "We're not in some 1950s sitcom here. If you're going to worry about a thousand boys wanting me, you should be worried about Will, too."

"I *was* until he became besotted with young Jonas over there."

We watched Will and Jonas slowly retreat as Mom lectured them about being in a relationship and the importance of communication and listening and if, god forbid, they weren't going to listen to good sense and reason, condoms.

Poor Will.

Dad and I shook our heads at the same time.

Smiling, I tried (and failed) to take a deep breath. "Look, Dad, if boys notice me, it's only going to be for my quick wit and excellent collection of flannel shirts."

Dad started to speak, then stopped himself.

"What?" I said.

His eyes dropped to his feet. "When Will's mom died, I read this W. H. Auden poem over and over again."

"The one about the clocks stopping, right?" I slid my arm around his waist so we were standing side by side, watching Will and Jonas turn various shades of beet and tomato.

He nodded. "That's what I wanted: to 'pack up the moon and dismantle the sun.'"

"Even though you had Will."

"Even though I had Will. But then I met your mom."

"Pregnant with me," I inserted.

"Pregnant with you," he agreed. "And I felt so sorry for her. Losing your father—I knew what it was to be too young to be widowed. But I was too tired and too sad to help."

"But she wanted to help you," I said.

"She wanted to help *Will*," he corrected me. "He was the only thing that gave her peace. Made her smile."

"Until I was born."

"I've told you this story once or twice, have I?" He squeezed my shoulder.

"I like this story," I said, leaning into him. "Keep going."

"Well then, you know that your mom went into labor during one meeting of our grief group. The old ladies took baby Will and told me to go with your mom. I didn't think I could—but she looked me in the eyes and said—"

"'You are doing this for me, dammit,'" I interrupted.

He laughed.

"And that was the beginning of everything," I finished.

He reached for the brim of his cap. "Not . . . quite."

I looked up at him skeptically.

"That wasn't the moment when there was no turning back," he said. "I've never told you this next part . . ."

I pulled away and faced him, frowning. "What else is there?"

"Zelda-belle." He exhaled sharply, folded and unfolded his arms, then took my hands. "Your mom loved Will, and I . . . I couldn't take the sadness anymore. I was thinking about . . ." He raised his eyebrows, willing me to fill in the blanks.

Frowning harder, I cocked my head, trying to find the answers in his face. Then a cold wind swept over my body. Did he mean . . . he was thinking about killing himself?

He must have seen the shock of comprehension on my face because he smiled sadly. "Grief, no sleep, no family nearby—I felt hopeless. It's not an excuse—it's . . . an explanation."

Stunned, I shook my head. "Then what?"

"Then you slid out of your mother's body—"

"Gross, Dad."

He smiled and began to tear up, "Not gross—magic, baby. You were magic."

He gathered me in his arms, and I closed my eyes, breathing in his familiar warm Dad-ness. "You raged, entering this world. You demanded the name of the person who so rudely evacuated you from your nice, warm home. There was going to be hell to pay . . . And I saw a sliver of sunlight. You kicked and screamed a crack into my burrow of sadness. And I loved you for it."

Now I was tearing up.

"You saved my life," Dad said, "you and your Zelda magic. I didn't know I loved your mother yet. I wouldn't know for a while. But I knew I loved you. You are inherently lovable. Without trying. So forgive me," he said, looking around, "if I'm a little worried about all of these boys."

I hit him again, and he gathered me back into his arms.

"That is not the same, and you know it," I said, laying my head on his shoulder and disappearing into his embrace. I knew he was okay now, but I hugged him extra tightly, as if I could infuse him with more Zelda magic, whatever that was.

"Promise me," he said, pulling back from our hug, "promise me you'll be careful. And remember the prime attack zones: spectacles and testicles."

"Goodbye, Dad," I said loudly. He grinned and held me one more time, chin resting on top of my head.

Then Will and Jonas freed themselves from my mother and hugged Dad, too.

The three of us watched them both walk over to the passenger side of the car and laugh, Dad forgetting it was his turn to drive. He

shook the keys at us as he rounded the car, then in a parting gesture to me, pointed at his eyes, and with a weird sort of head movement, nodded toward his belt line.

Spectacles and testicles. I shook my head and grinned. *Hilarious.*

And then the Subaru turned over, Mom blew us kisses, we all waved one more time, and my parents were gone.

CHAPTER THREE

I dragged my duffle bag, backpack, and heavy suitcase up two wooden steps onto the well-worn porch of Gilda Radner cabin and huffed, catching my breath. Suddenly, faced with the prospect of meeting my fellow campers, this whole improv camp thing was becoming very real. I took some slow, deep breaths (both due to the altitude and in an attempt to soothe my nerves). I thought about pulling out *The Scene Must Win* for advice, but I worried that might make me look weird. Plus, I realized, I had Jane Lloyd's rules of improv practically seared to my brain:

> *Trust Yourself.*
> *Trust your Scene Partner.*
> *Say yes. Even better, say yes, and . . .*
> *Perform at the peak of your intellect.*
> *Make statements and assumptions.*
> *Raise the stakes!*
> *Balance giving and taking.*

Make active choices.
Be in the moment.

I loved the rules of improv for improv, but they were also really great rules for life. The one that best fit my current situation, I decided, was, "Trust yourself."

You can do this. I scanned the exterior of the cabin. It was comprised of logs stacked horizontally and painted dark brown, windows with wooden crossbars, and a well-used screen door.

I pushed open the screen door with my free hand, my eyes sweeping around the cabin as I hauled my luggage over the threshold. There were eight metal-frame bunk beds, a single bed (presumably for our counselor), and a dresser. Along with the wide floorboards worn smooth with time, this place felt like a cabin from the old version of *The Parent Trap*.

A giggle alerted me to the fact that I wasn't alone. Two sets of feet poked out from underneath a bunk bed: one clad in cheery-pink flats, the other in strappy leather sandals.

"Uh . . . need some help?" I called, abandoning my luggage just inside the screen door.

In quick succession, a thump, a yelp, and more giggles came from under the bunk bed as two people wormed their way back out.

The strappy leather sandals belonged to a tall, brown-skinned girl with long braids and glasses. She rubbed her head where she had hit it on the bottom of the bunk. "Hi," she said, smiling warmly. "I'm Sirena. And uh . . . We're not always hiding under the bed when we meet new people."

I chuckled. "Just sometimes?"

She laughed and thumbed in the direction of her much shorter, pink-shoed, pink-cheeked, blond friend. "Just when we're pretty sure we brought this CD and neither of us can find it."

"CD?" I asked, tilting my head. "Like a physical...*disc*? With music on it?"

Sirena's pink friend swept her bangs out of her face. "A physical disc, yes. But not with music on it."

"It's fifty-seven minutes of Pacific Coast whale sounds," Sirena said. "Emily thinks it's equal parts calming and hilarious."

"A whale sounds *CD*?" I couldn't let it go.

Emily shook her head, smiling. "I know, it's stupid."

"It's not stupid," Sirena and I said together.

"I'm just kind of surprised," I said. "It...do you *have* a CD player?"

"One." Emily picked it up off the bunk. It was a couple inches thick, a little bigger than a CD itself, and bright yellow. "My mom's old Discman. But we don't mind sharing." She turned to Sirena, beaming.

Sirena plucked a dust bunny off Emily's shoulder, showed it to her, and they shook their heads, laughing again.

"Maybe the CD's in the van still?" Emily wondered, dropping the Discman on the bed and combing her fingers through her hair, searching for more dust. Then she stopped. "Is that same van coming back to get us all? In two weeks, I mean? Or is *Pacific Coast Whale Sounds* lost forever?"

Sirena started picking dust out of her braids. "It's not in the van, because I was looking for it then, too. I totally needed it to distract me with Erick and Ty back there snoring away like a two-man lawnmower parade."

Emily threw her head back, laughing.

I realized I hadn't really introduced myself yet, but they didn't seem to notice. Sirena abandoned her braids and lolled her head to one side, imitating their snoring. Emily laughed so hard she clutched her waist and moaned, "Side ache!"

I smiled. Physically, these two were opposites: Sirena was a whooping crane to Emily's chickadee. But they belonged together.

"I'm Zelda . . . from Minneapolis."

They both looked at me like they'd forgotten I was still there. Quickly, though, Emily flopped down on her bunk which, in addition to the Discman, sported her sleeping bag, pillow, and a stuffed owl that looked like she had been sleeping with it since she was a baby. "I'm Emily. Oh, wait. Sirena already said that." She laughed a little and Sirena just smiled and shook her head, joining her on the bed. "We're from Denver. We came here with our whole team."

"Really?" I asked, plopping down on the bunk across from them. "That's awesome."

"Yeah. It's me and Sirena, and the guys are all in Eddie Murphy. Until after auditions."

Sirena pulled a backpack into her lap and poked around in it. "Thank god we have each other," Sirena said, pulling out some gum. Without asking, she tore a piece in half and handed it to Emily who wordlessly unwrapped it and popped it in her mouth. "I mean, we love our team, but sometimes those guys are idiots."

"Really?" I asked.

Sirena chuckled. "I don't think they mean to stereotype us—they just don't think. But I can only be Harriet Tubman so many times, you know? Emily's taken to starting every scene as a pilot."

Emily bumped her shoulder. "Not *every* scene . . . Sometimes I'm a cop."

I laughed.

"Or a neurosurgeon," she continued. "Otherwise, they make me somebody's mother. Every time. The minute you're kind of chubby and a girl, that's all you're good for, apparently."

Sirena elbowed Emily. "You're perfect the way you are."

Emily smiled shyly.

Sirena looked at me over her glasses. "You know what the guys call it when the two of us are in a scene together?"

I shook my head.

"'Chick-prov.'"

I frowned. "Then when guys do a scene together, do they call it 'Dick-prov'?"

Emily gasped a little, choking on a laugh.

"That," Sirena pointed at me, "is genius."

I smiled and tucked one of my legs underneath me on the bunk. "I'm just here with two guys from my team—one of them's my brother."

"Oh, wow! How's that? Performing with your brother?" Sirena asked as Emily combed her fingers through her own hair, still apparently on the search for rogue dust particles.

"It's good. We get along really well . . . mostly."

Emily smiled.

"Who's older?" Sirena asked.

"He is, but just by four months."

Their confused look is one I've grown accustomed to over the years. "It's a second marriage for both of our parents," I explained. "So we're not twins, but we're in the same grade."

They nodded slowly.

"So . . . you two just picked a bunk?" I asked, eyeing the one by the window.

"Yeah," Sirena said. "The Eddie Murphy counselor told our guys to sleep anywhere since everyone's getting switched around after casting, but we haven't seen the Gilda Radner counselor yet." She shrugged. "We figured it probably wasn't that big of a deal."

"Well, *Sirena* figured it wasn't that big of a deal," Emily amended. Apparently satisfied she'd picked out all the dust, she started braiding her hair over her shoulder. "I was sure we were going to get into super big trouble or whatever, but—"

"But I finally made you see reason." Sirena smiled, handing Emily a hair binder for her braid.

Emily smiled back, taking it.

"I'm sure it'll be fine," I assured her, needlessly pulling at my own curls. "And if it's not," I said, "I'll take the blame." I put on a voice. "Emily tried to hold me back! She pinned my arms to my sides with her exceptional strength, but she was no match for me . . . The Incredible Hulk of Unpacking!"

They laughed. Sirena nodded a thank-you at me. I smiled and retrieved my luggage from near the screen door. After throwing my backpack on top of the bunk by the window, near Emily and Sirena's, I unzipped my duffle and pulled out my sleeping bag and pillow.

"So," Emily said, picking up her stuffed owl and tucking it into her lap. "Are you the only girl on your team back home?"

"What?" I released my bright turquoise sleeping bag from its compression sack and arranged it and my pillow on the mattress.

"No. There's like...I don't know. Half my team is girls, I think. My coach is a woman, too."

"Lucky," Sirena said, shaking her head.

"Yeah, I don't really have a problem with our guys," I said, trying to decide what to do with the stuff in my suitcase. "We actually do a lot of sketches, and I write most of those...I don't know. Maybe with our coach being a woman and all those girls on the team..." I decided everything else could stay in my suitcase under the bed since I was probably moving tomorrow anyway. "Maybe she just shuts that sexist stuff down without us realizing it."

"You are super lucky," Emily said. "Our team needs some serious help. Like from Oprah."

I grinned. "Oprah?"

Sirena raised an eyebrow. "Emily thinks Oprah can solve anything."

I squinted. "You could do worse than to love Oprah, I guess. What—she built a school, created a publishing boom, launched a media empire—"

Emily interrupted me. "She's smart. And brave."

"Too bad she isn't here," I said, sitting on the bed across from them.

Emily and Sirena offered me identical quizzical looks.

I smiled. "Cuz I bet *she* could find your CD."

CHAPTER FOUR

"I can't believe I left the schedule at home!" Emily moaned on our trek to the Main Lodge. I had assumed there would be cell reception, so I'd left my paper copy at home, too. We had been walking three wide, but the dirt path narrowed, so I dropped back.

Sirena put her arm around Emily's shoulders, and Emily peered up at her like a flower seeking the sun. Sirena's voice was so gentle, I almost missed it. "All you need to know is the next thing on the schedule, right?"

Emily bit her lip a little and nodded.

Sirena hip-checked her. "Well, then, I'm sure we can beg *someone* to tell us when it's time for dinner."

I took two quick steps to catch up to Emily's other side as the path widened again.

"And short of that," I assured her, "I'm really good at sneaking food out of kitchens."

Emily flashed me a small smile and nodded. "I just don't want to be late. Or get into trouble."

Sirena gently tugged on Emily's braid. "We're not going to get into—"

But Sirena was interrupted by a voice that sounded like a DJ announcing the bridal party at a wedding reception. "Paloma! Do you hear that? Real. Live. Actual. GIRLS!"

All three of us jerked our heads to the right where two girls were dragging their luggage down the intersecting path toward us.

Sirena and Emily and I waved and walked over to meet them halfway. As we drew nearer, I couldn't help but stare at Announcer Girl. Her skin was white. But not white-person-white. Not pink-ish or olive-ish or even just super pale. Actual White. At first, I didn't notice her hair because she was wearing a baseball cap, but when I looked more closely, I realized her ponytail was white, too. She wore dark sunglasses, jeans, and a light gray long-sleeve button-up shirt layered over a striped tank top.

I felt like I was staring at this shockingly white girl forever, which felt rude, so I smiled. "I'm Zelda."

"Zelda!" she spluttered. "Is that seriously your name? Holy god, I thought I was going to be the one to stand out, but you? You're named after a video game about an elf!" She took a step closer to me. "And that hair! It's so curly! Geez. I bet people want to pull it and watch it spring back all the time. That would annoy me." Before I could respond, she turned her attention to Sirena and Emily. "Are you two named after video games, too?"

Her friend, shorter and olive-skinned with bangs and long brown hair pulled back into a ponytail, put a hand on her arm. "Hanna," she warned, "we want them to *like* us."

Hanna waved her away. "They'll like you, Paloma. You're going to take care of us all. And they'll like me, too. I can tell. We've been talking for two whole minutes, and no one has called me an albino yet."

I choked on the words in my throat.

Hanna's friend rolled her eyes. "Hi. I'm Paloma. Please excuse Hanna. She's actually very nice once—"

"*Actually?*" Hanna protested, dropping her backpack on the ground and putting her hands on her hips. "I'm *actually* very nice? I'm *already* being *extremely* nice."

Paloma grabbed Hanna's arm and marched her a few steps away from us, her voice low and full of reprimand.

I turned to Emily and Sirena, who were both staring at Hanna with their mouths open a fraction of an inch. It looked like they were trying to translate what she was saying from another language.

"She's a little intense, huh?" I muttered.

That snapped them both out of their staring. Emily crossed her arms over her chest and Sirena exhaled sharply, tucking her hands in her pockets. "A little," Sirena admitted.

Before we had a chance to regroup further, however, Hanna sighed. "Okay!" she huffed at Paloma, putting her hands up defensively.

I tried to exchange a look with Emily and Sirena, but they were already having their own wordless conversation.

Paloma walked briskly back over to us, Hanna dragging her feet a little behind her.

"Can we start over?" Paloma asked.

We all nodded.

"This," Paloma said, gesturing at Hanna, "is Hanna. She is funny and fun and deeply loyal. She often speaks before she thinks, but you

can't help but forgive her over and over because at her core, she is the best of humankind."

Hanna actually looked a little embarrassed.

Paloma bumped her shoulder into Hanna's. "She also has oculocutaneous albinism, Type 1. That means her body doesn't produce melanin, which gives our skin and hair color."

While this information sunk in, Hanna said, "Is it my turn now?"

Paloma nodded.

"This," Hanna sighed, gesturing at her friend, "is Paloma. She's fifty feet tall and only eats purple food. She's from Milwaukee, Wisconsin. She can milk an elephant."

Shaking her head, Paloma said, "*One* of those things is true."

"Ah, but which one?" Hanna said in a spooky voice. Then she mouthed "elephant" and pointed at Paloma.

Sirena and I laughed a little.

"Hey," Hanna dropped her voice. "Did you know Gilda Radner doesn't have a counselor?"

"What?" Emily asked. She was a cat with its fur standing on end.

Paloma picked up Hanna's discarded backpack and handed it to her. "She canceled at the last minute. Got cast on a Second City touring company. They're scrambling to replace her, but since there's only five of us—"

"We're the only girls in the whole camp?" I interrupted, stunned. "There's like two hundred people here."

"Yup," Hanna said. "And since I am really more ghost than girl—"

"Hanna." Paloma grabbed her wrist. "You do not look like a ghost."

Hanna smiled. "It's okay. I'm eternal." She turned to the rest of us. "Paloma here is my biggest defender."

Paloma shook her head. "I mostly defend you against you," she said and slung her own bag over her shoulder.

"Make the first joke, then they laugh *with* you," Hanna said, shrugging.

"What are we going to do without a counselor?" Emily asked, shifting from one foot to the other. Sirena wrapped her arm around her shoulders.

Hanna shrugged again. "We've got Paloma. After I met her, I told my mom I didn't need her anymore."

Emily's mouth dropped open.

"She's joking," Paloma assured her. "I'm just good at keeping a schedule."

Emily brightened. "Really? You know where we need to be next?"

Paloma smiled at Emily. "Yeah. Dinner's at six at the Main Lodge. Hanna and I should drop our stuff off at the cabin. We can unpack later. And auditions are tomorrow at nine a.m. Are you all auditioning?"

We nodded and Paloma said, "Good. I thought we could warm up together before we go. And make sure you have some protein at breakfast. It'll keep you full through the morning."

"See?" said Hanna, wriggling her eyebrows at us. "Hope you needed a mom here."

"I'd love one," Emily said. "I just don't want to play one." She grinned as Sirena and I laughed.

Emily and Sirena and I helped Paloma and Hanna with their luggage, and we all turned to follow the path back to Gilda Radner.

A few steps in, Emily's shoulders relaxed and her face went smooth again. Paloma's surety about the schedule seemed to have calmed her anxiety. She took a deep breath and asked, "So...Hanna... albinism...that's why you look like Elsa from *Frozen*?"

I inhaled sharply, but Hanna laughed.

"Her skin is way pinker than mine, but yeah. I always say I'm more Elsa than Elsa. But I've been her for Halloween like fifty times."

"Me, too!" Emily grinned.

Paloma rolled her eyes. "Hanna keeps trying to make me be her Anna, but that whole Nordic scene doesn't really jive with my coloring."

"Ditto," Sirena chuckled, and she and Paloma high-fived.

"Yeah, so instead, Paloma's been that uni-brow artist Frida Kahlo for Halloween fifty times," Hanna teased her.

"Sirena's always Katherine Johnson," Emily said.

"The human computer?" I asked. "From NASA?"

Sirena beamed at me. "I love that you know who Katherine Johnson is."

"Hey! *I* knew who Katherine Johnson was," Emily interrupted, hands on her hips.

"We watched *Hidden Figures* together." Sirena shook her head at her. "I'm talking—"

"You guys? I have something important to say." Hanna abruptly stopped walking and her face pulled into a worried look. We all held our breath. She clapped a hand on Emily's shoulder. "We're seriously in a rut when it comes to Halloween."

By now we were all laughing. But a tiny little voice whispered in my head, *No one asked, so no one here knows you're always Hermione Granger for Halloween*. I shook my head to silence the voice.

"For the record, Hanna," Emily piped up, "I don't think you look like a ghost at all."

"Now, see, Paloma, you can sheathe your arrows." Hanna linked one arm through Paloma's and the other through Emily's. "My fellow Elsa here thinks I look firmly of this world."

Dragging suitcases and lugging backpacks, the five of us trooped back to the cabin along the dirt path. I wanted to look up at the mountains, but I kept tripping over tree roots. It was going to take a while to get used to the terrain.

CHAPTER FIVE

By the time we dumped the luggage, walked over to the Main Lodge, and climbed the steps up to the wraparound porch, I was breathing surprisingly hard.

"It's the altitude," Sirena said, watching me clutch dramatically at my chest. "Drink lots of water so you don't get altitude sickness. It'll get easier to breathe when you acclimate."

I took a giant slug of water out of my bottle, crossed the porch, pulled open the front screen door, and found myself in a large, open room. A range of mountains was on display through the floor-to-ceiling windows on one wall. On the far end, a hip-high stage ran the width of the room. I took a deep breath—that must be where the final show would be performed. Twelve large tables with folding chairs arranged around them filled the space where I expected an audience to be. *The tables go away for the show,* I decided. I looked up in search of stage lights and found a couple rows of rigging near the stage, but the rest of the A-frame roof featured ceiling fans and round globes that illuminated the dining area. It was clear this place had been retrofitted for theatre, but it was wonderful nevertheless.

I must have gazed around a little too long for Emily's patience because she slipped past me with Sirena's hand in hers and scooted through the crowd to sit with their team. Hanna and Paloma waved at a group of guys who waved back. I hadn't realized they'd also come with a group.

Paloma glanced over her shoulder at me. "You want to join us?"

There were only enough chairs for two more, so I waved her away. "I'll find my brother. See you later!"

I scanned the room, looking for Will. He and Jonas were seated at an all-guys table and looked very settled in. My heart lurched a little. How did I go from knowing six people to sitting with no one?

Trust yourself. Trust your scene partner.

One table was still empty, so I slid into a seat. Maybe someone would join me. Since I didn't have my phone to entertain me, I looked around, trying to make friendly eye contact with passersby to no avail.

Finally, someone tapped my right shoulder. I turned right, but no one was there. When I turned to my left, I jumped—it was Thor/Ben, the blond Scandinavian god/coach.

"Gotcha," he said.

I hate that middle school trick, but I didn't want to come off as a jerk, so I pretended to laugh as he flopped in a chair two down from me.

"Hi," I said. "Did you get sent by the powers that be to talk to the super-awkward loner?"

He laughed. "No. I came to make sure you were going to audition tomorrow. You were funny before."

He thought I was funny before? When? At the car? What had I even said?

"Uh, thanks. Yes. I am totally going to audition. I sent in my sketch last month."

"Which one was it?" He settled an arm over the chair between us.

"The one about the zombies suing the creators of *Walking Dead* for defamation of character?"

A slow smile spread across his face. "That was you?"

I turned my body to face him. "You remember it?"

He nodded slowly. "Oh, I remember it. The part where they eat the brains of the IT guy for taking too long to set up the LCD projector?" He reached over and poked my bicep. "*That* was funny stuff."

I grinned. "Thanks."

He poked me again and my stomach flipped over. "Why are you all alone . . . uh . . . I can't remember your name?"

"Zelda. And you're Ben."

He laughed. "Good memory. Zelda . . ." He made a confused face. "Like the video game?"

I nodded, used to this. "And the Fitzgerald."

He stared at me blankly.

"F. Scott Fitzgerald's wife was named Zelda."

He shook his head.

"He wrote *The Great Gatsby*?"

He frowned. "With Leonardo DiCaprio?"

"The movie is with Leonardo DiCaprio. Yes. It's also a good book. And F. Scott Fitzgerald's wife, Zelda, wrote and danced and was an amazing artist in her own right. But it was the 1920s, so she didn't get the attention her husband did." I could feel myself rambling. And lecturing. I tried to rein it in and shrugged. "My mom loves Zelda Fitzgerald."

He nodded and gazed over my shoulder.

I was losing him.

Balance giving and taking.

"Who's named Ben?" I blurted.

He quirked his head. "Huh?"

My cheeks reddened. "In your family. Is some relative named Ben? Or are you Ben for Ben Franklin?"

He laughed. "Now *him* I've heard of. No, I'm Ben because my dad liked the name Ben. But maybe I should make something up." He folded his super-muscular arms across his chest. "I'm Ben for . . . that clock in London. Big Ben. Tall, important, great at telling time."

Big Ben is actually the name of the *bell*, not the *clock*, but after the failed Zelda Fitzgerald history lesson, I decided another one back-to-back wasn't going to win me any fans. Keeping it positive, I just smiled. "Those are definitely qualities you want for your child."

He laughed again and met my eye. "Funny girl . . . You're dangerous."

Dangerous? Was he flirting with me? He couldn't be flirting with me. No one flirted with me.

"Too dangerous to eat dinner with?" I asked, shocked at my own forwardness.

One corner of his mouth drew up. "I could risk it. If you promise me one thing."

I couldn't tell for sure if my shortness of breath was Ben or altitude-related, but I had my suspicions. "Yes?"

34

"Promise me—"

He kept talking, but his comment was drowned out by the squawking feedback of the PA system as a round man in his sixties with a deep tan and salt-and-pepper hair took to the microphone.

"Hello, hello, sorry about that. Okay. Got it? Do we have it?"

I looked back to Ben, but he was eyes-forward on the speaker. I really wanted to know what I was supposed to promise him, but he was all business.

"Hello, everybody. Paul DeLuca here. And this other old guy is Paul Paulsen. Welcome to the thirtieth summer of Rocky Mountain Theatre Arts!"

Everyone whooped and clapped. Paul DeLuca basked in the applause as a tall, balding Paul Paulsen climbed on stage to join him. Paul Paulsen clutched a clipboard in one arm and nodded at us, his pinched facial features attempting a smile under bushy eyebrows.

I couldn't believe I was seeing Paul DeLuca and Paul Paulsen in person. They had started RMTA with Jane Lloyd all those years ago. The only thing better than seeing them would have been seeing Jane.

Paul DeLuca held up a hand to quiet us down. "We're very excited for your two weeks with us in these beautiful mountains. And to maximize that enjoyment . . . we have a few rules."

We all chuckled at his joke, and his smile broadened at the acknowledgment.

"One, drink water. Drink more water than you've ever drunk before. We have a slogan up here—'Pee Clear.'"

The crowd tittered. I looked over to catch Ben's eye, but again, he was focused on Paul.

"Altitude sickness is very real and very painful, so stay hydrated.

There are big orange water jugs on the front porch. Just refill your water bottle whenever you pass by. P2?"

P2? . . . Oh, I realized, *Two Ps. Paul Paulsen.*

P2 regarded his clipboard and leaned over the microphone. "Two, curfew is at nine p.m. Later than that, and it gets very dark."

Paul DeLuca smiled and added, "Much darker than city kids are used to."

We chuckled again and his chest puffed up. "Rule Three. The Boy Scout camp is across the road. They come through here to access some hiking trails and to see our shows—"

There was a single whoop from someone, and everyone laughed. It was a bigger laugh than Paul DeLuca had gotten. A tiny frown of annoyance flashed across his face, but it was quickly pushed down by a theatrical smile. "In turn, this year, for the first time, we are going to get to use their high ropes equipment for team building and whatnot. So be nice to the Boy Scouts."

Paul Paulsen leaned back over the mic, his voice tight. "Lastly, we have a very strict physical violence policy. If you get in a physical altercation, you will be sent home. No exceptions."

"Well," Paul DeLuca drawled, "unless it's in a scene."

Paul Paulsen raised disapproving eyebrows at Paul DeLuca. Noticing them, Paul DeLuca held up a hand and forced a chuckle. "I know, I know. I'm joking." He grinned at the audience and wagged a thick finger at us. "Keep those fight scenes to a minimum."

Paul Paulsen's eyes returned to his clipboard, and he slid a pencil behind his ear and sighed.

"Now, dinner is almost upon us—" Paul DeLuca began.

More cheering from the crowd.

"But before we eat, we are very excited that we have *five* girls at camp this year. So girls: welcome!"

My eyes sought out the other Gildas. Five was *exciting*? I thought about all the girls who did improv back home. Plus, Jane Lloyd had started this camp, and she was a girl.

What was up with this place?

I leaned over to Ben. "How many girls have there been in the past?" I whispered.

He shook his head, eyes front.

I gave him a look, but then shrugged. Maybe he didn't want to be rude to Paul.

Paul Paulsen climbed down the steps away from the stage as Paul DeLuca continued. "Okay. Anyone who wants to audition for the upper-level teams, that starts right here at nine a.m. tomorrow morning. You'll be in team cabins by tomorrow night. Well, except for the girls. You'll all stay put in Gilda Radner. And now! Let's eat!"

Chatter and scraping of chairs echoed through the Lodge as groups stood up to get in line for food. I frowned a little. Everyone would be in a cabin with their teammates except for the girls? We'd miss out on so much. I could already imagine the inside jokes piling up.

On the other hand, with only five girls, what else could they do?

I looked over at Ben, who was watching Paul DeLuca amble out of the room. Then he turned to me and smiled. "The Pauls seem nice, but they're pretty intense rule followers. Sorry if I seemed rude. Just trying to fly under their radar. Especially P2's."

"Paul Paulsen?" I asked.

Ben nodded. "Last year, someone missed curfew twice, and the Pauls sent him home."

I raised an eyebrow.

"It's weird," he said. "This place is so laid back in a lot of ways. You'll find you have quite a bit of freedom, schedule-wise. But there are few ways they're super strict. Curfew's one."

"Well, Gilda Radner doesn't even have a counselor, so—"

"Laura's not here?"

I shook my head. "She got a last-minute touring gig for Second City."

His face tensed for a moment and then he smiled. "Good for her. I hadn't . . . heard that."

I nodded, watching him. His jealousy was clear. "How long have you been coming here?" I asked. I took in a short breath. "You didn't meet Jane Lloyd before she died, did you?"

"No, that was before my time." He ran his tongue over his front teeth. "It's my first summer coaching," he said, "but I came as a camper for years before that. I've been doing film and television and performing—"

"At UCB. I remember. You told my dad."

He smiled. "That's right. I did." He slid into the empty chair between us and planted a hand on my shoulder, which burst into flame at his touch. "Now. Are you ready for some turkey tetrazzini?"

"That sounds . . ."

"Terrible. It's terrible. I'll spare you the suspense."

I laughed. "But wait—you said I had to promise you something."

He let his hand drop as he drew his eyebrows together. "I . . . don't remember." But then he brightened. "Oh. Yeah. I just wanted to make sure you audition tomorrow. Promise me you'll audition." He shook his head. "You wrote 'Zombies v. *Walking Dead.*' I'll be watching for you."

My stomach turned in on itself.

Then Will appeared. "Hey, Zelda! I figured you were with the Gilda girls. But here you are." His eyes flicked to Ben. "Hi," he said neutrally.

"Hey," Ben said.

I watched them eye each other for a weird hot minute.

Make active choices.

"So . . ." I said, standing. "Should we get in line?"

"You know," Ben said, pushing his sleeves up to his elbows again, "I better actually go talk to the other coaches. We're doing a short show after dinner. If I don't see you later, I'll catch you tomorrow at auditions."

Charlie Brown feelings of disappointment swept in as he swept out.

"What's . . . what's going on there?" Will asked in a low voice.

I shook my head. "Nothing. We were just talking."

"And grinning. And giggling. And touching."

"What? Look, Will, I am not denying he is all kinds of hot—"

Will spluttered.

"But he was just making sure I was auditioning tomorrow. He liked my zombie sketch."

He sighed. "He's a coach, Z."

I frowned. "I know that."

"A coach you were flirting with."

I scoffed. "I wasn't flirting. Or," I said at his look, "if I was, he certainly wasn't flirting back."

I glanced at the table where Ben had found the other coaches. His muscular back flexed as he pointed at some papers on the table. None of the guys I knew looked like Ben. He was only three years older than me, but he radiated . . . confidence. Adulthood.

Will snapped his fingers in front of my face. "Zelda. Are you seriously that much of an idiot?"

"Hey!" I protested, knocking his hand away.

He shook his head as Jonas slid between us and flirtatiously elbowed Will who elbowed him back.

"Hi," Jonas said to Will.

"Hi, yourself." Will smiled.

For all intents and purposes, I had disappeared.

"What's the holdup?" Jonas asked. "Aren't you hungry?"

"Zelda's got her flirt on," Will said, crossing his arms and moving a quarter inch closer to Jonas so their biceps and hips were touching.

"Don't say 'flirt on.'" I rolled my eyes. "You sound like Dad."

"Whatever. Ben's a coach," Will repeated.

"I was just—"

"You were flirting with a *coach*?" Jonas asked, scandalized.

I folded my own arms and stared at the ceiling. "Just drop it. It's nothing. He remembered my zombie sketch and liked it. That's all."

"Well," Will began, "as your older brother—"

"Four lousy months does not make you an older brother. Girls mature faster anyway, so as your more mature sister—"

"Guys!" Jonas interrupted.

We looked at him.

"Isn't *anyone* hungry?"

"Okay, RMTA! Are you ready for some improv?" Ben clapped his hands to get the crowd amped up.

The tables had been removed and the chairs reconfigured to face the stage. There were ten coaches—all guys—standing in a line. They introduced themselves, but as I whooped and clapped, surrounded by the other Gildas, my eyes were glued to Ben.

"As I'm sure you all know," he said, fists on his hips, "improv is completely made up on the spot. You give us suggestions, we build characters and scenes out of thin air. We're going to play a little, just for fun, and give you a chance to get to know us." He dropped his voice and gave his fellow coaches a slow smile. "Hopefully we won't embarrass ourselves."

The crowd chuckled, and he stepped forward, chest first. "To start us off, I'd like a location where two people might run into each other."

"Coffee shop!" someone yelled.

"I heard rocket ship!" Ben said. Over the laugher, he grinned. "Just kidding. Coffee shop!"

Half of the coaches jogged off in one direction, the rest in the other. They lined up in the wings on each side of the stage, facing one another—some standing, some bending over like they were preparing to pounce. Jenn, my coach back home, called this "clearing to neutral." But Ben stayed where he was. I frowned for a millisecond. Why wasn't he clearing to neutral with everyone else? The person who gets the suggestion doesn't automatically start the scene ... I glanced up and down the row I was sitting in to see if this was

bothering anyone else, but everyone was either watching Ben or whispering to the person next to them. *Huh. Maybe this is just one of those extra-polite things Jenn insists on*, I decided.

"FredrickSON!" Ben bellowed. A couple coaches made brief eye contact, and one of them nodded. Then he hunched over and limped onstage to meet Ben.

"Yessir," he said, his voice hissing like a snake.

I grinned. What a great vocal and physical choice. He reminded me of Dr. Frankenstein's assistant, Igor.

"Ah. There you are, Fredrickson." Ben whipped around to face him, miming holding a cup of coffee. "What is *this*?"

"Fredrickson" shuffled from one foot to the other, his eyes avoiding Ben's. "Your nonfat, no-whip, skinny soy latte, sir."

Ben huffed. "*That* was my order *last* week. The campaign is ramping up, Fredrickson. So what do I need?"

"Uh . . . a different order?" Fredrickson whispered.

"Of course!" Ben raged. He stomped in a circle around Fredrickson, who cowered a little more with each step. "I have speeches to give! Hands to shake! Babies to kiss! You think a nonfat, no-whip, skinny soy latte is going to fuel THAT?"

"Uh . . . no, sir?"

"Correct, Fredrickson!" Ben mimed dumping the coffee in the trash and then flipped something that looked like a dog treat into the air. Fredrickson jumped and "caught" it in his mouth. Like Fredrickson, the crowd ate it up.

"So . . ." Ben put his hands on Fredrickson's shoulders and glared down at him. "What's my coffee order *this* week?"

Fredrickson trembled. "A ... full-fat, full-whip, whole-milk cappuccino?"

"With?"

"Those little shaved chocolate curlicues?"

"Aaaaand?" Ben tapped his foot.

"Ummm ..." Fredrickson's face twitched, and he lowered his voice. "If I guess right, can I have another treat?"

Ben stepped back, affronted. "Of course. What am I, a monster?"

I giggled and caught Sirena's eye. We leaned our shoulders into each other's and grinned.

"Of course not, sir. All right then, sir. A full-fat, full-whip, whole-milk cappuccino with chocolate curlicues ..."

"Aaaand?"

It had to be something that made sense in the world of coffee but was also a little unexpected. My brain automatically started making a list: *cinnamon, extra napkins, sprinkles—*

"A twisty straw?" Fredrickson asked.

Perfect, I thought.

Ben patted Fredrickson's head like a dog. "Who's a good boy?" He threw another "treat" into the air, and Fredrickson twisted around to catch it in his mouth again.

The lights blacked out, indicating the ending of the scene.

We cheered and applauded as the lights came back up again. Ben grinned, soaking it all up.

"They were so good!" Emily said, leaning across Sirena.

I nodded, my chest swelling. I knew I belonged up there with them. And tomorrow, I was going to get a chance to prove it.

CHAPTER SIX

"Ah, the relief of nightfall," Hanna proclaimed, banging open the screen door to Gilda Radner. She stripped off her button-up shirt, throwing it and her baseball cap onto her bunk. She examined her arms. "Now that I'm sleeveless, we won't need a night-light in here. And bonus—if anyone wakes up to use the bathroom and gets lost wandering around in the woods, the glow of my arms will help you find your way home."

Emily looked to Sirena. "Am I going to get lost in the woods?"

Sirena and I just smiled and shook our heads.

"With me around, there's no chance of it." Hanna threw her arms up in the air and slowly turned in a circle. "Boop. Boop. Boop."

I glanced back at Emily. Her face was twisted with worry. Couldn't Hanna see that her joke was making Emily tense?

Paloma kicked off her sandals and glared sideways at Hanna.

Hanna continued to boop and rotate. "I'm a bear-proof lighthouse."

"Bears?" Emily bit her lip.

"Hanna," Paloma warned her, turning on the wall-mounted heater by the door. "You're making our new friends nervous."

I was glad Paloma was here to temper Hanna. I wasn't sure what to say.

Hanna pulled flannel pants out of her suitcase and squinted one eye. "If all my jokes are albinism-related tomorrow, do you think that'll make me *more* or *less* likely to get on the top team?"

Paloma pulled her hair out of her ponytail. "Ignoring you."

Suddenly, Emily gripped the bunk and started taking in quick, shallow breaths. Before I even realized something was wrong, Sirena was at her side. "I breathe in one," she said softly, a hand on her back, "I breathe out one. I breathe in two . . ."

Emily nodded, and struggled to match her breath to Sirena's words.

"What's the matter?" Hanna turned around. For the first time since I'd met her, she was completely serious. Paloma looked up from brushing her hair, startled.

Sirena held up a "one-minute" finger and continued counting for Emily. "I breathe out three . . ."

I exchanged a look with Paloma, and she snagged Hanna's sleeve.

"I breathe in four," Paloma said, raising her eyebrows.

Hanna and I nodded. "I breathe out four," we said.

Paloma kept brushing her hair, and Hanna and I took her lead in not staring and changed into our pajamas. We continued counting breaths in and out for Emily until she released the bunk bed and stood up straight.

"Thank you," she said. "That was really nice of you. I'm sorry I freak out, I just—"

"*I'm* sorry." Hanna interrupted her. She twisted her hand around awkwardly. "Part of my albinism is my eyesight is pretty crappy, so I can't always read facial expressions. Sometimes I don't know when to stop."

We all just sort of stared at each other with half smiles on our faces. Finally, I said, "I think we just had our first Gilda bonding experience."

"You're right!" Paloma exclaimed, reaching for her toiletry kit. "Let's go brush our teeth, because then I think we're ready for our next bonding experience: 'My First.'"

"Dental hygiene be damned," Hanna said, climbing on the bed and pulling Paloma down after her. "Let's do this now."

"My first what?" Sirena asked. She knotted her robe at her waist and sat on the bottom bunk across from Hanna and Paloma.

All pretense of us getting ready for bed was swiftly abandoned. Picking up her stuffed owl, Emily clambered next to Sirena, and I sat on the floor.

"Pick a category," Paloma instructed. "Like, my first job. Then everyone says what their first of that thing was. I can start. My first job was babysitting the next-door neighbor's twin three-year-olds. It was horrible. They used pee as a weapon."

We all groaned, except for Hanna, who grinned evilly, clearly having heard this story before.

"Not sure if this counts," I said, tapping my fingers on the floor as the groans died out, "but *technically* my first job was tutoring my slightly older brother in telling time."

"This was last week?" Hanna deadpanned.

I chuckled. "Third grade. He got so angry when any adult tried to help him, so my parents told me they'd let me pick out five books at the bookstore if I could get him to learn to tell time."

"Nerd." Hanna coughed into her fist.

"Just wait until you hear what one of the books was," I said, climbing onto my knees.

"*Chess Strategies for Kids?*" Paloma joked.

I shook my head. "*Mastering the Art of French Cooking* by Julia Child."

"What? What were you thinking?" Hanna demanded, laughing.

I peered up at the ceiling. "It was really hard, teaching Will to tell time. That book was *big*. I think I wanted my money's worth."

"Did you go on to become a child prodigy in cooking?" Sirena asked.

I shook my head. "The closest that book ever got to the kitchen was on the seat of my dining room chair. I was a really short kid."

I looked around at four beaming faces. My brain felt all buzzy and warm. I liked it here in Gilda Radner, I decided. I was glad we'd be staying together.

"My first job was super boring compared to Julia Child over here," Hanna said, thumbing at me. "I just bussed tables at a brew pub."

"I bussed tables!" Sirena exclaimed. "At my parents' restaurant."

"My first job was *also* working in Sirena's parents' restaurant," Emily said, smiling at Sirena. "Washing dishes."

"That's how we met," Sirena said. She glanced at all of us quickly, then back at Emily. Emily returned a tiny nod. Sirena took a breath. "Then we started dating like two months later."

"Oh!" Paloma cooed, clasping her hands together. "That's so nice! I had a feeling, but I'm so glad to know for sure."

"That's awesome," I agreed. I hadn't really thought about it, but now that I knew, their closeness made even more sense. I couldn't help but ping a little with jealousy—they had a person, the way Will and Jonas had each other.

"Thank you," Emily said, blushing. "My mom says we're lucky to be both girlfriends and best friends. She loves my dad, but her best friend lives in Baltimore."

"*My* mom likes to pretend we're *only* best friends," Sirena said, rolling her eyes. "But Dad's cool. We're working on Mom together."

That sucked. I took a moment to be grateful for Will and my parents.

"Maybe you should tell her she should be happy about it because neither of you is going to accidentally get pregnant," Hanna said.

Paloma moaned. "*Hanna.*"

Hanna looked at Paloma, shocked. "*What?*"

Sirena and Emily laughed, so I joined in. "I've tried that one, actually," Sirena said. "No dice." She took Emily's hand. "It's okay. It's better than it was. And the guys on our team are . . ." She looked to Emily for the right words.

"Less grossly into us being together than they used to be?" Emily suggested.

Sirena pursed her lips. "Yeah. Sometimes."

"Well, I think that sucks," Hanna said. She threw up a hand. "*You* don't suck. Let's be clear, Paloma. The situation sucks." She gestured to Emily and Sirena. "The situation should be if you two are happy together, everyone else should be happy for you. And not gross-happy."

Sirena and Emily cracked a smile.

"We love the guys on our team," Emily insisted. "And we love improv."

Paloma nodded. "But just being a girl is hard enough without also being . . . Do you have a label you like?"

Emily beamed. "Thanks for asking." She turned to Sirena. "Isn't that nice? To be asked?"

Sirena chuckled, squeezing Emily's hand and nodded. "Yeah, it is." She looked at their clasped hands and smiled. "We like 'gay.' And 'lesbian' is fine, too. In certain contexts, 'queer' makes the most sense. Right, Em?"

Emily nodded. "I did have a boyfriend freshman year, and he was really nice to me, but dating him felt mostly just weird. Like I was playing a part? And then I met this girl during the play, and at first I was like, 'She's really cute. Oh my gosh, do I like girls?' and then I was like, 'Yes, I do, because, *this* is what kissing is supposed to—'"

Sirena coughed. Paloma and I caught each other's eyes and grinned.

Emily giggled and leaned her head on Sirena's shoulder. "Sorry! Sirena doesn't love me talking about Bailey. I'm Sirena's first girlfriend."

Sirena shook her head and smirked. "Not true. Tiana in *Princess and the Frog* was my first girlfriend."

We all laughed.

"Anyone else have a label they like?" Emily asked.

"I've never had a boyfriend or a girlfriend," Paloma said, gazing at the ceiling, "but I'm pretty sure I'm straight."

"It's a shame it's such a long label," Hanna joked, "because 'I've never had a boyfriend or a girlfriend, but I'm pretty sure I'm straight' doesn't really fit on a T-shirt."

"If you could manage it, I'd order one," I said.

"Me, too," Hanna said, pulling her shirt close to her face. "Maybe if we make the font smaller . . ."

As the laughter died down, Paloma sat up straight. "How have we not talked about this yet? *Five* girls showed up here. Out of two hundred campers. And the Pauls are *excited!*"

"Yeah . . ." Hanna said slowly, straightening her shirt. "That worries me, too."

Sirena reached for a large satin scarf in her robe pocket. "And we're all here for the first time. Does no girl ever come back?"

"People get busy," I said. "It could be just a coincidence."

"Maybe," Sirena said. She folded the scarf into a triangle and tied it around her braids. "But did anyone talk to you about not having a counselor? Is *that* related?"

We shook our heads.

"The freedom's nice and whatnot," Paloma allowed, "but it seems a little irresponsible."

Now we were all leaning forward.

"I talked to one of the coaches," I said, not mentioning Ben's name on purpose. I mean, even with all this openness with the Gildas, after Will and Jonas's reaction, I wasn't sure there wasn't another round of flirt-shaming in my future. "He was surprised that Laura— who was supposed to be our counselor—wasn't here. The gig was super last minute, I guess."

"Huh," Paloma said, tapping her knee with her pointer finger. "I kinda wish she was. We'd have someone to answer questions, you know?"

"Like auditions tomorrow," Sirena said. "Are we all going to make the upper-level teams because we're good? Or because they need women?"

We were silent for a moment.

I sat on my hip and tried to channel Will's encouragement from the car. "Come on," I said, "we can't think like that. We're good. It'll be fine. We'll just go in, stay out of our heads, and be in the moment."

Sirena exchanged a look with Paloma.

"What?" I asked.

"It's just . . ." She sighed. "Sometimes, when I get an opportunity, I wonder—is it because I deserve it, or because I help fill a quota?" Emily took Sirena's hand again.

I frowned. "A quota?"

Hanna smirked. "Yeah. Did they ask me to be on Student Council because I'm smart and have good ideas, or because vampire girl helps Student Council look diverse?"

Paloma whacked Hanna on the leg but nodded. "You can go crazy asking yourself questions like that."

My shoulders dropped. "That sucks."

"I mean, I definitely have a distinct point of view that's important," Hanna added. "It's smart to include me."

I caught Paloma's eye, and we smiled.

"I feel that," Sirena agreed. "But the thought occurs to me, too." She sighed and laced her fingers through Emily's.

Paloma cleared her throat. "We shouldn't think too hard about it. Zelda's right. We're all going to be great. Okay?"

We nodded and voiced our agreement, but I couldn't totally shake off my unease.

CHAPTER SEVEN

Will was nowhere to be seen.

And predictably, neither was Jonas.

But loads of other people were—all of Gilda Radner, plus probably fifty or sixty guys. Some people were doing vocal warm-ups, others were stretching, and a small group of guys were circled up playing zip-zap-zop. Once again, my fellow Gildas had drifted off to be with their home teams, and so once again, I was alone.

Still, I was sure Will and Jonas were on their way. I signed all three of us in and sat in the middle of three chairs at the end of an empty row. I put my Second City tote bag on one and flung my arm over the other to save them for Will and Jonas's inevitable arrival. Because they *were* coming...right?

Ben plus two other guys in their early twenties hopped up on stage. The zip-zap-zop guys collapsed their circle, everyone found seats, and the crowd fell silent.

"Okay," Ben said with an authoritative voice, "Welcome to auditions."

Some guys called out, "Wooool Ben!"

Ben smirked and continued. "I'm looking for six to eight people for the Varsity team and Roger and Dion here are looking for eight to ten people on each of the Junior Varsity teams. Anyone who doesn't make Varsity or JV, as well as everyone else who isn't auditioning, will be put onto Skill-Building teams. Every year, JV performs a show the second-to-last night of camp, and the Varsity team performs the final night for everyone at camp as well as for reps from Second City, iO, and UCB."

None of this was news to me, but every time someone mentioned the final show, I got the shivers. I imagined myself up there, sweating under the lights, deep in the moment, sharing the stage with other great performers.

But there wasn't time to get lost in my daydream. Ben pressed on. "No matter what, you will be a different performer at the other end of two weeks."

I twisted around, searching for a glimpse of Will or Jonas. Were they seriously going to miss this?

Ben took the pen from behind his ear and tapped it on his clipboard. "Based on this list of everyone who signed in, we'll split you up into groups of six, and we'll just do some Montages to start." He made a notation, replaced his pen behind his ear, and pushed up the sleeves of his white, long-sleeve T-shirt to his elbows. This shirt was tighter than yesterday's and showed off some serious muscle definition in his arms. Between the missing lover boys and this specimen of male perfection, focus eluded me. I closed my eyes and tried to ground myself.

"When your group's called, have one person get an audience suggestion," Ben continued, "and then you can all go straight into your Montage. Feel free to employ call-back scenes that go forward or backward in time. Give us a minute to make groups, and then we'll start."

I nodded, eyes still closed, and flexed my hands. *Trust yourself.*

"What's a call-back scene?" Emily hissed in my left ear. I jumped and moved my arm to make room for her.

"'What's a call-back scene?'" I repeated.

She nodded, eyebrows furrowed.

I looked up at Sirena, who naturally, was with her. Already I was starting to recognize Sirena's sympathetic Emily-just-needs-to-hear-it-again-out-loud look.

"Okay," I said, tucking my curls behind my ears. "Let's say the first scene is about a teacher and a student arguing . . . over a test score. You take some element of the first one—maybe testing in this case—and it inspires the next scene to be about . . . cheating on the ACT. The third scene is inspired by that one. Maybe it's people who are cheating on their spouses."

"Because it picked up on cheating from the second scene," Sirena added.

I nodded. "So, a fourth scene could build on that last one, or it could 'call back' an earlier scene. Like, the teacher and student. But now their argument has gone so far they're on *Judge Judy.* That last scene *calls back* to the first one, putting it forward in time. Call-back scene."

"Oh god," Emily twisted her cardigan in her hands. "That sounds so hard. Is it hard?"

Sirena put a hand on her back. "This is like a Harold—a series of related scenes. That's all. We call it Harold, they call it Montage. You're fine."

"I'm fine. It's just a Harold. It's just a series of related scenes. I'm fine."

"Breathe, Em."

"Okay, I'm breathing."

"Don't *talk* about breathing—just breathe."

Emily let out some shuddering breaths.

Sirena moved her hand to Emily's lower back and put the other one on her stomach. "Deep breaths, Em. Down here."

I didn't mean to stare, but the calming power in Sirena's voice and touch and Emily's now-smooth face and breaths showed a complete trust that made me wish for that kind of connection. I skimmed the room looking for Will and finally caught his eye. I gestured for him to come and sit in my remaining saved chair. We'd have to grab another for Jonas.

He wove his way through the chairs. "Sorry I'm late." His lips were very pink and his hair was unusually messy and—

"Will," I muttered, moving my bag for him, "your T-shirt is on inside-out."

His cheeks flushed. "Seriously?" he asked in a small voice.

"Yes. Is Jonas waiting a few minutes so it doesn't look like you were—"

"Shut up, Zelda."

I sighed and shook my head. Suddenly love was everywhere.

But moping wasn't going to help me out. I elbowed him. "I'm happy for you. I really am."

He looked at me sideways, then suppressed a pleased smile. "Thanks, Z. He's . . ." He sighed. "I don't even know. I think he really likes me."

I laughed. "Well done, Sherlock. I've known that boy liked you since January."

"What?"

"We came back from winter break, and you got that shawl-collar cardigan for Christmas, and he couldn't take his eyes off you."

"Seriously? Why didn't you say something?"

"I—I don't know. I should've, I guess." Why *hadn't* I said anything?

Will shook his head. "Well, I guess it doesn't matter now—"

"Hey."

We looked up. Jonas's brown eyes melted into my brother's.

"At least *your* shirt's on right-side out," I said.

Jonas brushed the back of Will's neck and fingered the tag of his T-shirt. He gave him a slow smile. "I wonder how that happened?" he asked.

"Okay, grab a chair, boyfriend," I muttered.

"Shhh—" Will said as Jonas flashed him a look of concern and peeled away to find one.

"What?" I whispered.

Will looked around. "We're not . . . *out* . . . here."

I shifted in my chair to frown at him. "What do you mean? You've been out since middle school." I glanced at Emily and Sirena, who were still lost in their own little world.

He tugged at his earlobe. "But I don't know if this place—Jonas has only been out a few months. I guess someone said something in his cabin yesterday that was kinda homophobic, and he's nervous. It's fine. We just have to test the waters a little. Put some feelers out. Jonas said at his last school that improv was a major bro zone. And just look at how few girls there are here. We might have to be Will and Jonas, Excellent Friends."

"Instead of Will and Jonas, Passionate Lovers?"

"Shut up," he groaned. "You never get to say the word 'lovers' again. Ever. Who says 'lovers'?"

"Well, you've just said it twice." I grinned. "Okay. I get it. I'm sorry I didn't think about what it might mean for you to be out in a new place."

He leaned back in his chair. "Thanks."

Jonas returned with the chair and slid in next to Will. I watched them fold their arms and find comfort in making contact shoulder to shoulder, knee-to knee.

I turned to my left to introduce my new friends to Will and Jonas, but Emily and Sirena were talking to each other in low voices. I looked around at everyone in small groups, chatting. I assumed Hanna and Paloma were sitting with the rest of their team. Everyone had someone but me.

All three coaches climbed back up on the stage. Ben clicked his pen. "These will be your Round One Long Form groups. Then we'll take a break and come back for Short Form structures. Finally, we'll close with some One-Liners."

The coach to Ben's right was a tall, goofy-looking white guy with a mop of light, curly hair. The previous night, he'd played this really funny post office worker who could only give directions using zip codes. He waved good-naturedly. "Uh, in case you forgot from last night, I'm Roger, by the way."

The crowd chuckled. Roger smiled crookedly. "I've been doing a few shows here and there in Chicago. First summer here. Happy to see you all."

"And I'm Dion," the other coach waved. Even taller than Roger, Dion had dark brown skin and wore his hair in a fade. He'd been great at voices in the show—at one point he'd played Kermit the Frog, and I'd nearly fallen off my chair. "Also here from Chicago," he continued, "also my first summer. Careful for Roger," he nodded in his direction. "He's terrible at Frisbee."

In a faux-hurt voice, Roger said, "Hey, now."

Dion grinned. "Rest assured—Frisbee in his hand, you will get hit." The crowd laughed. "Super excited to get started."

Roger and Dion looked like string beans standing next to each other. Their easy smiles made *me* feel excited to get started.

"Right. And most of you already know me. I'm Ben Porter," Ben added. He paused like he was waiting for another cheer but there was only light applause and a delayed whoop. I tried to catch his eye, but if he saw me, he didn't respond.

Ben called off six names, including mine and Hanna's. As I climbed the stairs to the stage, my stomach flopped over. I grabbed Hanna's hand and squeezed it, but none of the other guys would look at me. I frowned. Improv is all about trust. You're getting on stage without a script or even characters. It's all about eye contact and nonverbal communication. How was I going to be able to show the coaches the kind of performer I was when most of my scene partners wouldn't even look at me?

"Whoa!" One of the people in our Montage pointed at something on the horizon and started pacing back and forth.

No one jumped to join him.

"What is that?"

Hanna leaned next to me and whispered, "There's a winner of a start."

Clearly, this guy had no idea what he was doing. *Or,* I considered, *maybe he just clapped the last scene out on a high note and jumped in without an idea for the next one. Maybe he was sacrificing himself.* I took a deep breath. *Okay. What's something he could be pointing at? . . .*

I mimed holding onto a tray and put on my best popcorn vendor voice. "Eclipse glasses!" I called out, joining the guy on stage. "Get your solar eclipse glasses here!" A rumble of laughter rolled across the audience.

"Who are you?" he asked.

"I'm—"

"What are you doing here?"

My scene partner had interrupted me, which happens sometimes, but the bigger problem was he had just asked three questions in a row. Questions can be the death of an improv scene because it makes the other person do all the heavy lifting. Luckily, I was up for the challenge. *Make statements and assumptions.*

I clapped a hand on his shoulder. "Why, sonny, the solar eclipse is coming in less than three minutes."

"Solar eclipse?"

"Yes! It's a meteorological marvel! But if you stare into the sun, you'll go blind—so get your eclipse glasses right here! Only twenty bucks!"

"Twenty bucks?"

This guy was either super nervous or a parrot. I raised my voice. "Perhaps you're hard of hearing! The solar eclipse is coming! And I did say twenty dollars!"

The audience laughed.

"What do I need eclipse glasses for?"

Oh my god. So many questions. Okay. Time for my foolproof fallback: knowing the guy. "Wait a minute. Jerry?"

"Huh?"

"Jerry Feldemeier?" I mimed setting down my tray and turned to him so we were eye to eye. "Look at you, son! You've grown so much! I remember when you were knee-high to a grasshopper! Tell your mom Agnes Ruffles says hello!"

"Yeah, yeah. Yeah, I will."

"And for old time's sakes, kid, take a pair of eclipse glasses on me."

In the end, our Montage went fairly well, but it wasn't my best work. We did get a big laugh in the last scene when I called back Agnes Ruffles, though. The scene took place in a movie theater, and I came out as Agnes Ruffles selling 3-D glasses to the moviegoers. That's one of my favorite things to do in Montage. Most people have nearly forgotten the earlier scenes, and so the audience gets to experience the joy of remembering coupled with the warm feeling of an inside joke. I love it when it works out.

"You are very funny," Hanna rumbled in my ear as we climbed off the stage.

"So are you." I smiled and high-fived her. "You have amazing timing."

"Thanks, but *you*, Zelda-girl, *you* have something special."

I blushed a little. "That's really nice of—"

"I didn't know they let vampires in here," a guy in the next group said to his friend, passing us on their way to the stage.

I frowned, but a quarter-second too late, realized the vampire jibe had been directed at Hanna.

"He—" I began, pointing behind me at the guy.

Hanna lowered my hand and just shook her head. "It's fine, Zelda-girl. Normally I'd skewer them, but today I'm saving my best lines for the stage."

I laughed. "You are awesome, and those guys are idiots."

"Damn straight." Hanna high-fived me and retreated to Paloma and her crew, and by the time I returned to my seat, Will was already in position for his Montage group. Emily was up, too.

Unfortunately, Emily was too anxious to be her best self. At one point, she played a really funny newscaster who was so nervous, she couldn't remember any of the news, and later managed a spot-on Irish accent, but the guys she was performing with mostly sidelined her. After the third scene, where she played someone's mom, a guy behind me whispered, "That fat girl is really bombing."

His friend chuckled and whispered back, "What did you expect?"

I frowned, wishing I was the kind of person who would just turn around and pummel those asshats. Instead, I looked over my shoulder and threw eye-daggers at them.

Peering out from under their baseball caps, the one with a gap

in his front teeth grabbed his crotch and the one with close-set eyes glared back and flipped me off. I looked to the coaches to see if anyone was paying attention to the cretins, but the coaches were spread around the room, eyes on the stage.

Geez, I thought. *Bro zone doesn't even begin to cover it.*

Two hours later, it was time for the One-Liner round.

I turned to Will for reassurance, but he was digging through my bag.

"What are you doing?" I hissed.

"Jonas has a nosebleed."

I leaned forward to look at him, and sure enough, Jonas was pinching his nose and tilting his head back, but blood was running down his chin.

"Good god—take that blood faucet to the bathroom." I pushed Will to standing. Leading Jonas by the elbow, Will helped them edge their way out.

As I watched them go, my group was called. I took a deep breath and trotted up on stage. Unfortunately, Crotch-grabber and Finger-flipper stood on either side of me. My weakest aspect of improv next to two sexist body-shamers. Awesome. With the Gildas distracted by their teams and Will and Jonas gone, I looked up for some support from Ben, but his eyes slid past mine.

"Last round," Ben said, looking at his clipboard. "Most high schoolers don't play this game because it involves . . . a bar-going culture, but I think you can handle it. It's called 185."

"We play it!" Hanna and Paloma's group shouted.

"You do?" Ben asked. "Where are you from?"

"Wisconsin, baby!" Hanna yelled. The rest cheered.

"Ah, well, there you go." Ben smiled.

They mostly missed trying to give each other high fives.

"Okay, it goes like this," Ben continued. "You get a list of occupations from the audience, then the controller doles them out. For the purposes of the audition, we'll skip that part, and I'll just give you the occupations."

"Or I can do that," Dion offered.

"I'll do it," Ben insisted.

Dion shrugged and leaned back against a pillar.

"So, I'll say 'doctors,' for instance. When you're ready, you step forward and say, '185 doctors walk into a bar. The bartender says, "We don't serve doctors here," and the doctors say_____,' and then you insert a pun. Like, 'We only wanted a shot!'"

This line earned Ben some groans and a few laughs. "It's just an example," he said, grinning. "Okay. Got it?"

I nodded, my stomach suddenly home to a kaleidoscope of butterflies.

"Okay. 185 . . . lawyers," Ben called out.

Crotch-grabber stepped up. "185 lawyers walk into a bar. The bartender says, 'We don't serve lawyers here,' and the lawyers say, 'Then how will we pass the *bar* exam?'"

Crotch-grabber smiled, all his teeth showing, seeming pleased by his laugh-to-groan ratio.

Finger-flipper stepped forward. "185 lawyers walk into the bar. The bartender says, 'We don't serve lawyers here,' and the lawyers say, 'Objection!'"

The crowd was warming up now. I started to step out, but

Crotch-grabber stepped in front of me. "...And the lawyers say, 'We'll be brief!'"

I jumped out again, but Finger-flipper cut me off. "And the lawyers say, 'We'll be the judge of that!'"

I was out before Finger-flipper even finished his joke, but Crotch-grabber was already talking. "185 lawyers—"

The crowd began to murmur in response to the tension building between the three of us. Some guy yelled out in a falsetto voice, "Get it, girl!" A bunch of guys laughed.

Now I looked out at the crowd. I spotted Emily and Sirena and Hanna and Paloma, urging me on with their eyes. I bit the inside of my cheek. Crotch-grabber delivered his punchline.

I hesitated. Crotch-grabber and Finger-flipper looked at each other and grinned. One of them turned to me in a sort of courtly bow. The other mirrored him.

I could feel my cheeks flush. My heart was a hammer against my sternum. They'd taken all of the low-hanging-fruit jokes. There weren't any lawyer puns left. I looked to Ben to switch the occupation. It was clearly time. Roger leaned over to Ben, probably to tell him the same thing. But Ben shook his head. He glanced up at me like we were strangers. He clicked his pen and waited.

I stepped forward. The crowd cheered. I searched for Will, but he and Jonas hadn't returned yet.

"185 lawyers walk into a bar," I began.

Jenn, our coach back home, tells us anything can sound like a joke if you sell it like it's a joke.

I increased my volume. "The bartender says—" I racked my brain for lawyer puns: *defendant, prosecutor, bailiff*—"'We don't serve law-yers here,'"—*opening statement, verdict*—"and the lawyers say—"

My brain popped. It was empty. Totally empty.

I backed up. "And the lawyers say—"

"That girls aren't funny," Crotch-grabber muttered only loud enough for everyone on stage to hear. The performers snickered.

I shuddered an exhale, but with my full voice, boomed, "The law-yers say, '*We'd* like a lawyer because we're going to sue you.'"

Next came the last sound any improviser wants to hear: polite applause.

The scene was called, and I was furious. Furious at Ben, at those asshats, and at the three other guys who didn't step forward *at all*. And mostly at myself for going blank up there.

I couldn't just walk out of the Lodge, even though I wanted to. Then they'd win. I sat carefully in my folding chair. Will and Jonas were still gone and, assuming they'd stopped Jonas's nosebleed, were probably making out somewhere. Sirena and Emily were in the next group.

Crotch-grabber and Finger-flipper didn't say anything to me as they took their seats. They didn't have to. They knew they were in my head.

CHAPTER EIGHT

I had to show my face at lunch. The Gildas invited me to sit with their teams, but I sat with Jonas and Will instead because they didn't know about the one-liner disaster. I wanted to be in a space where I could forget it had happened.

The third time Jonas kicked me under the table in an effort to slide his foot next to Will's, however, made me shift into lunch-inhaling mode. Once I disappeared my soup and sandwich, I pulled on my stocking cap and said, "I'm going for a walk. Shake off the morning."

"Team lists are up in an hour, right?" Jonas asked. At my nod, he turned to Will and gave him a secret smile. "Do you want to 'go for a walk,' too?"

I messed up Will's hair as a parting gesture and took the steps two at a time down to the main path. Inhaling the pine scent (and any air, really) as deeply as I could, I turned in the opposite direction from the cabins. Time to explore this place a little.

A couple minutes later, the dirt path narrowed, and the trees grew denser. They were skinny and white and looked almost like birches.

Birds chirped and the wind cooled my skin. I pulled the flannel out of my bag, put it on, and buttoned it up.

You can do this, I told myself. *Improv is your thing. This is where you belong. Maybe you've been coddled too much back home. This is the real world. Time to toughen up.*

I jumped up and down a few times and shook out my hands.

"Hi." A low voice startled me, and I whipped around.

Three guys who looked about my age in matching navy blue T-shirts and khaki cargo shorts smiled back at me.

"Sorry," two of them said.

"We didn't mean to scare you," the one in front continued. He had a warm grin and dark brown skin and big brown eyes for days.

"It's—I'm fine," I stammered, both because of the surprise, and how cute he was. "Just—I, uh—"

"Are you lost?" A white guy behind him popped out. The sun glinted off his braces and his red hair.

"No, I'm—sorry. Um. I'm just thinking. You startled me. You're . . . Boy Scouts? There's a camp nearby, right?"

They nodded. The redhead stepped off the narrow path. "Are you *sure* you're not lost?"

The cute guy smiled. "Don't listen to Murph. He's trying for his orienteering merit badge—"

"And I'm *this* close!" he exclaimed, holding up two fingers an inch apart.

"He's not that close," the cute guy whispered loudly.

My laugh felt different here than it did back at auditions. Freer.

"I'm Zelda," I said. "I'm . . . uh, at improv camp."

They nodded. "We gathered that," Murph said. "You being a girl and all."

I blinked.

"We're *Boy* Scouts," he continued. "No girls. Well, except the nurse. And we *know* her."

"Of course!" I exclaimed. Geez. How stupid was I?

"I'm Jesse," the cute guy said. "That's Ernest Murphy." He pointed at the redhead. "We call him Murph."

"Because naming a kid 'Ernest' is cruel and unusual punishment," Murph said, rolling his eyes.

"I have a great-uncle named Ernest," I countered.

"Is he a hundred years old?"

"Well—"

"Case closed."

Jesse and I caught each other's eyes and grinned.

Murph pointed behind him. "This last guy doesn't matter, so—"

"Hey!" the third guy exclaimed.

Everyone laughed again.

"Ricky." A dark-haired guy with olive skin and glasses reached out and shook my hand. "Sorry." He pointed at the dirt on his hand and tried to wipe it off on his Boy Scout–issued shorts.

"Always picking up rocks, that one." Jesse chuckled.

"And putting them in *my* backpack!" Murph complained.

Ricky just smiled.

"You're off on a hike?" I asked.

"We take this hike over lunch most days," Jesse said, tugging at his backpack straps.

"Gets us out of lunch duty," Murph added.

"Smart," I said. "I love hiking."

"Join us some time," Jesse offered. He caught my eyes again and held them.

"Really?" I blurted. "Is that allowed?"

The others nodded.

"Of course. Two hours up, lunch, one back." Jesse grinned. "You're welcome any time."

"That's awesome!" I said. Suddenly, I didn't feel so cold anymore. "I don't know what the rehearsal schedule is going to be yet, but I'd love a good hike if I'm free . . . It's . . . nice to meet you."

"You, too." Murph reached out and high-fived me. "And, uh, improv camp is back *that* way," he pointed.

"Thank you," I said solemnly, "I feel very oriented now."

"Doesn't count," Jesse called over his shoulder as they hiked on.

"It does!" Murph protested. "Ricky?"

Ricky unzipped the side pouch of Murph's backpack and inserted a rock.

"Ricky!"

Their boots thumped on the path, and their voices faded away. The birds and the breeze replaced them. I stared up into the trees.

It's just improv, I told myself. *It's not brain surgery . . . or orienteering.* I smiled. *You can do this.*

My name was second from the top. On the Varsity list. With Ben as my coach.

"See? I told you. I knew you'd make it!" Hanna exclaimed, leading me away from the bulletin board in the Main Lodge. "What did I say? I mean, I'm funny, but *you*? You're *really* funny."

I was still speechless.

"That one flub was nothing compared to the rest of your morning," Sirena assured me, joining us as we pulled further away from the mob of people crowding the lists. "Right, Emily?"

But Emily was close to tears. "We're not together," she said to Sirena.

My eyes widened at her reaction. I mean, I knew everything was a little bit harder for Emily, but still—she was going to *cry* because she and Sirena weren't on the same team?

But Sirena was clearly very used to all of Emily's big feelings. She took her hands. "Hey," she said.

Emily looked at her shoes.

"*Hey,*" Sirena said gently. Emily's eyes met hers. "We're both on JV." Sirena smiled. "I bet we'll practice together sometimes. And you've got Hanna."

"*Yeah*, you do," Hanna said. "And as I have well established by now, I am a *very nice person*." Hanna flung an arm around Emily's shoulders, but with Emily so much shorter than her, it was more like Hanna's armpit resting on Emily's head. "We're the Elsas, okay?"

"Okay . . ."

Hanna threw her other arm around Sirena. "Don't worry. Em an I are going to build an ice castle to protect us from idiots. It's going to be great."

As I trailed behind the three of them making their way toward the front door of the Lodge, I tried to imagine being in Sirena's shoes. Would I be so willing to acknowledge Emily's feelings as she always was? My family was comfortable with a lot of emotions, but this wide-open vulnerability? We didn't really do that. You pushed that serious stuff down. Made it into a joke.

Maybe that's why Dad had never told me how dark things had gotten for him when Will was a baby. Or why Will hadn't told me he liked Jonas. I caught the screen door to keep it from slamming into me and watched Sirena and Emily find seats on a bench together on the porch. Maybe they were onto something.

"You're funny and smart, Emily. You're going to be fine," Sirena promised.

"Okay." Emily nodded little nods.

"And you've also got Jonas," I added, finding my voice. "He's my brother's . . . friend." *Almost slipped there.* "My brother's and my friend. He's maybe not quite as nice as Hanna . . ." I grinned at her.

"Is anyone?" Hanna wondered, peering at the sky.

"But still super nice," I assured Emily.

Paloma threw open the screen door and marched up to us, handing everyone a schedule. "We start rehearsal right away. Come on." She gestured for us to come inside, and we followed her back into the Lodge. "Congratulations, Zelda. You kicked so much ass this morning. You totally deserve it!" Paloma gave me a high five as we all circled up by the stage.

"Thank you!" I shook my head. "I still can't quite believe it. And hey—you and Sirena are with my brother, Will. Give him hell for me."

Paloma nodded. "Done." Her forward trajectory halted upon seeing Emily's face. "Are you crying?" She turned to Sirena, concerned. "Is she crying?"

Emily shook her head. "No. I'm fine. I promise. Just surprised. I hadn't—I didn't prepare myself for—I don't know why I assumed—"

"We're fine." Sirena tucked an arm around her.

"Okay." Paloma looked unconvinced. "Because there can be crying in Gilda Radner, but if these guys are going to take you seriously, there can't be crying in improv."

"I think that's baseball," I joked.

"True. Also, improv." She stared at Emily. "You *sure* you're okay?"

Emily nodded, fiddling with the cuff of her shirt.

I squeezed her shoulder. "Would this have been a moment for the *Pacific Coast Whale Sounds* CD?"

Emily coughed on a laugh. "Yes." She flashed a small smile at Sirena who pulled her into a hug.

"Youuuuu're so braaaaaaave," Sirena said, imitating a whale.

Emily laughed and hugged Sirena tighter. She let out a slow, deep breath. Then she let Sirena go. "I'll be fine," she assured us.

Paloma tilted her head. "Good." She turned to me. "I'm glad it's you, Zelda."

I opened my mouth to ask her what she meant, but Roger and Dion whistled and waved for their JV teams to follow them. The Gildas dispersed just as Will and Jonas ran in from opposite doors. Seriously. Who did they think they were fooling?

They stared at the list on the bulletin board. Seeing they were on opposite teams, they glanced at each other, then down, then back, then both folded their arms awkwardly. I wished they could turn to one another for comfort like the girls did. But instead, Will and Jonas just exchanged shy smiles of disappointment and trotted off in opposite directions.

With the JV teams gone, I looked around the dining/stage area at who was left: seven guys who had done really well at the audition—two guys who looked black, and five guys who were probably white. Then my stomach dropped. Two of the white guys were Crotch-grabber and Finger-flipper.

"Hey, *counselor*," Crotch-grabber said, sauntering up to me. "Get it? Counselor? Cuz camp? And cuz you're a lawyer?"

I grimaced. "Got it. But if you have to explain your joke, then it's not a very good joke."

"Whoa! Kitty wants to fight!" Finger-flipper made a meow sound and clawed the air, crossing over to us.

I frowned. I was just standing up for myself. Plus, Crotch-grabber had started it. Wasn't *he* the—

Ben clapped his hands, and everyone turned to give him their attention. "Congratulations and welcome to Varsity."

The team whooped and hollered.

"As you know, my name is Ben Porter—"

More whoops and hollers.

Ben nodded and smiled. "And in addition to teaching and performing at UCB, as well as the film and television I've been doing in LA, I've had the great privilege to study with Marcus Holland right here at RMTA."

Clearly a bunch of these guys had also studied with this Marcus Holland person because they stomped their feet and hollered even louder at the mention of his name.

Ben held up his hands to quiet them. "He was a successful stand-up comedian for more than twenty years, was a coach here for ten more, and taught me everything I know about improv. In his retirement, I am honored to take his spot as the Varsity coach, and my hope is to transmit his improv wisdom to you."

I looked around at the faces next to me: determined, fearless. I smiled.

"So, lots of work to do," Ben said, hopping off the stage, "and no time to waste. Let's get started with the warm-up version of What Are You Doing?"

He strode through the room grouping people up.

"Are we all going to introduce ourselves?" I asked Ben when he paired me with a pale guy with short brown hair and extra-large ears.

Ben's eyes were glued to his clipboard. "Everyone else already knows each other." His eyes flicked around the room and he gestured at each of the pairs. "Brandon and Xander are over by the window—" That was Crotch-grabber and Finger-flipper to me. "There's Cade and Donovan—" A big white guy with scrubby facial hair who looked closer to thirty than eighteen pretended to mow a lawn as his partner, a light-skinned black guy with chin acne, beautifully mimed shooting an arrow into the sky. "And then Trey"—he pointed at a round guy with dark brown skin miming lifting something heavy over his head—"and the other Jake." A short, muscular white guy pursed his lips and fanned himself.

Ben clapped a hand on my partner's shoulder. "And this Jake can introduce himself."

Ben walked away, and I tried to exchange a look of, "Isn't this a little weird?" with my partner, but he didn't meet my eye. In fact, if I was being paranoid, he didn't seem terribly excited to be paired with me at all.

"Hi, Jake. I'm Zelda," I said and smiled.

"Hi," he said, nodding at me.

"How many years have you been coming here?" I asked.

"This is my third. Second on Varsity. I had Marcus as a coach last year."

"Oh, cool. He was a big deal, huh?"

"Yeah. He really loved Ben. What are you doing?"

For a second, I thought he was challenging my asking him questions. Then I realized he had already started the game. So much for team building. "Uh, okay . . . rowing a boat."

He began to mime rowing a boat.

"What are you doing?" I asked.

"Painting a picture," he responded, still rowing the boat.

I mimed dipping a paint brush onto my palette. "Ah, the lilies this time of year!" I cooed in a terrible French accent.

"No," Ben stepped in. "There's no talking in What Are You Doing? It's about listening and space work."

"Oh," I stammered, "O-okay. It's just that I was taught—"

"The high school version talks," he cut me off. "But I'm training you to be professionals."

I nodded and shook out my hands. "Okay. Got it."

I watched him stride over to another pair of actors without a second glance in my direction.

Will had been totally wrong thinking Ben was flirting with me at dinner last night. He was basically pretending we'd never met. Or maybe meeting me was so unimportant that he wasn't pretending— he just didn't remember.

"Hey—what are you doing?" Jake asked.

What was I doing indeed.

Three hours later, I was flabbergasted. We'd worked on voice development. We'd worked on building characters through movement. We'd worked on miming objects and handing them off to one another. And every time I thought I knew how a structure worked or the purpose of an activity, Ben had shut me down. Now we were on to scene work.

"No," Ben commanded me. "You've done three scenes in a row, and you've assumed a relationship each time. You can't *always* know who your scene partner is."

"Really?" I asked. *Make statements and assumptions* was one of Jane Lloyd's rules, and this was *her* camp. Plus, that idea had been hammered into me back home. Assume the relationship. Start the scene in the middle.

"Really," he said. "It's a crutch."

A crutch? It just seemed like common sense. When your characters already know each other, you don't have to waste time with introductions. You just cut to the chase of what the scene's about. Plus, I had seen him do it himself last night when he called on Fredrickson.

". . . Okay," I said, frowning. "Start again?"

He nodded. "Your suggestion is fast food."

The other Jake and I cleared to neutral and began again.

I stepped out onto the stage and mimed a counter, wiping it down.

Jake 2 stayed in the wings, frowning.

I called him on, offering, "Can I help you, sir?"

He didn't move.

Figuring that he must not know what I was doing, I wiped the counter again and turned to the "grill" and flipped a burger to give him some more information. *Make active choices.* Still nothing. "Guess I was hallucinating," I said, trying to justify his unresponsiveness. "Maybe a customer will come in soon."

If Jake 2 hadn't figured out that I had established a fast-food counter and was a fast-food employee after seeing my space work and getting the suggestion "fast food" from Ben, I wasn't sure what else to do to help him.

"No." Ben. "You're not giving Jake the opportunity to create his reality. You've decided for him."

Was I in an alternate improv universe? What did Ben want me to do?

Jake 2 was frowning. He wasn't moving.

"Uh . . . he seemed to need some help," I said, trying to be gracious.

"Her space work was confusing," Jake 2 complained.

My space work was—

"Well, then." I tried to smile. "You can come on stage and *tell* me what I'm doing," I said. "I'm sorry if it wasn't clear to you, but if you don't come into the scene, then it's my job to establish—"

"NO." Guess who? "Improv is give and take, Ellie."

Ellie? Who was Ellie? I looked around. Did he mean *me*? By the time I realized he was shortening "Zelda" to "Ellie" of his own volition, he was well into a lecture about me being a "taker" and not a "giver."

"Also," he continued, "I am the coach. Don't give your fellow improvisers notes."

I stood agape on stage, my cheeks blazing. "Sorry," I said finally. It seemed to be what he was waiting for.

"Again." He clicked his pen. "From the top."

CHAPTER NINE

I had to find Will.

I stuck my head in Bill Murray, but it was empty. Then I made a beeline for Jonas's cabin, Dan Aykroyd, but it had been vacated as well. Seriously. How did anyone find anyone before texting? Did our ancestors just wander around for days looking for each other?

I drummed my fingers against the Dan Aykroyd doorjamb. I needed Will. I needed to be reminded why I was putting myself through this. I needed to talk to someone who believed in me.

Hoping Will was looking for me in Gilda Radner, I took off toward my cabin. But as I rounded Dan Aykroyd, I plowed straight into Ben.

"Whoa, there," he said like he was a cowboy, and I was his runaway horse.

My face flushed, and I stumbled back. He was the last person I wanted to run into—literally or figuratively.

"I'm glad I found you," his warm voice rumbled. "Let's take a little walk."

"I'm looking for my brother, actually," I said, flashing him a dismissive smile.

"JV's not here. They're at Boy Scout camp doing high ropes. Team building."

I sighed.

"Come on. It's a beautiful day. Keep me company." This sweet, charming Ben was completely different from who he'd been at rehearsal. "Just a quick walk. What else do you have to do?"

I shrugged. "Wash my hair? Re-lace my hiking boots? Take a chipmunk census?" I bit the inside of my cheek. I could be funny *now*? Where had that been during rehearsal?

"The latest chipmunk census was just filed last week."

I closed my eyes and shook my head.

"Ten minutes," he cooed. "Tops."

I took one more look around, hoping that I'd see Will returning from high ropes. Then I did a quick calculation. If I refused to go with Ben at this point, I'd come across like a baby who couldn't handle a Varsity rehearsal. Not a great first impression. So even though I wasn't in the mood for a "Chin up, kiddo, you're really talented, but you just need guidance" speech, I reluctantly fell into step beside him.

His flip-flops and my Chaco sandals padded on the dirt path.

"Tough rehearsal," he said, pushing up his white long sleeves.

I nodded. Here it came.

"But you've got a lot of talent."

Predictable. I made a noncommittal sound and ducked under a pine bough.

"It just needs molding."

Did someone release a how-to book for these speeches? I rolled my eyes.

"Hey." He took my arm and stopped me. "Look at me."

I sighed and did as I was told.

"You. Are *bursting* with talent. It's really normal, what happened today. You've only been on a high school team with gentle, high school rules. You just have to toughen up a little." He squeezed my arm then released it.

I grabbed my elbow. It was what I had told myself earlier in the day. But it didn't make me feel any better.

"Give me another day or two and you're not going to believe how much stronger of a performer you'll be. I promise. Remember, I teach and perform at UCB. Plus, I had Marcus as my coach for years. He's a genius. He throws off the rules of improv that weaken a performer and just goes rogue out there. It's exhilarating. Trust me—I know what I'm talking about."

He had me there. What did I have? A decades-old book on improv? My coach, Jenn, back home? Sure, she'd done improv in college and had performed at HUGE Improv Theater in Minneapolis, but as great as HUGE was, it still didn't have the clout that Upright Citizens Brigade did. Plus, he'd been so great last night in the show— he'd run circles around everyone else. Maybe it was time to set aside my ego and just trust him.

He must have seen something shift in me because he said, "Come on. I want to show you someplace cool I bet you haven't found yet."

"I . . . I think I just want to be alone for a while."

"Look, you have nothing to be embarrassed about. And I promise we won't talk about improv. I just want to show you something I think you'll like."

Being with him was a constant reminder of all of my missteps this afternoon. I couldn't figure out a way to gracefully extract myself, though, so I nodded, following him down a narrowing path that made a sharp turn behind a bush I probably wouldn't have noticed on my own.

He didn't say anything for ten more minutes as he made seemingly random turns right and left.

He'd better not try to kill me, I thought. *Because I am never finding my way out of here by myself.*

"Okay, close your eyes."

"Close my eyes? You'd better be showing me like a freaking hidden Niagara Falls or something."

Ben barked a laugh. "It's not Niagara Falls," he said, "but it's still pretty cool. Come on."

I grudgingly squeezed my eyes shut and let him lead me around one last corner. When he told me to open them, I gasped. A slow creek meandered through the clearing and thousands of tiny flowers dotted the wild grasses. A cliff formed a wall to one side. It looked like one of those nature paintings they turn into puzzles that grandmas buy. I could feel myself softening toward him as he led me up onto a flat part of the cliff ten or so feet above the ground.

"This. Is my place," he said, sitting and stretching his legs out in front of him. He gestured like a waiter. "Ta-da!"

My heart was still beating fast from the climb. I tried to take in a slow, deep breath to calm it down as I sat, crossing my legs underneath me. "It's . . . beautiful."

We sat in silence for a while, watching the birds and chipmunks and listening to the creek. I tried to focus on the nature, but I was very aware of the warmth of his body sitting next to mine.

"Did you know that aspen trees are all one huge organism?" he asked.

I was confused. "Aspen trees?"

He pointed. "The white ones."

"Oh," I said. "The ones that look like birch trees."

He nodded. "All the aspens are connected by their root system underground. Cool, huh?"

I smiled. "Like a metaphor for improv."

He turned to me with a quirked eyebrow. "I thought we weren't talking about improv."

I smiled. "Improv *theory*. Not specifics. I'll allow it."

"Okay, your honor." He folded his arms. "How are aspens like improv?"

"Well, their root systems are all connected . . . Like, no one person can stand on their own in improv. They need the team. The interconnectedness of the root system. Trust. Unity."

He just sort of nodded vaguely.

"Sorry." I smiled, feeling like I was losing him. It was Zelda Fitzgerald all over again. "English teacher father, Theater professor mother. They see symbols everywhere . . . And now, it seems, so do I."

We were quiet again.

Seriously. Could this afternoon get any more embarrassing?

He stretched his arms into the sky and then leaned back on his elbows. I pretended to stare at the creek, but I was watching him out of the corner of my eye. With that blond hair and sculpted body, he looked like he belonged in an REI catalogue. Well, except for those flip-flops. Beach shoes on a mountain? Come on.

I swiftly forgot my criticism when a breeze picked up and blew his hair around. He swept it out of his eyes.

My own eyes felt strained from the work of staring out of their corners.

I shook my head. What was I doing? Sure, Ben was definitely good-looking. But he was my coach. Plus, guys weren't into me like that. There wasn't a universe in which this older, super-hot guy was going to be into me. Especially not after this embarrassing afternoon.

Still . . . he had taken me alone to this very pretty spot. With flowers and trees and cliffs and a freaking water feature. He'd taken me to *his* spot.

I sighed. Making out with a hot older guy in a remote, gorgeous, secret nature spot was something that happened to other people. Hiking with a hot older guy to a remote, gorgeous, secret nature spot out of pity to make me feel better about my disastrous afternoon rehearsal was much more along the lines of something that happened to *me*.

So maybe I should make the most of it.

"You say 'no' a lot as a coach," I said, still staring out at the creek.

"Well, today I did," he said, "but again—it's super normal early on."

"Okay. But a lot of what you say seems . . . opposite of what I've been taught. And the opposite of Jane Lloyd's book. I mean, she helped found this camp. 'Make assumptions.' 'Trust your scene partner.' 'Say yes.'"

"Marcus says those rules are just there to help beginners," he said, sitting up. "I'm trying to prepare you for the professional world. I'm taking away your safety net so you develop a heightened awareness. So you can be more aggressive. By the time I'm done with you, you're going to be on fire."

I rubbed the worry lines that had emerged on my forehead with my index finger.

"You want to get better, right, Ellie? You want to be as great as I know you can be? You want *Saturday Night Live*?"

I hesitated. How did he know that was my dream? Or was it just everyone's dream around here?

Scooting closer to me, he wrapped an arm around my shoulder. His scent—something spicy mixed with fresh air and clean sweat— overwhelmed my senses.

I inhaled him again. If this was what feeling sorry for me smelled like, then I'd take all the personal disasters, thank you.

We sat there for what felt like forever, his arm draped over my shoulder. It seemed much more intimate than a coach/performer gesture, but I had been me long enough to know better.

But then he said, "Turn around. I made you tense today. Let me loosen you up."

I hesitated. *Coaches give back rubs?*

"Come on, Ellie. Relax." The corners of his mouth turned up in a way that made me feel I was being ridiculous. "Give me those stiff improv shoulders."

What was I going to do? If I refused, it might make him feel like I didn't trust him, and improv is supposed to be about trust. So, I turned.

I groaned as he began working the knots in my shoulders.

"Holy—"

His laughter drowned out my cursing.

"Hey," I managed. "Why do you keep calling me Ellie?"

He stopped rubbing my back.

"Oh, you can't massage *and* talk? I pick massage," I joked.

He laughed again. "I can do both." He resumed his work on my lower back. I froze when he lifted the bottom of my shirt to access a spot near my spine. Seconds later, though, the warm pads of his fingers on my bare skin tripped something new in my nervous system, and silently, I urged him on. I became buried in the feeling of wanting his hand to touch me everywhere.

"Ellie suits you," he murmured. "I like calling you Ellie."

Before I could fully consider whether or not *I* liked him calling me Ellie, he placed his warm, open palm against my cool, bare lower back.

"Huh..." I managed, all of my focus on the skin his hand was massaging.

He exhaled. "You are...," he began, softly.

Suddenly, he climbed to his feet.

My body felt cold where he'd abandoned it.

"Time to head back," he said loudly, fully breaking the spell of the moment.

I was incapable of speech the rest of the way back to camp. I was what? I was... I tried to fill in the blank. Why hadn't he finished his sentence? If it was a normal, improv coach to improviser thing to say, he just would have said it, right? *You are funny; you are going to be okay; you are learning* . . . But he didn't think he should be saying whatever it was. That was why he'd cut himself off, right?

You are . . .

Was this what it felt like to be Will and Jonas? Or Sirena and Emily? Was Ben saying he liked me? Nothing even remotely close to this had ever happened to me before. I was relying on books by Rainbow Rowell and Nicola Yoon and Maurene Goo and on movies like *The Princess Bride* and *Love, Simon* and . . . that was it, actually. Just on books and movies.

What else could make him cut himself off?

I followed him wordlessly for ten minutes, but before the last turn, his feet stopped and so did my heart.

"Don't . . ." He turned to face me and put a hand on my shoulder. Then he looked down, his thumb slowly tracing a path back and forth. "Don't, uh, tell anyone about today. We don't want anyone to say the only reason you're on Varsity is because . . . well . . ."

My body stiffened. "Is what?"

He chuckled and dropped his hand. "You know."

Is because he likes me?

"It isn't, though, right?" I asked, avoiding his eyes and biting my thumbnail.

"God, no. But you know how guys can be. I'm just trying to protect you. Give me a couple minutes before you follow, okay?"

He took my other hand, squeezed it, and left, leaving me to wonder what the holy freaking hell had just happened.

CHAPTER TEN

In trying to make sense of my day, I wandered. There were probably trees and paths and flowers and buildings and people, but I was distracted by the questions in my head.

Did Ben like me? Or was he just looking out for me?

Either way, he was in my corner . . . right? I hadn't just made the team because of a quota? Because I was a girl?

I wandered so much, by the time I decided to stop, dinner was over.

When I opened the door to Gilda Radner, there was a party going on. By the looks of it, both JV teams were squeezed inside.

"Zelda!" Emily shouted. "You were right! Jonas is so nice! And Hanna is so nice! And everyone is *so*—"

Beyoncé was blaring loudly, and I lost Emily's last word. "What?"

"NICE!" she yelled near my face. "WOOOO!"

"Typical white girl," Jonas smiled, sidling up next to me as Emily danced away. "Can't handle her Beyoncé."

I laughed. "It's so good to see her feeling more comfortable."

He nodded as she twirled to the music. "Yeah. Today was really good for her, I think."

My eyes sought Will's as he reached for Jonas. "Be happy for us, Z, because, baby, we are *out*!" Will shouted and the cabin cheered.

Grinning, I sought Sirena's eyes, and she grinned back at me.

"Kiss!" someone yelled.

"Not *that* out!" Will shouted again. Everyone hooted. He took my hands. "Dance, Z!"

I shrugged and joined in.

It still hurt to breathe, but the music sort of made me forget that for a while. As I danced, I tried to push all thoughts of Ben and Varsity out of my brain, focusing on these people, this joy. *Be in the moment.*

Between songs, Paloma shouted, "Water break, people!"

Hanna put her hands up in protest. "Come on, Mom!"

"You'll thank me when no one gets altitude sickness!" she retorted.

"But we won't thank you when we get up five times in the night to pee!" Hanna said.

We laughed as Hanna turned down the music and people flopped on beds, mainlining water.

"Hey!" a JV guy exclaimed, jumping up from the bed he'd just sat on. "What's this?" He held up a flat, square, plastic case.

"Our *Pacific Coast Whale Sounds* CD!" Emily exclaimed. "Where did you find it?"

The guy probably explained, but I watched Emily, who beelined to her suitcase and pulled out the bright yellow Discman. Wordlessly, she slipped the CD inside, then connected a double-ended aux cable to the Bluetooth speakers. Soon, lonely moaning filled the cabin.

Hanna put her hands on her hips. "What circle of hell is this?" she demanded.

"It's peaceful!" Emily and Sirena insisted, but they were already giggling.

As the debate continued about whale sounds (relaxing or slow torture?), I clambered up on my bunk and gestured for Will and Jonas to join me. They followed, settled in next to each other, and leaned against the window.

"So . . ." I looked around at the groups of twos and threes alternately hydrating and laughing. "What—how was—"

"Z." Will grinned. "We had the best day. These are the BEST PEOPLE!"

Half the cabin cheered. The other half was busy adding their two cents about the CD. "It sounds like the whales are lonely!" "It sounds like drowning cows." "It sounds like trombones are being *murdered*."

Ignoring the debate raging below us, Jonas tilted his head back on the window and closed his eyes. "Dion and Roger are amazing."

"Yeah, we basically spent the whole day together," Will agreed. "It was all trust building, all day."

That. That was what I was used to. Team building. Improv through trust.

"Sounds awesome," I said, reflecting on my own day, feeling my cheeks redden all over again. I put my hands on them in a vain attempt to cool them down.

"It was." Jonas shifted on the bunk. "They brought everyone together and turned off all the lights and we sat back-to-back in a circle. Each one of us was invited to say something that was true."

"At first it was stuff like, 'I'm wearing a red shirt,'" Will said, "but then it got deep. Someone said—" He looked at Jonas. "Oh, I'm not—I really shouldn't say. It was all supposed to stay in the room."

I nodded, understanding. That's how those things go. But it didn't stop me from feeling a little left out.

"Anyway." Will gestured at Jonas. "You tell this part."

My eyes widened. Telling a story with Will was like combat—you fought for control. Jonas was softening him. I smiled.

Jonas did, too. "People were dropping some serious secrets, and as I sat there, it just felt like the secret of Will and me . . . didn't need to be one. Especially once we realized Sirena and Emily were together. I reached over for Will's hand in the dark. And he let me take it. And then he squeezed mine. And then—"

Will's face started to redden. "I didn't quite realize we were going to go through the entire play-by-play here."

I laughed. I liked seeing this vulnerable side of Will.

Jonas elbowed him. "It's part of the story. You said I should tell this part of—"

"I know, I know." Will elbowed him back. "Go ahead."

He smiled. "And then when it was my turn, I said, 'Will is my boyfriend.'"

I grinned.

"And I was next," Will said, "and I said, 'I'm Will.'"

I laughed and wrapped my arms around both of them in a messy hug. "Did everyone laugh?"

They beamed.

"Yeah," Will said. "The good kind."

"And after," Jonas continued, "it was . . . normal. It feels so good to not have to hide this part of who I am."

"I'm so glad you felt safe," I said, laying my head on Will's shoulder.

"Me, too," Jonas agreed, laying his head on Will's other shoulder.

"What about you?" Will asked, poking my leg.

It was as if a cold rain blew in.

"Well . . ." I lifted my head. I wasn't sure what to say. Will had already been shocked about my alleged flirting yesterday. What would he think about Ben's hand on my naked back? About our walk? About my promise not to tell anyone? Earlier, I'd been desperate to confess all of my embarrassment, but now it seemed so wrapped up in the walk with Ben. I wasn't ready to be lectured about a thing I wasn't even sure was a thing.

"It was very . . . serious. Ben is unlike any coach I've ever had. Intense. He says he's preparing us for the professional world. And seeing as how he's been teaching and taking classes at UCB, not to mention the film and TV he's done, he must know what he's talking about."

"Oh." Will frowned. "But you're having fun, right?"

Fun? Uh . . . "It's . . . it's good," I said. "It's going to be good."

Normally, Will would never let me get away with that level of evasiveness, but he was distracted by Jonas, whose eyes were suggesting things to him a sister did not need to see.

"Those whales moaning kind of sound like something else to me," Jonas said, raising his eyebrows at Will.

"Go. Get out of here. No one wants your love!" I tried to push them off my bunk.

Will laughed and kicked me a little but climbed down with Jonas. Hand-in-hand, they tried to sneak out of the cabin, but Emily spotted them. "I love you two together!" she shouted. Sirena slid an arm around her waist and kissed her cheek, and she giggled. "Go kiss under the moon!"

Will shook his head, and Jonas grinned behind his hand as they darted out of the cabin.

"Zelda," Hanna demanded, hands on her hips. "Your brother is a gay Korean American almost-twin, and you didn't tell us? What other interesting secrets do you have? What else are you hiding?"

She had no idea.

CHAPTER ELEVEN

"Okay." Ben tapped his pen on his clipboard. "We'll run a couple Montages, then we'll split off and write cold open sketches based on ideas we generate from the scenes. The Pauls told me this morning that Michael Edelheit is coming from Second City Toronto, and he's specifically on the lookout for fresh writer-performers. Play your cards right, and it could be you with his business card in your hand. Got it?"

Now *this* was more my speed. I love improv, but I might love comedy writing a tiny bit more. And a Second City business card in my hand? I'd say *yes, and* to that. I smiled at Ben, but he clicked his pen and scribbled something on his clipboard.

Part of me hoped he'd be a little kinder to me after our walk yesterday, but today it was business as usual. At least I knew that under his facade, he thought I was worth something.

"Let's get started," Ben said, sitting backward on one of the folding chairs. "Somebody get a suggestion."

Xander jumped forward and clapped his hands once. "For this next series of scenes, I need a suggestion for something you hate to do."

"Go to the doctor," Ben said.

As Xander cleared to neutral, I mimed slinging a stethoscope around my neck and hurried on stage. "Nurse?" I called out. "Send in my next patient."

No one responded as my nurse, but Xander mimed opening my office door. "Doctor? Oh! Not my usual doctor!" He gave me a slow smile. "Well, hello there, lady doctor. How lucky am I? Should I drop my pants now, or now *and* later?"

My stomach twisted—how was I going to get around this?

Perform at the peak of your intellect.

Squinting, I tried to stay in the scene in character. "Lady doctor? I guess that makes you my gentleman patient." I looked down at his "chart." "Ah! I see you've had a series of brain injuries that make you say inappropriate things. Well. We should get you some heavy drugs to suppress that."

Some chuckles rolled in from the wings.

"Who do I have to talk to," Xander said, ignoring me, "to make sure I get you every time?" He circled around me. "Because I need a *full* checkup."

"Well!" I said, my throat tightening. "Well, yes, see, the thing is, I'm really only an intern, so I don't do full checkups. I'll have to get my supervisor!" I skittered off stage and Xander moaned in disappointment.

That was only the beginning.

The next time I was in a scene, there were some allusions to my character being a porn actress, but it wasn't the focus of the scene, so I let it go.

Then, four scenes in a row, I was basically relegated to being a sexy secretary.

"Okay, one more before we break for writing," Ben said.

Determined to drive this Montage in a more pro-Zelda direction, I hopped up on stage to take charge. "Ben, are you going to give us a suggestion for this one, or can I—"

Brandon stepped in front of me. "You're walking through the woods and you trip over something. What is it?"

Ben barked out a laugh. "Good hustle, Brandon. Okay . . . you trip over a dead body." Brandon turned and gestured for me to join him.

I hesitated for a split second, but Jane Lloyd's voice was in my head: *Say yes*. So, I joined him.

He pointed at the floor.

Ah. I was the dead body. Well, at least this way I wouldn't have to talk to him.

I lay on the floor, arms and legs akimbo. I heard Brandon clear back to neutral, then clomp on stage.

"Whoa! A dead hooker!"

Everyone burst out laughing. My patience bubbled over, and I turned my head toward Ben. "Seriously?"

"*Not* a dead hooker!" Brandon jumped back.

Ben shrugged. "Don't deny the reality that's been established," he said. "No matter what."

"Even if it makes me uncomfortable?" I asked, squinting at him.

"Hey, baby, don't be ashamed. It's the world's oldest profession!" Brandon said, still in the scene. "What will you do for . . ." He mimed looking through his wallet. "Twenty bucks?"

"I'll kick you in the shins for free," I said, *not* in the scene.

"Kitty got claws!" Xander meowed.

"What is wrong with you?" I asked. "Every time I stand up for myself, you do that. I'm a cat? Is that what you're saying?"

"This hooker is feisty." Brandon mimed lifting his backpack on his back.

And damn him, his space work was excellent.

"Ben," I said, sitting up, "it just feels like over and over we keep doing scenes where I'm—"

"Stay in the scene, Ellie."

"But—that doctor scene—"

"Ellie. Quit being so sensitive and stay. In. The scene."

"But—"

"Ellie. If I were Marcus, you'd be done for the day. You are a hooker in the woods. Quit being a child."

A child? I pursed my lips. "Fine." I climbed to my feet, turned to Brandon, and reminded myself to *Trust your scene partner.*

Brandon smirked and raised one of his eyebrows, daring me to fight back.

I bit my lip. While I believed in Jane Lloyd's rules, *both* scene partners had to trust each other in order for the scene to win. I didn't see how this was going to work if the only person trusting their partner was me.

Still—Jane had never let me down before.

I took a deep breath. "I'm a hooker in the woods," I said in a monotone voice.

"Well, well, well," Brandon drawled, looking me up and down. "Isn't this my lucky day?"

I sighed.

"Since I'm low on cash, will you take Venmo?"

Everyone laughed.

Xander hiked on stage, joining us.

"Oh, look! A woods hooker! I think I'd like to see a dance," Xander said. "I'll be the pole."

Perform at the peak of your intellect. "I'm . . . I've got a broken arm," I said. "And there's no signal out here, so no Venmo, either. If you don't have cash, there's no deal. And I'm expensive. Five thousand dollars minimum." I turned to Brandon. "As you've already established there's only twenty bucks in your wallet," I grimaced and nodded at Xander, "and I can tell *you* aren't carrying a wallet, I guess we're out of luck." I shrugged. "By the way, I also garden. Care to see what I've done with the squash?"

"I'm more interested in what you've got going on with the cantaloupes," Brandon said and sidled up next to me.

Stepping back to avoid him, I knocked into Xander, who wrapped his arms around me. "Me, too," he cooed. "I love a good pair of cantaloupes."

I struggled my way out of his grip and turned around to face them.

"Hey!" Xander snapped. "This hooker's a lot of trouble."

My breathing was ragged. I had never felt less safe on stage. So even though I knew Jane Lloyd would not approve, I couldn't see another way out: I mimed pulling out a gun. "Soon you'll be dead. How's that for too much trouble?" I asked and promptly shot Brandon and Xander in the chest.

They remained standing.

"Ellie, we don't kill off our scene partners," Ben reprimanded me.

"Oh, that's not a crutch? A high school rule?" I asked, dangling my mimed gun off my pointer finger. "I know we don't deny reality. You told me that. And yet I shot these asshats, and they're still standing." I mimed flipping the gun around on my finger and shot them again. "Die, asshats."

They folded their arms. "Bulletproof jackets," Brandon said with a smug look.

Everyone guffawed.

I mimed pulling back on my gun to reload it. "Heads don't have bulletproof vests," I said and aimed.

"Okay, okay, let's cut the scene. Clearly, you're very emotional, Ellie," Ben said.

"*I'm* emotional?"

"Take five, everyone." Ben clapped his hands.

I stood still, stunned by what had just happened as everyone cleared out. One guy said "period," and I just about lost it.

"Put down your weapon, Ellie." Ben smiled as he climbed on stage.

I looked down at the mimed the gun I'd been "holding." Exhaling sharply, I shook out my hand.

"Always set down mimed objects," he said quietly. "Then you'll stay more aware of your space work in general."

I hated to admit it, but that was actually good advice. But I was still mad. I crouched down, picked up the "gun," looked him in the eye, put the whole thing in my mouth, and swallowed it.

He chuckled. "So much fire, little girl."

My eyes bulged. "I am *not* a little girl—"

He put his arm around me, and I hated myself as I melted. Damn his good scent.

"I know you're not . . . Trust me. I just mean you're feisty. But you have to stop taking things like this personally."

"*Personally?*" I pulled away.

"This is what it's like out there," he said, tucking a curl behind my ear. I twitched. "You need to decide if you can play with the big boys or if you're going to run home crying to mama."

I bit my lip and exhaled fire through my nose. "You're saying I'm overreacting."

He shrugged. "They're just playing. They don't really think you're a hooker."

I scoffed. "I know that."

"Just let it go. Let more go. You'll be surprised how not alienating your team—"

"*He* started the hooker scene," I protested.

"And there are lots of guys like Brandon. Are you going to throw a fit every time someone does something like that?"

My mouth fell open. "Uh, yes?"

"Then you're not going to have a long career in improv."

I scoffed. "Are you serious? I have to be willing to be sexy secretaries and hookers to have a career in improv?"

"They're just playing around," he said. "And as a woman, you need to know how to harness your sexuality on stage. Have some fun."

My throat was clogged with questions, the biggest one being, *What if this isn't fun anymore?*

"Look, Ellie. Show these guys you earned your spot on the team.

Get out of your head. You *want* a spot on this team, right? You want to meet Nina Knightley?"

The world stopped spinning on its axis. "Nina Knightley is coming?"

He nodded.

"*Saturday Night Live* Nina Knightley. *Nina on Her Own* Nina Knightley," I clarified.

He nodded again. "It's the thirtieth anniversary of RMTA, so in addition to the reps from iO and UCB and Second City, big-deal alumni are coming back. There's never been more pressure to have an amazing final show. Think of how huge it will be to be on the top team when you meet Nina Knightley."

I bit the side of my thumbnail.

The Jakes came in with beef jerky and topped off water bottles.

"Think about it," Ben said, clapping me on the shoulder. "Can you relax a little for a chance to impress Nina Knightley?"

I sighed. Maybe I *was* overreacting. It was just a scene. Or five. But ultimately, it was small potatoes in the grand scheme of things. I nodded. "Okay." Ben smiled and squeezed my shoulder. The heat where he'd touched me cooled as he walked out into the hall.

I turned to the Jakes, determined to start fresh. "Hey," I said.

"Hey," they muttered.

One of them pushed the other as he was drinking his water, and it spilled on his shorts.

"Dude!" Jake 1 yelled.

"I won't tell anyone you couldn't make it to the bathroom," Jake 2 promised.

And *I* was the child?

Jake 1 squirted water on Jake 2's shorts. "Now I won't tell either."
Jake 1 grinned.

Brandon and the other guys came in.

"Bathroom's right over there." Brandon smirked.

The Jakes squirted water at Brandon.

"Hey!" he yelled. Then he turned to me. "You up for a wet
T-shirt contest?"

I opened my mouth to retort, caught Ben's warning glance as he
walked back into the room, and closed it again.

"Let's get back to those Montages," Ben called out. "Ellie? Do you
have anything you need to say first?"

I knew he was testing me. Did I have the strength to be an adult?
To be on Varsity?

I stared back at him. I wanted this so badly. I had to show them
I was strong.

I shook my head at Ben, pursed my lips in a straight line, and
cleared to neutral.

CHAPTER TWELVE

I tapped my pen on my notebook and shifted my back to find a more comfortable place to lean against the aspen tree. Maybe my sketch could be about a different kind of dead body.

A nonprostitute kind.

Setting: Woods, modern day.
                    MAN 1
    (Putting his pack down)
    Wow! This hike has been crazy!
                    MAN 2
    (Joining him)
    Right? So many...

I chewed on the end of my pen a little. *So many what?* I wondered. *Leaves? Trees? Of course there are trees. Everyone knows the woods have trees.... What might be surprising about being in the woods?*

A little yellow bird landed on the path in front of me. It cocked its head, hopped twice, and then flew away. I took the pen out of my mouth.

MAN 2

(Joining him)
Right? So many different types of birds!
MAN 1
I haven't seen this many birds since...

I closed my eyes. *Does anyone actually care about birds? Do people talk about birds in real life? This is so dumb. It's stilted. It sounds like robots talking.* I shook my head to quiet the editor in my mind. Back home, my coach, Jenn, says there's a time for the editor, but only after the writer has had free reign. *Press on*, I reminded myself, *you can revise later.*

MAN 1

I haven't seen this many birds since we went to the bird-feeder convention.
MAN 2
Holy cow! Is that a dead body?
MAN 1
A dead body? Like a dead bird body? There weren't any of them at the bird-feeder convention. What are we going to do? Do you have a shoebox? We could bury it...
MAN 2
No! A human body!

MAN 1

That's not going to fit in a shoebox.

I sighed and ran my pen off the paper. The bird-feeder convention maybe had potential. But where was this going? What was the point of the scene?

I tore the page out and stuffed it into my bag.

What was a funny kind of dead body? Who could be dead, and we'd be okay with it? I could hear Jenn saying, "Punch up, not down." She means it's funny to make fun of people more powerful than you—not less.

With that in mind, I flipped my notebook to a fresh page and made a list:

Funny Dead Bodies:
1. Not actual dead bodies—just bodies you think are dead and then when they wake up and everyone else freaks out, they're calm and are named Jeff or something.
2. Super-mean substitute teachers . . . Eh. Usually mean substitute teachers are just mean because kids are mean first. Though sometimes they're straight-up jerks. Still. Still feels like punching down.
3. Hitler? That's punching up. Or other things Nazi-adjacent? . . . But what are decades-old Nazi bodies doing undecomposed in the woods?

I shook my head, dropped the notebook and pen, and stood up to stretch. I paced around a little, shaking out my hands. Maybe there was something wrong with the premise. Dead body...What was funny about dead bodies? Suddenly, I imagined my biological father and Will's biological mother scowling at my abandoned list on the ground.

"Come on, Zelda," I muttered, rolling my eyes at my overly dramatic daydream. "It's a comedy sketch. It's not real life." I whirled around, pointed at my notebook, and proclaimed, "Okay, you. Let's do this. No messing around this time."

I settled back against the tree again as I propped the notebook on my knees.

Tap-tap-tap. *Maybe I should just write a palate cleanser. Something non-dead-body-related.*

Tap-tap-tap. *Or maybe I can push the boundaries of the premise.*

Setting: Mount Rushmore, modern day. We hear "Hail to the Chief" play as a group of politicians walk and wave.

Okay. Presidents. What's unexpected for a president? I chewed on my lip.

POLITICIAN 1

Thank you! Thank you! It's so great to see so many of you here today at Mount Rushmore, where we've carved dead presidents' faces into sacred Native American rock face and called it a national park! Please put your hands together for the next president of the United States, Moose MacPhearson!

I threw down my notebook.

I needed to talk to some sane people. I particularly needed to talk to my parents, but they were hiking.

Will was sane and here. He'd be sympathetic to my flailing in the deep end of the hypermasculine pool that was Varsity. But after he warned me about flirting with Ben, I worried he wasn't going to be interested in helping me figure out what Ben's mixed signals meant. Still. . . . Maybe I could just tell Will about the weird dude teammate stuff and omit the weird Ben stuff. Where was JV rehearsing? The Main Lodge?

I reached for my cell to text Will and ask him where he was, but quickly remembered that the Rocky freaking Mountains were a freaking cell phone tower dead zone.

Sighing, I tucked my pen behind my ear and slipped my notebook in my bag. *Make active choices.* It was time to find Will, and the Main Lodge seemed like a good enough place to start looking.

Retracing my steps, I turned down the path that would eventually cross in front of the Main Lodge. As I neared the edge of the woods, someone shouted, "Watch out for the Bludger!" I smiled at the Harry Potter reference, and when I emerged from the trees, 150 guys—probably the Skill-Building teams—were playing the nonflying version of Quidditch in the field in front of the Lodge. There were like eight games going on simultaneously. It felt like everyone was laughing.

My stomach twisted in envy as I watched a short blond guy dressed all in yellow leap over the fence. *He must be the human form of the Snitch,* I mused. He was chased by a much taller guy, giggling and straddling a broomstick. *Sure. And that guy's the Seeker.*

The Snitch zoomed past me and I yelled, "You know where JV is?"

The Seeker was close on his heels. "They're playing Capture the Flag back by the cabins!" he called over his shoulder.

"Thanks!" I said, but my voice was drowned out by the celebratory cheer of the Seeker's team as he tackled the Snitch.

I watched as the whole team barreled after their Seeker, piling on top of him. I tried but failed to imagine Varsity having this much fun together ... but before I could wallow in too much self-pity, I squared my shoulders. *Remember, you're going to meet Nina Knightley.* I forced myself to look away from the Quidditch festivities and turn back toward the cabins.

Nearing Gilda Radner, I heard voices coming from inside, so I picked up speed and threw open the screen door.

"Hi!" I said, eager to be greeted by any familiar face, but hoping against hope Will was there.

Startled, the Pauls stared back at me.

"Hello," Paul DeLuca recovered first.

"Uh, hi," I said again. "What ... what are you doing here?"

"We came to meet your new counselor," Paul Paulsen said, drawing his shaggy eyebrows together into a wooly caterpillar, "although I'm not sure if she's showing up."

"Give her time." Paul DeLuca waved away the concern, but he patted the sweat off his forehead with a folded handkerchief.

"We've been waiting for an hour," Paul Paulsen insisted. "She's not coming."

Paul DeLuca sighed, his girth seeming extra-large squeezed into the small cabin. "We should head back and check the voicemail." He turned toward the door, then changed his mind.

"How are you girls getting along?" he asked, doubling back and peering into my eyes.

"Uh, great," I said. I put a hand on one of the top bunks and patted it. "Yeah, we're good."

Paul DeLuca raised his eyebrows at Paul Paulsen, whose own eyebrow caterpillar seemed confused. Finally, Paul DeLuca turned to me again. "We're really struggling to find a young woman to come up here at such late notice to be your counselor. What if . . ."

"Paul," P2's voice was low and urgent.

Paul DeLuca waved away this concern, too. "I checked the forms. Sirena's eighteen. Technically an adult. Plus, there's only five of them." He gestured around the cabin as if to show how empty it was.

"What about curfew?" P2's lips were thin.

Paul DeLuca turned to me. "Was anyone late for curfew last night?"

I shook my head.

He smiled broadly and turned back to Paul Paulsen. "They're girls! What trouble are girls?"

I made a sound of protest, not sure how I felt. It *seemed* like a compliment, but I found myself frowning.

Paul Paulsen's eyes studied the cabin, then me, and then he sighed. "Lock the door at night, okay?" He pointed a pencil at Paul DeLuca. "We'll keep looking," he said. Then Paul Paulsen turned away and peered through the window. "If Marcus was still here, we'd have a female counselor," he muttered. "He always managed to find one."

Paul DeLuca nodded and caught my eye. "Say. Are you having fun? Making new friends?"

I opened my mouth. Maybe this was who I could talk to about the weird guy dynamic on Varsity.

"Well," I began, raising an eyebrow at P2. "The guys on my team are . . ."

"It's not too often we have a girl on Varsity," Paul DeLuca interrupted me. "It might take them a little bit to get used to the estrogen in the room."

I cocked my head like the yellow bird that had landed on my path. "I—"

"But don't worry." Paul DeLuca clapped a hand on my back. "Ben's got it all under control. Marcus trained him well. Plus, Ben and Laura were really close for a while. He's used to funny girls. Good, good." He filed out of the cabin, P2 close behind.

Before he joined the other Paul, P2 looked back at me. "Please tell us if anyone comes back late."

"They'll be fine!" Paul DeLuca bellowed.

Mouth open, I watched them go. Why did they ask me how things were if they weren't interested in my answer? Clearly, the Pauls were *not* the sane people to talk to.

It's okay. Just plant yourself here and sooner or later, someone is bound to come by. And in the meantime, write.

After I climbed up to my bunk and took out my notebook, I decided that even though traditionally sketches are supposed to be inspired from the scenes we create together, I didn't have to be married to the dead body premise. After that, I managed two or three minutes of a sketch about a sleepwalking bear. As I read it back to myself, the rhythm felt good. The jokes needing punching up, but it was a start.

I flipped over to a fresh sheet of notebook paper when Paloma and Sirena practically fell through the door, gasping for breath.

"Oh my god, they're going to find us!" Sirena hissed to Paloma. Her braids were flying everywhere as she pressed her glasses on her face to keep them from falling off.

"Who?" I asked.

They both screamed.

"Zelda! Geez!" Paloma clapped a hand over her heart.

"I heard a scream from Gilda Radner!" a male voice called from some distance away.

"I'm sorry!" I whispered. "What's going on?"

"Capture the Flag!" Sirena grinned, shaking a blue-and-red square of nylon at me. "And we've captured it!"

"Oh, that's right! That's great! Well, hide!" I exclaimed. "I'll cover for you."

They buried themselves: Paloma under a crumpled-up blanket and Sirena behind the door.

I stayed in my bunk like nothing had happened.

"Got you cornered!" Jonas exclaimed, banging into the cabin.

"Guilty as charged!" I smiled.

Jonas jumped and braced himself against the door frame. "Zelda? What are you doing here?"

"Writing." I tapped my pencil against my notebook. "We were sent off to write cold opens, so I've been reading mine out loud, doing all the voices."

His face fell. "That was *you* screaming?" he asked.

Oh, sweet, earnest Jonas.

I nodded and fixed an innocent look on my face. "Why?"

He flopped down on the bottom bed of the opposite bunk—a foot away from Paloma.

"Capture the Flag," he said. "Dion's team versus Roger's."

I tried not to sigh. "That sounds like fun."

"It is," he agreed. "I'm glad for you that you're on Varsity, but I wish you were with the rest of us."

"Me, too," I said wistfully.

Paloma shifted on the bed and it squeaked.

Jonas's eyes darted around. "But you're . . . uh, good?" he asked.

"Well . . ." Jonas could be my sane person, right? He'd at least smile sympathetically. "They're jerks, actually." I felt lighter saying it out loud. "All of them. Pretty big jerks."

"Really?" Now his eyes were on mine.

I nodded.

"Are you going to quit?"

I opened and closed my mouth.

"You can't quit!" Paloma threw off her blanket. Jonas screamed so loudly, it made Paloma jump. He also fell off the bed onto the floor. I laughed until tears streamed down my face.

"Jonas? Are you okay?" It was Will's voice.

"He's—*"gasp"*—fine!" I was still laughing. "Oh my god, Jonas—the look on your face!"

"I'm sorry!" Paloma said, trying to help Jonas up off the floor. But he was laughing too hard to be moved.

"I'm fine!" Jonas said, waving her away as Will barreled into the cabin. Jonas took my brother's proffered hands and stood. "I'm not sure if I should be pleased or embarrassed that you recognized my scream."

I laughed again. "Pleased, I think," I said. "Clearly, he loves you."

"Z—" Will shot me a look.

"Oh come on, Will." I threw my legs over the side of the mattress. "You are on opposite sides of Capture the Flag and you revealed your position to check on him. You. Mr. Competitive. Mr. Monopoly-Money-Launderer. Mr. What-Battleship-Up-My-Sleeve? You *revealed your position.*" I shrugged. "Only two explanations—you're sabotaging the game so you don't have to run at this altitude, or you love him."

"You were dead before, and now you're going to be double dead," Will moaned, closing his eyes and covering them with both hands.

Jonas removed Will's hands from his eyes and gave him a soft smile. "I'm glad that you're here."

Will was a puddle.

Paloma turned to me, arms folded. "Zelda, promise me you won't quit," she said.

Now it was my turn to moan. "Why?"

Will still held Jonas's hand, but he frowned at me. "Quit what?"

I made a disgruntled sound. Telling Jonas was one thing, but telling Will made things . . . real. And although I wanted to talk to him, I wasn't sure I was super jazzed about my growing audience. Still, there really wasn't any getting out of telling him now. "Varsity," I groaned. "The guys are gross. And Ben's . . . weird. Kind of mean? I can't explain it. And maybe it's not important, but you guys are having way more fun than we are."

"But you're on Varsity." Paloma climbed up on my bed and sat on her knees. "Do you know how long it's been since a girl was on Varsity?"

I shook my head.

"Fifteen years. When Nina Knightley was a camper here."

What? Paul DeLuca said it wasn't very often girls were on Varsity. I didn't realize "not often" meant every decade and a half.

"You have to stick it out. Be better than those jerks. Just be awesome and funny and ignore them. Look, I saw your audition. You didn't make it just because you're a girl. You made it because you deserve to be there. *You have to stay on Varsity,*" Paloma stressed each word. "For us. Promise me."

My mouth was still hanging open. I closed it and swallowed. "Nina Knightley," I repeated.

She nodded. "Be our Nina Knightley, Zelda."

I took a slow breath in and out, trying to adjust to this new weight on my shoulders. "Okay," I said. How could I turn back now? If Nina Knightley had to go through this challege for her career, then maybe I would have to, too. "I promise."

"Yay, Zelda!" Sirena shouted, bolting out from behind the door, the screen door banging shut behind her.

Jonas jumped and screamed again. Will steadied his arms to keep him upright. "Has she been in here the whole time?" Jonas demanded, shaking off Will. He was on fire now.

Paloma and I smiled sweetly.

"And," Paloma added, "she's got the flag."

"Dammit!" Jonas yelled. He tore after Sirena. Paloma hopped down to follow him. Will looked like he had itchy feet, but he squeezed my leg. "You can do this, Z," he said, "you're a warrior."

I bit my lips and nodded.

I had to stay on Varsity to get on *SNL*.

Plus, the Gildas needed me.

And Will believed in me.

I nodded again, afraid if I said anything, I would start to cry. I picked up my notebook and pen and set my face. *Trust yourself.*

I had to show those asses what I was made of.

CHAPTER THIRTEEN

"They have coffee cake!" Paloma called from the front of the line.

"At lunch?" Sirena called back. "*That* is my real reward for capturing the flag."

"Well, well, well!" Hanna was right behind Paloma up in front. "Gosh, I sure am hungry. This whole tray of crumbly, brown-sugary-cinnamon goodness looks like just the right amount for ME."

"Don't you dare, Hanna!" Sirena warned her. "If I can capture a flag, I can certainly capture that coffee cake."

Emily ran up to Sirena and hugged her. "I heard it was you!" she squealed.

"You can't cheer for the enemy, Emily." Hanna marched over, holding the whole tray of coffee cake.

"Yoink." Sirena smiled and stole two pieces in quick succession.

"I can cheer for whoever I want to," Emily insisted, smiling as Sirena handed her half of the stolen booty. I found myself nodding, encouraging Emily's emerging confidence. "Plus," Emily continued, "she's not the enemy anymore."

Hanna shook her head and handed the tray off to Jonas. "J, will you put this on our table? I gotta grab a plate—"

Brandon and Xander walked by and lifted the whole tray out of Jonas's hands without breaking a stride.

"Hey!" he and Hanna exclaimed. But not very loudly.

I gave them a wan smile. "Those are my teammates. Feel sorry for me. Just a little."

I felt a tug at my elbow. Expecting Will, my eyes widened when it was Ben instead. And even though I was confused and irritated with him, my brain ignored those logical feelings and zeroed in on the contact his warm fingers were making with the sensitive skin on the inside of my elbow. My heart started beating so loudly, I was sure Ben could hear it.

"We got high ropes rescheduled for right after lunch, so wear clothes you can move in. We'll read sketches tomorrow," Ben said. His words meant business, but his eyes locked on mine. He was still holding my elbow.

I nodded.

Neither of us spoke.

Then suddenly, he released me and ran his fingers through that shaggy blond hair. "Meet at the gate. One o'clock."

I nodded again. He turned on his heels and left.

"I don't like that guy," Will muttered.

"Where have you *been*?" I asked, ignoring his declaration.

"Changing out of sweaty Capture the Flag clothes," he said, eyes still fixed on a retreating Ben. "He likes you."

"This again," I muttered, moving toward an open table with my tray.

"Uh, yes. Because you don't believe me. He likes you. That is gross."

"Thanks," I said flatly.

"*You're* not gross," he said, following me across the dining hall. "Well," he amended, "you're my sister, so yes, you are. But other people don't think you're gross. He's your coach. *That* is gross." He set his tray down across from me. "Be careful with that guy."

I rolled my eyes. "You sound like Dad."

He shrugged. "I'm a guy. I know *that* guy likes you. Be careful."

I shook my head. "He's nice to me. Sometimes. Well..."

"He's not nice to you?" his voice increased in volume. The rest of the JV teams started to fill in around us.

"No, he's—he's ... argh." I exhaled and lowered my voice. "Ben knows what it's like in the professional world. He's making me tougher. To get me ready for it."

Will stared at me. I stared back. For a moment, we were six years old in the back of our old Volvo station wagon in a staring contest for domination.

"Don't ..." He paused and dropped his voice so only I could hear him. "Don't let that guy change you."

I rolled my eyes again, but he kicked me a little under the table.

"Seriously," he said. "Don't."

What would that even look like? I was totally myself: Zelda ... or Ellie ...

I frowned.

"What?" Will asked.

Jonas leaned over. "What's so serious?"

My eyes flicked between the two of them. I shook my head quickly. "Just eat. Then we are stealing back some coffee cake."

Jonas high-fived me, but I could tell Will wasn't 100 percent satisfied.

I jogged over to the gate after lunch dressed in yoga pants and a pale gray long-sleeve shirt, my purple knit hat crammed over my curls. The sun was buried underneath thick clouds that promised rain.

I slowed to a walk when I realized Ben was the only one already there.

"Hey, you." He smiled, crossing his arms over his chest.

"Hi." I flashed a quick grimace.

"I can tell you're mad at me again," he said, quirking an eyebrow, still smiling.

I couldn't meet his eyes. "I'm . . . not *mad*," I managed. Frustrated, yes. Bewildered, sure. I looked over my shoulder to see if anyone else was coming down the road yet.

Ben gently kicked my sneaker with the toe of his, turning my attention back to him. "Hey, you did a *good job* in that last Montage before we broke to write. That scene with you as the neighbor obsessed with her lawn? Inspired."

Tentative, I met his eyes and nodded a little. I'd spent that scene crawling around stage on my hands and knees miming a ruler and a pair of tiny scissors, clipping each blade of grass so it matched its neighbor.

"You're always listening. I watch you. You're so committed to the scene—you're in it from the moment the suggestion comes until I call the blackout. I've never seen a camper as focused as you."

Tension crept into my jaw. I wanted to smile, to enjoy his compliments—they were evidence I was growing, right? I looped my hand over my elbow. "Why can't you say those things in front of the guys?" I blurted.

Ben sighed and scratched the back of his neck. "I don't know... It's my first year coaching... And some of those guys were my teammates and I just..." He sighed again. "I don't want to get into a situation where they accuse me of being soft on you because you're a girl."

I frowned.

He shook his head. "I'm not explaining myself right." He squinted and peered over my shoulder like the right explanation was hanging in the trees. I shifted my weight onto the other foot, hoping he would find the words he was looking for. Then, seeming to make a decision to quit searching for them, he gave me a brief, sad smile. "Just know. I'm looking out for you. I am. With all those alumni coming, this show is going to be huge. I want to make sure it's perfect."

I studied his face. Was this vulnerability real? Or was he just putting on a show for me?

He seemed to know I wasn't buying this promise because he bit his bottom lip and looked at the ground. "Look, Ellie, it's ... weird not performing. I'm used to being able to control the show on stage, and suddenly I don't get to be up there. And it's really weird without Marcus here... He had all the answers. Now I'm supposed to have them..."

I knew what that felt like. That's what camp felt like to me. I missed my parents. Missed having Will at my beck and call. Missed the comfort and predictability of how improv with Jenn worked. I smiled a little and shrugged. "That's what they pay you the big bucks for, right?"

His lips twitched. Then he blinked and caught my gaze, holding it long enough for heat to wrap around my throat and the whole world to disappear around us.

"I'm sorry for not standing up for you during the prostitute scene."

The tension in my jaw released. "Thank you," I said. "Thank you for saying that."

He gave me a half smile. "Things'll get better. I promise. Forgive those guys. It's really my fault. If you're going to be mad at someone, be mad at me, okay?"

"I'm not mad at you," I said, meaning it.

Now he gave me a full smile. "Good. Oh, hey—here they come. I wish we had a few more minutes, just for you and me." His eyes glowed. I nodded, swallowing around my unasked questions.

"You ready?" Ben asked, in a low voice meant just for me. I nodded again.

Ben broke eye contact and called out, "Hey, guys!"

I brightened, determined to be Nina Knightley, to be awesome, to make things right with my team. "Hi, Jakes!"

"Hey," they said, then peered up and down the road, ostensibly looking for the other guys. I racked my brain for a neutral topic of conversation to get the ball rolling, but came up empty. I exchanged a look with Ben—and I smiled, realizing it was the first time he'd allowed that with other people around.

Ben gave me a tiny nod. "Ellie, have you ever been on a high ropes course before?"

I raised an eyebrow. He was trying to help me. This was another change from the way he'd been behaving in front of the rest of the team. I dove right in. "Well, I've rock climbed a bunch. My parents are really into it. They've been dragging Will and me along since we could walk. And now that my feet have stopped growing, I even have my own climbing shoes."

Oh, NERD, Zelda.

"Cool," Ben said, even though I could tell deep down he didn't mean it. But he was trying.

"She doesn't need you to show her the ropes, then," Jake 1 joked, smiling so widely, it made his ears poke out even further than usual.

"Good one," I said, also trying. Trying very hard. "That's funny."

"I wouldn't go that far," Brandon rolled his eyes as he and Xander sauntered up to join us. He chucked his chin in Jake 1's direction. "You trying to jump his bones or something?"

I forced out a fake laugh. "I was just—"

"Cuz Jakey's game, right, Jakey?" Brandon poked him in the stomach. Jake laughed and pushed him back.

Xander joined in, grinding on Jake from the side. "Jakey's all, 'Do me, Ellie, I'm so funny.'" He made some grunting sounds.

Brandon ground on Jake from the other side and pitched his voice into a falsetto. "Oh, Jakey!" he tittered, apparently imitating me. "You're so funny! I love it when you do me!"

The grunting sounds increased, reaching a fever pitch.

I looked to Ben to put a stop to this, but he just shook his head, smiling. "Relax," he mouthed.

Jake was laughing, but was also looking increasingly uncomfortable.

I pursed my lips. *Perform at the peak of your intellect.* I couldn't just "relax." Putting my hands up, I tried to pitch my voice in a light tone. "Guys, come on—"

Xander reached a hand out imitating a cat paw. "Kitty likes to—"

"Can we *please* find another way to—" My voice came out louder than I intended.

"Ellie!" Ben reminded me in a slight singsong voice, "Team building, remember?"

Ben promised me things would be better. *This* was not better. Fire in my eyes, I met Ben's. He raised his eyebrows for a fraction of a second, then elbowed me. "We're going to have some fun on the ropes course, right?"

"Yeah, Ellie, we're going to have some fun." Brandon grinned. He slapped Jake 1 on the butt as a parting gesture.

I clenched my jaw. So, things *weren't* going to be different. Those guys were still going to be weird and gross and Ben was still going to do nothing about it. Why was I even putting up with this crap?

Varsity. Nina Knightley. Saturday Night Live.

Right.

"Yup." I nodded, looking at my sneakers, "Fun."

"Hey, Ellie. Come on," Ben said. "Smile."

"She doesn't have to smile if she doesn't want to."

Shocked, I turned around and smiled for real. Standing three abreast in matching olive shorts and wicking BSA T-shirts were my Boy Scouts: the cute one, the ginger one, and the silent rock one.

"Hi!" I exclaimed, relief washing over me. "How are you?"

"Good! Zelda, right?" The cute one grinned. "I'm Jesse?"

"Right!" I high-fived him. "And . . ." I looked at the redhead. "I want you to know I'm making a Ron Weasley joke in my head, but it's only in my head. I'd never say it out loud."

He smirked. "Funny enough, in *my* head, I'm making a Hermione Granger joke. But only in *my* head." He held his hand up for his own high five. "Murph."

"That's right," I said, slapping his hand. "Murph."

We turned to silent guy expectantly. He looked at his friends. They nodded encouragement. He gave me a hip-level wave. "Ricky."

"With the rocks," I said.

His eyebrows raised above his glasses in surprise. "Yeah," he said.

"Good memory." Murph smiled.

Ben took a possessive step toward me. "How do you know the Boy Scouts, Ellie?"

"We met in the woods," I said. "I was—"

Brandon snickered.

I glared at him. "What."

He shrugged nonchalantly. "Just imagining what goes on with you and three guys in the woods."

I opened my mouth and then closed it again. Restraint. It was taking every ounce of my self-control, but I would be the model of restraint. I would give them nothing to blame me for. I would be the embodiment of the high road. I turned to Jesse, whose strained face mirrored mine. "We're doing high ropes today." I smiled thinly.

"I know," he said, his smile somewhat dimmed from before. "We're belaying you . . . I'm sorry," he faced Brandon, "what are you suggesting?"

"About what? About Ellie? I'm just joking."

Jesse's eyes flicked to mine. I willed him to drop it.

But Jesse cocked his head. "It wasn't a very good joke."

The Jakes let out a "woooooah" that Brandon shut down with a look.

"Hey! The rest of the team is here," Ben said as Cade, Trey, and Donovan joined us. He turned to the scouts. "Are you guys it? They said we were supposed to wait until the Troop . . . Leader or something—"

Jesse kept his eyes on my team. "Troop Guide. That's me. We're all set."

"Okay, then," Ben said. "Let's go!" He lead the way and we fell into small clumps. Jesse and Murph flanked me.

"Who *are* these guys?" Murph asked in a low voice.

"Improv can be really bro-y." I shrugged. "I imagine Boy Scouts can be, too?"

Jesse grunted. "Yeah. It doesn't mean I like it. I just . . . I wish he wouldn't talk to you that way."

"JAKE-EEE!" Brandon clapped three times. "Don't fall, man!" Xander and the others hooted. "Though if you do, those ears will act like parachutes!"

I tried not to shoot a withering look at Brandon in the spirit of togetherness, but poor Jake 1.

"Don't think of it as thirty feet!" Brandon yelled. "Think of it as three stories!" They all laughed again.

Jake 1 was stranded. His feet were planted in the middle of a wood-slatted rope bridge high above us. It had taken everyone else thirty or so seconds to cross from one end to the other, but halfway there, Jake 1 had suddenly frozen. For the last ten minutes, no amount of coaxing or contempt had succeeded in luring him to the other side.

He wasn't thirty feet up in the air on that bridge alone, though. A climbing rope connected Jake's harness to a pulley on a cable over his head down to a belay device on Jesse's harness on the ground. Jesse's left hand gripped the rope coming down from the pulley, and the other stayed at his right hip, folding the rope feeding out of the belay device to brake it. If Jake fell, it would only be for a couple feet. Ropes, engineering, and Jesse's sure attention would prevent anything worse.

Still . . . I could see if you weren't used to being thirty feet in the air, it could be scary.

Ben sidled over to Jesse. "Can we do anything to get this moving along?"

"Move what along?" Jesse's eyes were locked on Jake, his voice to Ben polite, but cool.

"Him," Ben said. "What do you do when this happens?"

"This is where the 'team' part of team building usually comes in," Murph muttered. He was acting as Jesse's second, holding on to the loose rope as a worst-case scenario backup plan.

"Don't get so scared you pee your pants!" Xander shouted. "We'll all get wet!"

As if on cue, rain began lightly tapping on our helmets.

"Dude! Gross!" Xander yelled. The bros all laughed.

"We can get a second person up there," Jesse called. "What do you think, Jake?"

Jake shrugged.

"You want me to let you down?" Jesse asked. "You made it half-way. That's amazing."

"Amazing if you're a little girl," Brandon said, not quietly.

Murph looked at me. His eyes bulged in a Did-he-really-just-say-that? way.

I rolled my eyes.

Murph turned to Brandon. "Did you know that women's bodies can handle much higher levels of pain than men's can?"

Brandon didn't even acknowledge him.

"So," Murph continued, "when you call someone a girl, it's quite the compliment."

I couldn't look at Brandon to see his reaction. I just smiled to myself.

Then Ricky appeared. "Zelda," he said.

I turned, expectantly.

"You climb?"

I nodded. He gestured for me to follow him. We padded over wood chips toward the firecracker ladder, a braided rope with ladder rungs fed through its core. I flicked a look over my shoulder to see if Ben noticed where we were going, but he was focused on Jake 1.

Ricky pointed at the landing on top. "Talk him over."

I hesitated for a second. Did I really want to help Jake? He hadn't been directly terrible to me, but I certainly wouldn't have considered him an ally. I peered up at him, blinking at the sprinkles of rain falling on my face. Shaking, Jake lifted a foot halfway up to take another step and the whole bridge pitched to one side. He whimpered as he overcompensated and pitched the other way.

As the guys on my team hooted and laughed in response, anger bubbled in my stomach. I met Ricky's eyes and nodded. I'd have wanted someone to help if it was me stuck up there, but if I was being perfectly honest, a tiny, selfish part of me also wondered if my rescue mission might gain me some credibility on the team.

Ricky handed me the free end of the rope and I looped it through my harness in a figure-eight knot. Ricky double-checked the security of my knot, and I double-checked his carabiner gate to make sure it was locked.

"On belay?" I asked, reciting the standard climbing safety call-and-response.

"Belay on," he responded.

"Climbing," I declared.

"Climb on."

I grabbed the rope at the center of the firecracker ladder with both hands and heaved my body up until my feet balanced on the first rung. I felt Ricky take the slack out of the rope. I pulled myself to the second rung, then the third. When I reached the fourth, the rain started to patter harder.

"It's just supposed to rain a little, but if it gets any worse or I see lightning, I'll call it," Jesse announced.

My breathing increased as I hauled my feet to the sixth rung. That's also when Xander noticed me.

"Kitty can climb!" he shouted.

The rest of the guys catcalled. My arms started to shake.

"Hey! What is she doing up there?" Ben demanded.

What *was* I doing? I watched the raindrops pit pat onto my hands and roll down my arms. I willed them to stop shaking.

"Get down, Ellie!" Ben called. "We don't need you up there!"

I took a deep, steadying breath. "Just gimme a minute," I called back.

"Ellie," Ben warned.

"I'm going to talk him over," I called. "Trust me."

"Yeah, if anyone can get Jakey down, it's Ellie," Xander said. Then he and Brandon started grunting again.

Ben pretended to chuckle, and he folded his arms across his chest. I took his silence for permission.

My arms continued to shake. *Come on, come on,* I berated myself. *What's it going to look like if you can't get up there? It'll just be another thing girls can't do.*

"Zelda." Ricky's voice was calm. "You can do this."

I looked down at him. In improv, one of our mantras is "get out of your head." You're just supposed to trust your body, your instincts, and your partner. The same was true in climbing, so I set my jaw, emptied my mind, and pulled.

Soon, I lost track of how many rungs I'd tackled. Now there were just three left.

"Ellie's coming to save you, Jakey-poo!" Brandon called.

"Way to go, Zelda!" Murph hollered, his voice cracking a little with the effort.

Two left.

"You've got this, Zelda." Jesse's voice joined Murph's.

My heart thudded in my chest. I ignored my vibrating arms and legs and pulled myself onto the platform, my feet still on the final rung. Then, not too elegantly, I clambered to standing.

"Yeah!" Jesse called.

I looked down the thirty feet below to Ricky on the ground and met his eyes through his rain-spattered glasses. He nodded.

The rain picked up.

"Okay, Jake," I said, turning my attention to him. "You can do this."

Poor guy. He was really trembling now. The rain was spitting in his eyes and he was blinking fast to keep it out... or maybe he was crying.

"Jake?"

He turned to me.

"Just follow my voice. Jesse's got you. The bridge is going to rock a little, but you're perfectly safe. Just slide one foot. Then the other. Can you do that?"

Jake nodded. He slid a foot forward.

Everyone cheered. The only nonsarcastic cheering was coming from the Boy Scouts, but there was cheering nonetheless.

"Ellie?" Ben's voice called. I kept my eye contact with Jake. "It's raining pretty hard. You and Jake need to come down."

Jake took another step.

"Just a minute," I called. I had to get him across. For both our sakes. "One minute more." Then I dropped my voice so only Jake could hear it. "Do it, Jake," I whispered. With the increase in rain came wind. I shivered and gripped the rope attached to my harness. "Show them you can do this." *That* we *can do this.*

He nodded. He took another step.

"Guys," Ben called, "it's time for you to come down. Right now."

129

"It's okay," Jesse assured him. "It's not lightning."

"You're doing it!" I whispered, trying to ignore Ben. "Almost there, Jake!" I reached out for his hand.

"I don't care that it's not lightning—I *said* COME DOWN!" Ben bellowed.

Jake grabbed my hand, and I hauled him onto the platform with me, but the victorious moment was drowned out by Ben's roar, "BRING. THEM. *DOWN.*"

"Good job, Jake," I whispered, pride filling my chest.

He nodded. "Thanks." He only met my eyes for a fraction of a second, but in that moment, I felt like we were on the same team.

"Ricky? Ready to lower," I called as Jesse called up to Jake.

Soon, we were both drifting down to the earth. Ben's imposing figure grew larger the closer I got to the ground. My bravery and pride and connection with Jake were gone—replaced by dread of the tongue-lashing Ben was barely keeping restrained.

When I landed, Ben was there with a finger in my face. "When I say to do something, you do that thing. Understand? You don't always know my reasons, and I don't always owe you an explanation. Never. Second. Guess. Me. Again. Got it?"

I nodded, furious, eyes on my shoes. He practically stomped away.

Ricky fumbled with the figure-eight knot attached to my harness.

"He's mean," he said in a low voice.

I took off my helmet but didn't respond, afraid if Ben saw my lips move, I'd draw his wrath again.

We were quiet as Ricky rubbed his hands together to warm them up and get circulation in his fingertips. He tried the knot again. Nothing.

I poked at it myself, but I was even colder and wetter than Ricky from being three stories up in the air.

"What's the holdup, Ellie?" Ben stormed back over.

Murph and Jesse were on his heels.

"I've got fresh hands," Murph offered. He took Ricky's place and tried to make sense of loosening the tight, wet knot.

Then there was a flash of lightning.

"Let's go, let's go!" Ben barked. "You want to get us killed?"

The other guys were already scampering off back to our camp, their retreating forms following the road.

"Our lodge is closer," Jesse offered.

My heart leapt a little.

"No. Just cut her out," Ben said, fists on his hips.

"I've got it, I've got it." Murph slipped the rope out of its confines.

"Run back, Ellie," Ben commanded. "We'll return the harness later. I need to have a few words with their Scout Master."

I tried to flash thank you and apologies to the scouts with my eyes, but Ben snapped his fingers at me. "Now!"

I turned and ran, hoping against hope Ben wouldn't catch up with me.

CHAPTER FOURTEEN

Dripping wet all over the cabin floor, I slipped out of my tennis shoes and stripped off my socks, the harness, my yoga pants, hat, and long-sleeve shirt, leaving them in a pile. Shivering in my bra and underwear and trying to shake off the dread snaking around in my chest, I skittered across the floor and threw my towel over my shoulders, undressing the rest of the way. After struggling into flannel pants and a thermal long-underwear top, I climbed into my sleeping bag and wrapped the towel around my hair. Ben's voice was shouting in my head.

IT'S TIME FOR YOU TO COME DOWN. RIGHT NOW.

Despite my warm pajamas, my fingers, toes, and nose were ice cubes. I shivered and rubbed my feet together to create warmth.

Turning on my side and drawing my knees into my chest, I looked out at the rain through my window. It was coming down in sheets. The thunder boomed louder and lightning flashed longer than I'd ever witnessed.

WHEN I SAY TO DO SOMETHING, YOU DO THAT THING. UNDERSTAND?

I had made Ben angrier than I'd ever seen him. Was I wrong not to listen to him? I just thought I knew better—Jake was moving. Wasn't it going to mean more to him in the long run that he could walk across the whole rope bridge than it would bother him to get a little wet?

I blew warm air into my cupped hands.

I DON'T CARE THAT IT'S NOT LIGHTNING—I SAID COME DOWN!

Granted, it was pouring now, but it hadn't been then. Did Ben just really know the mountains? Could he tell what the weather was about to do?

But Ricky and Jesse and Murph also knew the mountains. They'd seemed cautious, but in the end, Ben had been right. The storm was worse than Jesse had thought it'd be.

LET'S GO, LET'S GO! YOU WANT TO GET US KILLED?

My nose dripped. I exhaled.

I knew two things for sure: those Boy Scouts did not like my team, and they did not like Ben. Their comments jumbled together in my head.

This is where the "team" part of team building usually comes in ... I just ... I wish he wouldn't talk to you that way ... When you call someone a girl, it's quite the compliment ...

They were right to dislike my team, but they didn't understand all the circumstances.

Look, Ellie, it's ... weird without Marcus here ... He had all the answers. Now I'm supposed to have them ... I'm looking out for you. I am.

Then suddenly all I could think about was the feeling of his warm fingers on the skin of my lower back.

Ben was just being protective, right? He was scared because of the rain. I hadn't listened when he'd told us to come down. *Balance giving and taking.* I'd have to talk to the Boy Scouts and help them understand . . .

When I next opened my eyes, the rain had stopped, my towel had fallen on the floor, and my body felt warm again.

The clock on the wall and my grumbling stomach both indicated that dinner was in fifteen minutes.

I felt heavy as I changed clothes and folded a scarf into a triangle and knotted it over my hair. How would it be seeing Ben again? Or Jake? Would he be grateful? Embarrassed?

Ben's angry voice echoed in my skull as I skirted the mud puddles. Distracted, I bumped into an aspen tree and all the water that had been resting on its leaves poured down on me. I sighed and peeled off my now-soaking flannel shirt. Ben's voice was replaced by Brandon's and Xander's voices, taunting me about a wet T-shirt contest.

God, those jerks. The sun came out as I tied the shirt around my waist and adjusted my tank top straps. Maybe I should have listened to Ben when he told me to get off the ropes course, but he was still wrong for not shutting down the latest round of Brandon and Xander assholery. I imagined opening two giant, empty Nalgene water bottles and dropping Brandon and Xander inside each and screwing on the lids. Smiling, I marched toward the Main Lodge.

As I climbed the steps, I wasn't sure I was ready to face Ben. I stopped off on the porch to refill my water bottle and rehydrate, using it as an excuse to peer through the window.

No sight of him. I exhaled relief.

As I threw open the screen door, I spotted Hanna. Grinning, I trotted over to her, and she threw an arm over my shoulder.

"And where did *you* get caught in the storm? Someplace cozy?" She smiled conspiratorially.

"I wish. You?"

"Just rehearsal, but we were working on characters. Emily and Jonas played squirrels frightened by their own tails." She smirked and shook her head. "Their space work was outstanding. Then a guy on our team made me a lifeguard, and I fireman-carried everyone across the stage, including Dion."

I laughed. I wished I been there to see it.

"I love character work," she said, pulling out a chair at one of the tables. "Sometimes it's nice to be someone else for a while."

Spontaneously, I grabbed her hand. "I like *you*. Who *you* are."

She chuckled, and we sat in the folding chairs. "From what I hear, you need that advice more than me, Zelda-girl."

I frowned. "What did you hear?"

Hanna waved me away. "That Ben of yours—"

Emily and Sirena flopped down across from us. "Ben of yours?" Emily mirrored my frown. "He's *yours*?"

"No!" I exclaimed. I felt like I was tripping over myself to get ahead of the explanation. "He—he spent all day yelling at me. He's not mine. I mean, he's beautiful, of course." For a split second, I imagined him running his hand through his hair and grinning at me. I shook the image away. "But he's my coach. My coach who never stands up for me. My coach who's always *yelling* at me."

Sirena and Emily exchanged a look out of the corner of their eyes.

"You guys," I pleaded, thumping my head on the table. "He's the worrrrrst." I was lying a little, but there was no room for nuance here.

"He does look at you a lot," Sirena said, her eyes catching my gaze, inviting me to confide.

"He's my *coach*," I repeated.

"Sure, but he looks at you more than he looks at those other guys on your team. And you *are* very talented," Sirena said. I opened my mouth to protest, but she cut me off with a hand. "*You are.* Sometimes I think about Agnes Ruffles and just start giggling out loud in public." She sighed dramatically. "Thanks to you, people think I'm very weird now."

I chuckled.

"And talent is attractive," Sirena finished, shrugging.

"Also, you're not very ugly," Hanna added, waggling her eyebrows at me. "Nothing major, anyway. No arms where your eyes should be, for instance."

Sirena and Emily smiled, but I shook my head. This part I felt more sure about. I might be thinking thoughts about Ben, but after what I did on the ropes course, there was no way he was interested in me like that. Had he ever been? He definitely wasn't anymore. "Guys don't like me like that," I said. "I'm friends with guys. I wish I could show you my phone. My texts are all, 'When's rehearsal?' and 'Who was that actor we were all talking about?' and 'I'm having problems with my girlfriend. You're the only one I can talk to.'"

"Well, you've never-had-a-girlfriend-or-a-boyfriend-but-you-think-you're-probably-straight, right?" Emily joked.

"Unfortunately," I said.

"Then why don't they like you back?" she demanded. "Look at

you! You're nice and funny and . . ." She blushed and sort of gestured at me.

Hanna smiled. "Emily means you have nice boobs."

"I do not! I just meant pretty in general! You're an overall pretty and nice and funny person!"

I laughed.

Sirena started unscrewing her water bottle. "Look. If you think guys aren't going to like you, they won't like you. You've got a lot going for you, Zelda. *Know* that. *Be* that girl."

I nodded. "Thanks. That's sweet of you, Sirena."

She smiled and took a swig of water.

"But don't be that girl for Ben," Hanna added, making a face at me.

"Why not? I mean—I'm not," I said, automatically searching for him among the tables.

Emily and Sirena simultaneously gave me side-eye.

"I'm not!" I exclaimed.

"See—you do that leaning in thing and your boobs just—" Hanna made jazz hands.

"I wear too many buttoned-up flannel shirts. That must be the thing keeping the boys away," I joked.

Paloma marched over and sat down with a thump. Three pencils fell out of her hair.

"Are those all mine?" she marveled.

We cracked up.

"Who needs that many pencils?" Hanna cackled.

"I don't need *three*," Paloma clarified, "I just keep tucking them in there and they get lost!" She shook her head. A fourth plunked on the table.

We were goners.

She chuckled good-naturedly as she gathered the pencils and tucked them into her back pocket. When we were down to the hiccuping portion of the laughter, she asked, "How was high ropes, Zelda?"

I coughed and blew some air through my lips. "Weird. Bad. Yelly. It feels like everyone hates me."

She pushed my shoulder. "But you're fighting, right? You're doing this for us?"

"Yeah," I said, wrapping my arms around my torso, "I'm doing this for us."

I felt him behind me before I heard him.

"Hey."

Ben. I took a deep breath and looked over my shoulder. "Hi."

Was he going to still be mad at me for not listening to him? Or would he apologize for yelling and then I'd apologize for not listening and then he'd apologize for not standing up for Jake and me?

"Where did you go after high ropes?"

At that moment, the dinner bell rang and the food was laid out at the buffet. Chairs scraped all around us. I stood up so we could hear each other, and he took my elbow and guided me a few feet away behind a pillar. Where did I go after high ropes? *That's* what we were talking about?

"I was wet." I shrugged. "I went back to the cabin. Changed. Took a nap."

"You took a *nap*?" He put his fists back on his hips like he had at high ropes. "You missed rehearsal."

"I didn't know."

"You didn't *ask*."

"You told me to run back."

"To the *Lodge*."

"You didn't *say* Lodge."

"I didn't say *cabin*, either."

"I was *wet*."

"So were *we*!"

I gritted my teeth and imagined lasers shooting out of my eyeballs.

"You need to make up that rehearsal."

I wrinkled my forehead. "When?"

"Tonight. After dinner. Upstairs in Rehearsal Room B."

My mouth opened to protest. Someone grabbed my hand and squeezed it. I jerked a quick look behind me. Paloma was holding my hand. She and the other Gildas were piled up on the other side of the pillar, eavesdropping on our conversation. I bit my lips and exhaled through my nose, turning back to Ben. "See you then."

Ben spun away. I wanted to bury my face in my hands, but didn't want to give him the satisfaction in case he looked back.

The Gildas circled up.

"He could have been nicer about that," Emily said, and everyone nodded.

"Where's Will?" I asked.

Paloma gave me a small smile. "He and Jonas were walking away from the Lodge when I came in. Picnic, maybe? They haven't seen each other all afternoon."

I barked out a laugh. "That long, huh?"

Hanna looped an arm around my shoulder. "Chin up, Zelda-girl. I know we're poor stand-ins for a real-life best-friend-almost-twin."

I shook my head and smiled.

"But we're here for you." Sirena squeezed my arm, and I looked around at the other Gildas, who nodded.

A warm ball of strength glowed in my belly. The Gildas weren't just my cabinmates anymore. They were my friends now. And I was theirs, too.

I'd never been up to the second-floor rehearsal rooms—Varsity had always rehearsed on the stage in the main room of the Lodge. This, of course, must have been where JV and the skill-building teams practiced.

I followed the hall to the right and found Rehearsal Room B. I tried the doorknob and it clicked open. The room was empty.

When I flipped on the lights, they revealed a large room with high windows, a hardwood floor, and a mirrored wall with black velvet curtains pulled across it, except for the last few feet. A piano stood tall in the corner and several black rehearsal blocks looked leftover from a living room scene.

Makeup rehearsal. I shook my head. If he had wanted me to go to the Lodge after high ropes, I wished he would have said something. I wandered to the piano and plonked on a few keys.

"You made it."

I looked up. Ben had changed into jeans and a flannel, the top three buttons undone and the sleeves rolled up below his elbows. Was this guy incapable of covering his forearms?

"Yup," I said, plonking a few more keys. "What do you want me to do?"

"Who/What/Where scenes." He folded his arms.

I folded mine, too and met his eyes. "Alone?"

He held them. "I'll be your partner."

My stupid heart started pounding. I broke eye contact and cleared to the mirror side of the room.

He entered raking the ground.

He was establishing the "what": yard work. It was up to me to name "who" and "where" we were.

I pitched my voice in a southern drawl. "You must really miss Grandpa, son, because this is the third time you've raked his grave this week."

"Scene," he said. "Again. Enter with an action."

I circled back and started pulling on what I hoped looked like a gorilla costume.

He swiftly joined me, miming holding a clipboard. "Mickey Mouse auditions, line up right here, please. The director will see you soon." Then he "set down" his mimed clipboard and said, "Scene."

Gorilla, Mickey Mouse—close enough. But I had that nagging feeling about relationships—if you don't know your scene partner, you have so much work to do to establish it. I couldn't believe assuming the relationship was a *crutch*. It—

Now he was chopping something on a counter.

I picked up my own "knife" and chopped next to him. "My boyfriend and his parents will be here in five minutes, Dad. If you finish up these veggies, I'll set the table."

"Scene."

I swept back around and came out tossing Frisbees.

"Quit throwing the dishes, Lisa!"

See, now there was another thing—telling someone not to do something shuts down the scene. Plus, he'd only established the "what." Now the "where" and the relationship of the "who" were my job.

I chucked the "dishes" even harder. "My mother left me this house, and I'll do what I please in it! You might be my husband, but it's my name on the title!"

He stilled my throwing hand with his right and wrapped his left hand around my hip. It flooded with heat.

"I pay the mortgage," he whispered.

What was he doing? We'd established the who/what/where. But I remembered how angry he'd gotten when I broke the scene at rehearsal the other day. I'd already made him angry twice today. What would happen if I did it again? Would I be off the team?

I stayed in the scene.

I glared at him. "Sure, you pay the mortgage. With your trust fund."

Now he lowered my dish-throwing hand and placed my palm on his chest. "You love my trust fund. Almost as much as you love me."

He took my face into his hands. His eyes darted back and forth between my eyes like they weren't sure where to land.

No. He wasn't going to—

And then he was kissing me. A real, live boy was kissing me. Kissing ME. I hardly knew what was happening. He wrapped an arm around my back and pulled me closer.

This muscly California boy was—wait. Was this real? Or was it just for the scene? Did people actually kiss in improv scenes?

That was his *tongue!* What was I supposed to *do* with that?

And then it was over.

"Good job," he said, all business. "Good scene."

I looked into his face. Was I a bad kisser? Did he stop because it was a scene and the scene was over, or would he have kept kissing me if I was a better kisser?

Not finding a quick answer, I turned away and covered my burning cheeks with my hands.

"Look. You could get into trouble with the Pauls for missing rehearsal, so because you came to this one, I'll just . . . forget to tell them. Okay?"

I nodded, confused.

"And hey." He gently turned me around. "About the high ropes course." He shook his head and touched my cheek. "You scared me up there. The rain and the lightning—I'm sorry I yelled."

I nodded again.

"We good?"

Apparently, all I could do now was nod.

He took a step closer to me. I closed my eyes.

"Good," he whispered.

When I opened my eyes, he was gone.

CHAPTER FIFTEEN

When I slunk back to the cabin, the Gildas weren't there. I pretended to be asleep when they returned—I just wasn't ready to talk about what had happened with Ben at that rehearsal.

But by the next morning, I'd almost forgotten about it because everyone on my team was sitting around a table in the Main Lodge, laughing.

At *my* cold open sketch.

"Did you write that, Ben?" Brandon asked, leaning back in his chair and flipping through the pages. "It's genius."

My heart glowed. We were all seated around one of the lunch tables piled with multiple copies of our various attempts at cold-open sketch writing. The sun was streaming in through the large Main Lodge windows. I tried to suppress a smile.

"Remember—these are blind reads. We won't identify writers until the end," Ben said.

"Man—that sketch was awesome." Trey shook his head.

I chewed on my lower lip to keep from smiling my face off. I felt vindicated. Valued. I tried to catch Ben's eye. "How many are left?" I asked.

Ben flipped open a folder. "Just one more." He passed out copies without making eye contact. "There are two parts," he said. "Brandon, will you read Mr. Phillips, and Ellie, will you read Marcy?"

Ha! I thought. *I guess there are perks to being the only woman on the team.*

Ben handed me my copy of the script. I tried to smile, but he still wasn't looking at me.

Brandon cleared his throat. "Uh, Ben, you gonna read stage directions?"

"That's okay . . . Xander?"

Xander shrugged and picked up the script. He cleared his throat. "We're in an office. Mr. Phillips is working late. Marcy knocks and enters."

"Where have you been?" Brandon as Mr. Phillips demanded.

"I left," I said as Marcy. "The meeting got canceled, so I got a manicure."

"You got a *manicure*?" Brandon thundered.

"You didn't say not to," I said.

"I didn't say you could! We were all here!"

"Well, I had things to do!"

"So did *we!*"

Something felt funny about this. Besides the stereotypical male boss/female secretary thing . . .

"I'm sorry, Mr. Phillips, it'll never happen again," I said, internally rolling my eyes.

"Damn straight it won't. Because you're fired!"

"What?"

"You heard me!"

"Oh, Mr. Phillips, please. Please don't fire me. I'll do anything!" My eyes flicked above the script to catch Ben's. Seriously? Also. Where were the jokes?

"Well . . ." Brandon read.

"Please! I'll—I'll juggle!" I said.

"Marcy picks up a stapler, a mug, and a pen and attempts to juggle them," Xander read.

"I'll sing!" I continued. "*Oh, they built the ship* Titanic, *to sail the ocean blue!*"

Not super-original jokes, but at least she's the one getting the punchlines.

"Look, Marcy," Brandon said, "there's nothing you can do to make it up to me."

"What if I do *this*?" My eyes flicked over to the stage directions. I froze.

"They kiss," Xander read. Then he looked up and cackled. "Oh man! Were we allowed to write porn? I totally would have written porn."

"Save comments for the end," Ben said in a clipped voice.

"I'm just saying," he muttered.

I stared at Ben. I stared until he couldn't not notice I was staring. He met my eye for a split second, then looked down at the script again.

Had he taken what had happened at our rehearsal and turned it into *this*?

"Hey, Ellie. Your line," High Ropes Jake said softly.

I glanced at him, then coughed and looked back at the script.

"How was that?" I asked flatly, as Marcy.

"I'll consider your reinstatement," Brandon said, "as long as you promise me one thing."

"Anything." *Seriously?*

Brandon waited a beat, long enough for us to assume Mr. Phillips would want more action from Marcy. "Teach me that juggling thing? Then I'll teach you how to kiss with tongue."

It was the punch line of the scene, but to their credit, no one laughed.

"Well?" Ben prompted.

I couldn't look at anyone.

That ass.

"I like the one before this one," Donovan said. He retwisted one of his twists. "This . . . the structure's there—I see the three acts. But the jokes are weak and the setup is clichéd. It's not saying anything."

I tried to catch his eye to thank him, but he continued to study the page.

"It's saying something—it's commenting on the cliché," Ben protested.

"Is it?" Brandon asked. "It just feels . . ."

"Boring," High Ropes Jake complained.

Ben shook his head.

"It's . . . Also, it's punching down," I said, finding my voice. "She—Marcy—is in a vulnerable position. Mr. Phillips takes advantage of her. Like, it's not that funny when the president mocks a homeless guy—the power imbalance just makes it feel mean. But if a homeless guy mocks the president..." I shrugged. "Punch up. Not down."

"You're being too sensitive," Ben said.

"Maybe." Brandon flipped the script pages back and forth, looking at them again. "But regardless, it's just not that funny."

"Who wrote it?" Ben asked. "Do you have something to say in its defense?"

I furrowed my brow. *He* wrote it. *Ben* wrote it. I opened my mouth, but then closed it again. What good was going to come from my challenging him?

He caught my eye. "Anyone?"

I shook my head.

No one said anything.

"Well, after that response, I don't blame you for not owning up," Ben said, "The clear choice is the sleepwalking bear sketch."

"You wrote it, didn't you, Ben." Brandon fired off a finger gun at him.

"Actually..." Ben shifted in his chair and cleared his throat. "Ellie did."

I felt every eye on me. I raised my eyebrows expectantly. They'd already said how much they liked my sketch. Now they were going to have to admit to my face that I was funny. I smiled in anticipation of their praise.

"Did your brother help you or something?" Xander asked.

Was he *serious*? I made sure my voice was firm and clear. "No, I wrote it by myself."

"*Ellie* wrote it?" Brandon frowned. "Wait. Ellie-Ellie?"

Now my eyes unfocused, and I just stared at the table. "So . . . we're all shocked I could write something funny by myself?"

"It's just—it was *really* funny," Xander said in a voice that sounded both surprised and impressed. "And girls usually aren't—well, the ones I've known—"

"Oh, so it isn't personal," I said, heat rising into my face. "It's not that we're shocked that *I* could write a funny sketch, we're shocked that a *girl* could write a funny sketch. Without her brother's help anyway. Is that it?"

"God, Ellie, quit freaking out about every little thing," Ben said.

"This is not a little thing! If anyone else here had written this sketch, would you have doubted *them*?"

No one would make eye contact with me.

"You know, improv has always made me feel good. Like I was strong and funny and smart. I was a part of something. But you guys—" I shook my head. "What you do isn't improv. It's a lot of one-upmanship and dick waving and you don't need me for that."

I stood up and shouldered my bag. "I'm leaving." I turned to Ben. "I'm done. So, I won't be at rehearsal. Makeup or otherwise."

No one tried to stop me as I left. As a parting gesture, I tossed over my shoulder, "Ben wrote the Marcy-the-sexy-secretary sketch, by the way. Way to go, champ!"

I didn't wait to hear the backpedaling. The "Oh, the secretary sketch isn't so bad after all . . ." or worse, the "Actually, now that I read it again, I'm not sure about the sleepwalking bear sketch . . ."

I thumped down the stairs, my full water bottle swinging from my Second City tote bag, banging my hip with each step. As I reached the path, a big gust of wind blew up and a flock of birds abandoned a nearby tree in unison. One of the birds flew so near my head, I flinched.

I set my teeth and marched, my Chacos kicking up rocks and dust as I went.

I was breathing easy. I wasn't sure if it was from breaking free of those dillholes, or if I was starting to acclimate to the elevation a little. Maybe both.

I swung my arms as I walked. Without me, they didn't have a solid cold open. Without me, they'd start picking on each other. Without me, they'd maybe even turn on Ben.

A few minutes into my sojourn, the wind died down, the chattering and chasing of the birds quieted, and a creeping worry sneaked into my periphery. If I had actually *quit* Varsity, what was I going to *do* for another nine days? Would they take me on JV? Or was I forfeiting that possibility? Would Ben tell them I was "too sensitive"? Would they put me on a skill-building team? Or would they tell me I had to go home?

What were the Gildas going to say? What about Will? My stomach dropped.

Nina Knightley.

My chest felt tight, and I slowed my walk.

What had I done?

CHAPTER SIXTEEN

What was I supposed to do now? Just pace in circles? Wear new paths through the woods? Staring at my sandals, I hesitated. Was there poison ivy in Colorado?

The sound of chattering drew my attention, and I watched a pile of middle school–age Boy Scouts hike down our road, trying very hard to maintain a straight line.

Boy Scouts!

Turning on my heel, I clutched my bag to my shoulder with one hand and braced the water bottle with the other. My Boy Scouts took the same hike for lunch every day, right? I'd been invited any time I wanted. I knew what path they'd started on at least. Jogging, I willed my lungs to acclimate more. *Make active choices. Be in the moment.* It was a little far-fetched that I'd find them, but what other plans did I have?

Before long, the path grew narrower. I alternated between jogging until I couldn't breathe and brisk walking. With every step, Brandon, Ben, and Xander's words echoed in my brain. "Ellie *wrote it?" "Did your brother help you or something?" "It's just—it was really funny. And girls usually aren't—well..."*

Tears threatened, but I blinked them away.

I stopped for a moment and closed my eyes, listening for signs of human existence, but all I heard were chipmunks chittering, birds chirping, and the breeze rustling aspen tree leaves.

Finally, I came to a crossroads. A giant rock held court at the Y in the path. This was as far as I knew. I could guess and take one of the paths randomly... Or maybe I could see ahead a little. I peered down one of the paths and for a second was sure I saw Jesse, Murph, and Ricky. But when I got a closer look, they were much too young (and loud) to be my scouts.

Maybe height would help. I climbed on top of the rock and hoisted myself up to standing. Blocking the sun's glare with my hand, I squinted, peering down one path, then the other. The thick foliage prevented me from seeing much farther than I could on the ground. "Dammit," I muttered.

Before I could firmly settle into a haze of disappointment, however, a male voice jerked me out of it.

"Zelda?"

I screamed so loudly, another flock of small birds vacated their tree in unison. Terrifying birds was getting to be a thing with me.

"Whoa!" Ricky's hands were raised defensively as he appeared at the foot of the rock. "Just me!"

I shook my head. "I'm so glad I found you. Though I'm not sure all those birds I traumatized would agree."

Ricky's smile was small, but when paired with his green eyes looking straight at me through his smudged glasses, it made me feel like we were on a warm, safe, two-person planet. Like he was really with me, right here, in this moment. Like that was important.

Before I had a chance to respond, however, Jesse and Murph came crashing through the underbrush. "Zelda!" they both exclaimed.

"What are you doing here?" Jesse blurted at the same time Murph asked, "How did you find us?"

I shrugged. "You said come hiking with you sometime. Can now be sometime?"

"Of course," Murph and Jesse said in unison. Murph pushed Jesse who grinned and pushed him back. They turned to Ricky.

"Okay with you?" Jesse asked.

Ricky nodded. "*I* found her," he said and turned up the path.

I laughed, and we followed him, Jesse and Murph flanking me like they had the day of the high ropes disaster.

"Seriously, though," Jesse said. "Don't you have rehearsal?"

Our feet marched lockstep—them in hiking boots, me, woefully underprepared in my Chaco sandals—and I debated how much to tell them. They had defended me back at the ropes course. I was sure they'd be on my side, but I really didn't feel like getting into it. For now. "Free morning slash lunch," I said, grateful we were hiking side by side so no one could see my lying face.

"I can't believe you caught up," Murph grinned, side-hugging me.

I squeezed him back. "I know! I'm so glad I found you guys."

"You bring a lunch?" Ricky called from the front.

"Nope," I said.

"Just sandals?"

"Yup."

"No backpack?"

"Just this tote bag."

"Water?"

"*That* I have."

He nodded and turned back to face front. "All you need, really."

I smiled.

Twenty minutes later, we started in on some switchbacks as we approached a tall ridge. As the altitude quickly increased, our conversation quieted as we conserved our breath for actual breathing.

Finally, we reached a plateau. I transferred my tote bag to my left side and prepared to march forward, but a hand stilled my shoulder.

"Look," Jesse whispered.

Turning around, I gasped. From the ridge, you had a perspective you didn't—or couldn't—notice on the switchbacks. Standing on the ridge enabled us to see the change from leafy aspens to pine trees to squat bushes and grasses punctuated by tall black . . . what—trees?

"Three years ago, there was a forest fire here," Jesse said. "It was crazy—everything was black and dead. It looked like nothing would ever come back."

"But it has," I marveled.

"Yeah," Jesse agreed. "It's my favorite part of the forest now. Every day it's a little different. And from summer to summer—man. The forest is reclaiming itself. Regrouping. But differently than it was before."

Murph joined us. "This is where regular Jesse becomes 'Jesse the Troop Guide,'" he joked. "'Would you like a lecture on the burn area? I am Jesse the Troop Guide! It is my duty to provide it!'"

I laughed, but locked eyes with Jesse. "I'm a lecturer, too. I love a lecture." He chuckled and rubbed the back of his neck. We all stood together staring at the view for a minute.

"Come on. I'm hungry." Murph grinned. "Almost there now."

Before long, we emerged from the trees onto a field of huge boulders.

"Wow," I marveled. "It's really stark suddenly. What's up with that?"

"Above a certain altitude, trees don't grow," Jesse said. "It's called the tree line. Above it, you can see for days."

Up until this point, my lack of hiking boots hadn't been terrible, but now that we were traversing a field of boulders, I regretted my morning's choice of footwear.

"Tighten your straps," Ricky told me. "Don't want to roll an ankle."

I nodded and paused, recovering my breath and pulled on my Chaco straps. As I began to clamber again, I could feel the difference. "Thanks," I called ahead to him.

He simply waved a hand back in acknowledgment.

Ten or so minutes later, we reached the end of the boulder field. "Now just up, huh?" I said.

They exchanged a look.

"It's really windy up there today," Jesse said, frowning.

"So?" I asked, but goose bumps were already rising on my arms. I rubbed them, urging their retreat.

"So, we'll be a lot happier if we eat lunch behind this rock face as a wind break." Murph smiled.

"But we won't get to the top," I protested.

"You can go," Jesse said, "but it's cold and windy . . . I don't know. I'd be pretty miserable."

"Isn't it worth it to say you've gotten to the top?"

Ricky handed me a small, smooth stone. It was warm. "Say to who?"

I hesitated, palming the rock and stroking it with my thumb. "I don't know . . . people?"

They shrugged.

"If you want, go right ahead," Jesse said. "We'll wait."

I gazed at the summit. It was so close after how far we'd come. *Be in the moment. Make active choices. Raise the stakes.* "I'm going to do it," I said.

Every few feet, it seemed to get colder. I buttoned up my flannel, but by the time I summited, my teeth were chattering. I would have given anything to be wearing my stocking cap. I couldn't feel my fingers or toes. Looking down, I watched Jesse, Murph, and Ricky laughing and stealing each other's food. I waved with my whole arm, but none of them noticed.

They were right—I *was* miserable.

I gave a quick look around—the view was spectacular, no doubt about it. Then I hurried down the path back to my scouts.

"Blue lips," Ricky said, pointing at mine.

Wordlessly, they stood up and circled me, standing shoulder to shoulder.

Jesse met my eyes and said, "Take my hands."

I did, and already, I felt warmer.

Murph took off his Boy Scout baseball cap and put it on my head. "You lose most of your body heat through your head," he told me.

"Oh, trust me," I said, teeth still chattering, "I'm from Minnesota. That phrase is practically our state motto. We should make T-shirts."

"Or hats," Ricky said from behind me.

I smiled. "Touché."

The warmth of their collective bodies soon restored the temperature of mine from freezer to refrigerator. Suddenly, however, cold shot through me, and I released a whole-body shiver. They each took a step in even closer. Jesse put my hands on his chest and covered them with his own.

"Is this what you do if someone gets hypothermia on a backwoods hike?" I asked, chattering a little and grinning.

They exchanged looks that said, *Do we tell her? You tell her. Should we tell her?*

"What?" I asked.

"You don't have hypothermia," Jesse clarified, "you're just really cold."

"But if you did . . . ," Murph began. He offered the rest of the sentence to Ricky who shook his head.

"If I did . . . ," I prompted them.

"If you did," Jesse reluctantly continued, avoiding my eye, "you're supposed to strip down their clothes, strip down *your* clothes, and climb into a sleeping bag together."

My mouth gaped. "This is a Boy Scout rule?"

"This is a *survival* rule," Jesse corrected me. "Body heat's magic."

At the word "magic," I flashed back to Dad in the parking lot the first day of camp. "You saved my life," Dad had said, "you and your Zelda magic. I didn't know I loved your mother yet. I wouldn't know for a while. But I knew I loved you." A pang of homesickness blindsided me. I shivered to keep from crying, but they all interpreted it as further evidence of my extreme cold and stepped in farther. Jesse wrapped his arms around me. I lay my head on his chest and gave myself over to his warmth and the smell of pine and coconuts.

"Did someone *bring* a sleeping bag?" Murph muttered, rubbing my shoulders.

"I don't have hypothermia," I promised, willing myself to be strong. And warm. "Plus," I joked, lifting my head, "then one of you would have to turn into Super Boy Scout and strip down with me in said sleeping bag." I waited for the laughter, but they were quiet. Never one to let a potential joke opportunity die, I tried again. "I mean, you'd be like, 'Boys, we took an oath to help those in need, but this one's going to take some self-sacrifice—'"

"Do you—" Murph interrupted me, then paused. "We'd do it. Any of us would do it."

"Well, sure," I said, "Life or death, you're going to help anyone out, but—"

"It wouldn't be a *hardship*," Jesse said. His face looked confused. "This is a very weird conversation," he admitted, then looked at Murph, then Ricky, then me. Jesse pressed on. "You didn't peg me as one of those people who says mean things about herself so other people will build her up."

"I'm not!" I exclaimed, pushing myself out of Jesse's arms and accidentally stepping on Ricky.

"So, you really think you're . . ." Jesse looked at Murph and Ricky again. They frowned back.

"Guys, it was a stupid joke," I said, my face warming.

Tentatively, Jesse reached for my shirt sleeve and tugged on it. "Those guys on your team are assholes. You know that, right?"

I shrugged, unable to meet his eyes.

"The way they treat you is . . . it's not okay," Murph added.

"Look," I said, "I love this utopian world of equity the three of you seem to live in, but in my world, it's just the way things are." I shook my head. "It's fine. I'm fine."

"Yeah, but," Jesse went on, "that's not . . . normal. It *shouldn't* be normal."

I laughed shakily to lighten the mood. "I'm a big girl," I said, squeezing Jesse's arm. "I'll be okay."

"But will you be happy?" Ricky asked, and with a raised eyebrow, added, "'Ellie?'" I winced at "Ellie" coming from Ricky's mouth. Ricky didn't speak much, but when he did . . .

"Happy?" I shook my head. "I'm on Varsity. That's . . . that's the dream." My stomach suddenly iced over as I remembered: I had quit Varsity. "Well." I dropped Jesse's arm. "I'm much better. Warmer. Thanks, guys."

They all stared at me. I felt like they didn't believe me. They were right not to believe me, of course, but I still wanted them to.

Then Ricky reached into his pocket and handed me a sandwich wrapped in wax paper. My breath caught, and my stomach ice melted a little.

"Lunch," he said.

I bit my lips and nodded, accepting the gift.

You'd think hiking *down* would be easier than hiking *up*, but it depends on what you mean by "easier." Sure, it's easier on your lungs. But your joints are another story altogether.

Every step started to feel like a punch to my knees.

Jesse caught me rubbing them on a water break. "Slamming a little too hard?"

I nodded. "Maybe."

"Be gentle with yourself," he said and poked me in the leg.

Murph stood up. "Hey, Zelda, you know what we should do? My girlfriend, Josie, taught me those riddles where you give a really cryptic line and everyone asks yes or no questions to find out what happened. I've already done them with these two—"

"Several times," Jesse inserted, smirking.

"What? No!"

"More than several," Ricky muttered, tucking his water back into his pack.

I grinned. "Well, I hate to be a downer, but you can't beat me at those. My parents love road trips, so I know 'em all."

Murph rubbed his hands together. "Challenge accepted. Let me see . . . Okay. The police find a dead man locked in a room from the inside. The only things in the room are rope and—"

"A puddle of water." I interrupted him. "The guy stood on a block of ice and hanged himself."

"Zelda!" Murph scooped up a pinecone and threw it at me. Laughing, I batted it away.

"Okay, okay . . . How about this one: A man is found dead in a field with an unopened package—" Murph began.

"Airplane. Guy jumped, parachute didn't open." I grinned.

"Come on!" Another pinecone.

Now Jesse and Ricky joined in on the laughter.

"Do you know the one about the man and the bar and the glass of water?" Murph asked.

"The gun one?" I shifted my tote bag. "Hiccups?"

Murph shook his head. "I'm out. That's all I know."

Jesse laughed. "Good thing there isn't a merit badge for riddles. You'd be short on that one, too."

Murph threw two pinecones at Jesse.

"We should go," Jesse said as he batted them away. "We're nearly there."

My grin faded a little. Once we returned to camp, I was going to have to figure something out.

"Ready?" Jesse smiled.

Trust yourself. I nodded.

We fell into a line and silence, all of us consciously or unconsciously slowing our pace. I don't think any of us wanted our lunch hike to end.

Murph called back, "Wait! A man pushes his car to a hotel—"

"He's playing Monopoly," I called back.

Ricky and Jesse laughed again.

We hiked in companionable silence for a few minutes. Then I felt a tug on my tote bag. I turned around to see Jesse's warm smile.

"Feeling better?"

I dropped back so we were side by side. "Much better. Thanks."

"I hope your near-hypothermic adventure hasn't scared you

away from coming with us on another lunch hike." Not meeting my eye, he adjusted his backpack.

I laughed a little. "I don't scare easily."

He nodded and flicked a glance in my direction. "I can tell."

I took a quick step ahead of him when the path narrowed, but fell back into step with him as soon as it widened.

Ahead of us, Ricky touched Murph's elbow and pointed at something in one of the pine trees.

"Ricky doesn't say a lot," I said, wishing some of the improv guys I knew could take a page from his book.

Jesse nodded. "One of those brilliant but shy types. He's actually talked way more to you than he usually does with new people."

"Really?" I asked, smiling up at him. "That's nice to hear."

"Do you ever have free evenings?" he blurted. We stopped hiking.

I frowned. Soon I might have free evenings. Free mornings and afternoons, too.

He misinterpreted my frown. "I just mean, this was so much fun. I—*we*—like hanging out with you. Ricky, Murph, me—we should hang out . . . all of us. With you. If you want to."

If I *wanted* to? I nearly burst into tears of gratitude. "Yeah, I—I like hanging out with you guys, too. I'll . . . check my skedj."

He grinned. "It sucks not having cell phones up here. I mean, what is this—the nineties or something?"

I laughed. "Yeah—how do I let you know when I'm free? Wait until another ill-fated high ropes course gets scheduled?"

He chuckled. "I hope not . . . I'm sure we'll figure it out."

We smiled for a moment, and then he looked over my shoulder. "We should probably . . . catch up."

"Right!" I turned around and jogged a little.

"Whoa—no need to win a land speed race or anything," he called.

I made a big production of bending in half and pretending to breathe hard. "Too bad," I fake-wheezed, "cuz I was going to totally beat you."

He pursed his lips together and his eyes widened. "Try me." He tore off ahead of me, but I was not about to hang back and let him win. He had me in height, but I had lighter shoes. And a lighter bag. And I was not above deception.

"Ow!" I hollered.

He stopped in his tracks and whirled around. "What's wrong?"

The hesitation bought me just enough time to blow past him at speed. "Nothing now!" I called.

I grinned at the sound of his laughter and boot footfalls thudding on the path. "You are never going to—"

I think I heard him say "win," but I was too busy flying through the air to be sure. Time slowed down as I splayed my arms out in front of me to catch my fall, but then time triple-sped up, and I was a pile of arms and legs and pain.

"Zelda!" Jesse caught up quickly. "Are you okay?"

I tried to move my toes, but agony shot up my legs and I hissed. I rubbed my hip and elbow where I'd landed. "I'm—"

Footsteps sounded from around the corner belonging to Murph and Ricky and—I swallowed hard: Ben.

CHAPTER SEVENTEEN

"Ellie?" Ben pushed past Ricky and Murph and lifted me up.

"Hold on," Jesse held up his hands, "You shouldn't touch or move her until we check to see if she's broken anyth—"

"I'm taking her to the nurse's office." Ben's voice was cold.

"Wait," I said, struggling a little to be put down.

Ben tightened his hold and looked at me, cheeks flushed, his eyes beginning to well with tears. "Do you have any idea how worried I've been?"

I stopped breathing. I couldn't speak. He wasn't mad at me— he'd been worried. Had I been too hasty? Was there a chance to fix what had been broken between the team and me—and me and Ben?

Our eye contact was finally interrupted by a cough. The Boy Scouts stood shoulder to shoulder. I stared at my knees.

Finally, I said, "Thanks, guys, for the hike."

Ben turned us toward the Lodge.

"Bye," they muttered as Ben walked us away. The last thing I heard was Murph ask, "Why would he have been *worried*? Didn't they have the morning off?"

Ben was quiet as he carried me down the path. I had a million questions—like, where was everyone else? How did he find us? But the peace felt too fragile to push it.

Now we were in sight of the Lodge. "The nurse's office is inside, just past the kitchen," he said.

I wasn't sure what to feel. He certainly seemed sincere with his concern. And while I knew I could be enjoying the warmth and closeness of being held in his California muscly arms, I held my body stiffly, looking around to make sure no one was watching. Thankfully everyone else must have been deep into rehearsal.

After a few steps this way, he quietly said, "It's okay to relax. I've got you."

His voice sounded so concerned, and I didn't want to hurt his feelings or make him angry. So, I took a deep breath and exhaled, willing it to diffuse my tense muscles. Gently, he held me even closer.

The stairs up to the Lodge slowed Ben down a little, but he resumed his speed after he wedged open the screen door with his foot, crossing into the main room. We turned down the back hallway past the kitchen and a door marked "Office." Probably the Pauls'?

"Can you knock?" he whispered when we arrived at what I assumed was the nurse's office. "My, uh, hands are full." One side of his mouth raised up, and he slowly met my eyes.

I nodded, heart beating in my throat. I rapped twice on the door. It didn't sound like anyone was inside. I tried the knob, and it opened, the door swinging into the room.

My eyes swept over a tall, white, two-door cabinet, a sink, mirror, and two army surplus cots. A rolling office chair was pulled up to the desk, which was in reach of a tall filing cabinet. It all looked old. Like it was straight out of *Dirty Dancing*.

"No one here," I said.

Ben strode to one of the cots and gently set me down.

"Let's see what we've got here," he muttered. I scooted back and sat on the end of the cot. "This foot?" he pointed to my left, and I nodded. The toes were bright red, but weren't swollen or anything. "Let's get this sandal off."

Lightning shot up my leg as he loosened the strap of my Chaco and slid it off, palming the arch of my foot. But the lightning wasn't pain. It was something else entirely. As cold as I had been on the summit of that mountain, I was equally warm now. He ran a finger across the top of my foot. My eyelids fluttered shut. This was—no one had ever touched me like this before.

"Feel okay?" he asked in a low voice.

I nodded, eyes still closed.

"Should we take a look at anything else?"

I pointed to my left elbow and opened my eyes a little.

He unbuttoned the cuff of my flannel and lowered it off my shoulder, gently guiding my arm out. Everywhere he touched me set off fireworks. Gently, he bent my arm back and forth. "Feel okay?"

I nodded.

"Anything else?"

My hip was going to be purple the next morning, I was sure, but there was no need for him to . . . well . . .

I shook my head.

"Good," he smiled, still holding my forearm. Then, he released it and picked at the sleeve of my flannel. "Ellie, I'm so sorry about what happened this morning. It stops now. I'll never let anything happen again like what happened today."

I nodded. "Good. Thank you."

He met my eyes. "We all talked. After you left. I know I shouldn't have written that sketch. It just wasn't funny."

"...And it was mean."

"Well, comedy isn't always *nice*," he argued.

I gave him a look.

"But that was ... it was a bad sketch." He sighed and tucked a curl behind my ear. "You ... I know I'm extra hard on you."

He cupped my cheek, and I closed my eyes again. "But it's just because you're so talented."

I scoffed.

He took his hand away, and I opened my eyes.

"It's true," he insisted.

Biting my lip, I picked at a thread in the cot. His compliment was nice, but—

"What about the rest of the team?" I asked.

"Best behavior." He raised his right hand like he was swearing in court. "They're writing apology letters in the cabin. Come back. Please. We need you."

This was all turning out much better than I could have hoped for. Still, I had reasons for being skeptical. "Let me think about it," I said.

In response, I expected him to nod or maybe talk me into saying I'd come back. I did *not* expect what happened next.

He dropped his head in his hands and began to shake.

My eyes widened. "Are you *laughing* at me?"

He looked at me straight in the eye. His own eyes were filled with tears.

Instinctively, I reached out to wipe one rolling down his cheek.

He covered my hand with his own and held it there.

"What's wrong?" I whispered.

He closed his eyes and shook his head slightly, still holding my hand to his face. "This—you—this is all my fault." His voice shook. "None of this would have happened if Marcus was still here."

I wasn't sure how to react to that.

"Now the Pauls told me that Calvin Paige is coming. We started here the same year, and he's already on a weekly Harold team at UCB and has had supporting roles in two movies. Plus, he just got a national commercial we were both up for. I know he's just coming to rub it in my face." He squeezed my hand hard. "It's *killing* me I won't be performing in the show. Plus, my..." he shuddered and lowered my hand. "My dad... died this spring."

"Oh, Ben," I murmured, gingerly adjusting my position on the cot so we were sitting hip to hip. "Come here," I said.

He laid his head on my shoulder, and I wrapped my arms around him.

"He had cancer. It went so fast. And when my dad talked about my career, he'd always say, 'My kid's going to be famous.' He'll never get to see that come true. *If* it comes true."

"Shhh..." I whispered, stroking his hair.

He hugged me back. "I'm sorry for dumping all of this on you. Plus, I've been such a jerk. I haven't been myself. I'm so sorry. Please forgive me. I want to be a good coach. I just—I can't—"

"It's okay," I assured him. Good lord. He'd just lost his *dad*? No wonder he'd been so hot and cold. I felt my anger cool a little.

"Ellie." He pulled back, his face wet with tears. "Please don't hang out with those Boy Scouts."

I frowned. What did it matter to him who I—

"Please don't leave me," he continued, squeezing my hands. "I can't bear losing someone else right now. Especially if that someone is you."

My heart flip-flopped.

"Say you'll stay. Please?"

I hesitated. Could he really assure me that his coaching style *and* the team's attitude had changed in three hours? I looked into his eyes. Deep pools of sadness pleaded back. Those eyes . . . he *seemed* sincere. Maybe no one had ever stood up to Ben before like I had. Mom always says kids feel safer with boundaries—maybe Ben was feeling extra vulnerable without his dad *and* without Marcus here, and the boundaries I'd insisted upon were just what he needed to feel secure enough to do the right thing. And the Gildas—I had to be their Nina Knightley. I wiped his tears with my thumbs. *Say yes . . .*

"Okay," I nodded. "I'll stay."

He cradled my head in both of his large hands and stared at me. His eyes flicked down to my lips, then back up. He leaned in slowly.

He was going to kiss me again. I panicked and grabbed his wrists to stop him.

"What?" he whispered.

"I'm not . . . good at this. You—wrote that sketch and I—"

He smiled. "I'll teach you."

CHAPTER EIGHTEEN

What had just happened?

After some . . . awkward kissing (seriously—I was the *worst*), Ben stood up and stretched.

"Well," he grinned, cracking his back, "why don't you head to the cabin, ice your foot, and just . . . relax."

I inspected my bitten-up fingernails and opened my mouth to ask if the kissing had been as bad for him as I was worried it had been, but he cut me off.

"Here, Ellie." He opened a drawer and chucked me an ice pack. "See you at dinner."

Then I was alone.

WillWillWillWillWill. I needed to find Will.

Swinging my leg off the cot, I tested putting pressure on my foot. It was tender, but the shooting pain was gone. I slid my sandal on, keeping the strap loose, stood up, and shifted my body weight back and forth. It didn't hurt to stand.

I smiled and stepped forward. Then I nearly collapsed. The

shooting pain had returned. When I experimented further, I found if I kept weight off my toes, I could limp a bit on my heel.

I hobbled as fast as I could out of the nurse's office and down the hall in pursuit of Will. Until Ben had carried me in this way, I'd never been back to this part of the Main Lodge. I limped past the Pauls' office and the kitchen, but when I reached the foot of the stairs heading to the second floor, I paused: laughter. That was probably JV rehearsing, so that's where I'd find Will. Using the railing, I hauled myself up the steps, pivoting on my heel. When I reached the top, I took a swig of water to reward my effort.

But now what? There were eight rehearsal rooms. I guessed I could just peek in each room until—but then I heard Will's distinct laugh: a donkey bray. He doesn't let himself go very often, and I was thankful in this moment he did.

I cracked open the door to Rehearsal Room C and peered inside.

Four people were frozen in a tableau. Paloma stood to the side in such a way that made me assume she was controlling the scene. Will and the others were shaking with laughter. Their coach, Roger, was crouched against the wall, his head in his hands. The more everyone laughed, the more pleased Paloma's face became. The players frozen in place began to shake from holding their positions for so long.

They were happy.

I didn't want to break that up.

Easing the door closed, I pivoted on my heel just in time to see Sirena bound up the stairs.

"Hi," I said in a low voice.

"Hi, Zelda!" she said, smiling as she put her hand on the door-knob to the rehearsal room. Then she took a second look at me and frowned. "What's wrong?"

I shook my head and rubbed my eyebrow. "Crazy morning. I was hoping to talk to Will, but they're neck deep in something hilarious. He'd never forgive me for pulling him out of that."

She nodded slowly. "Break's in fifteen. Or we might call it for the day . . . You want to come in until then?"

"No, it's okay. I don't want to interrupt." I pulled my bag higher on my shoulder and tried to fix my features into a no-one's-made-out-with-me-lately-especially-not-my-coach face.

Sirena stared at me for a moment with her head cocked. Then she pushed her glasses back on her nose and nodded at rehearsal. "I should get back in there—unless you want to talk or something."

I did—desperately—but I really needed Will first. I reached out and squeezed her forearm. "I'll be okay. Have fun."

"Okay . . ." She squeezed my arm back, nodded once, and slipped into the room.

Fifteen minutes. I slid down the wall and cracked my ice pack in half, propping it on my foot. I sighed with relief as the cool pressure tingled against my toes. Wiggling them experimentally, I decided I'd probably be fine in a day or two. They were achy, but I didn't think they were broken.

Not that there's much you can do for a broken toe. When Will and I were in fifth grade, Mom broke one as she was lugging climbing equipment out of the Adventure Closet in the basement. The doctor had just taped her broken toe to the one next to it. "Its buddy helps the broken one heal," she'd said.

I missed Will, my own buddy toe.

But soon, he slipped out of the door of the rehearsal room. "Hey, Sirena told me you—holy Jesus, Z, what happened to you?"

Then, for the first time since this whole thing had started, I began to cry in front of someone. It poured out of me in waves crashing onto the shore of Will. He gathered me in his arms and just sat there, holding me while I sobbed. I wiped my tears with the sleeve of my flannel, and pretty soon I was wiping my nose with it, too.

"Can you walk?" he asked when my tears had started to let up a little. I nodded. He helped me down the stairs and out onto the wraparound porch. We sat on a bench around the corner from the main door.

"Okay," he said, folding his arms, "did *he* do this to you?"

I furrowed my brow. "Who? Ben? No! He—" And then all I could think about was the weird, awkward kissing I'd just participated in. Something must have shown on my face because he tugged on my shirt sleeve.

"Tell me."

So, I did. I told him about rehearsals. The high ropes course. My makeup rehearsal. The kissing scene.

At that point, he pursed his lips so tightly they became a straight, hard line of disapproval. But I pushed on. I told him about my cold open that everyone loved. The terrible and embarrassing scene Ben wrote. My storming off. My hike with the Boy Scouts. My fall. Ben's rescuing me. The nurse's office.

"So, you're back on Varsity," he said evenly.

I nodded.

"And you kissed him."

I pulled at my sleeve and nodded again, not looking at him.

He sighed. "He's your coach."

"I know," I said, "I feel really stupid. But—"

"But nothing. It's a power thing. He shouldn't be taking advantage of you like that."

"He wasn't taking *advantage*, exactly," I protested.

"No? He humiliates you in front of your team. He doesn't stand up for you when they take their turn. He yanks you around, being all hot and cold. He *writes* a *scene* about how you don't know how to kiss—"

I buried my face in my hands.

"And it is *fine*, by the way, that you don't know how. You'll learn. With the right person, the learning is . . ." He couldn't push down the smile fighting at the corners of his mouth.

I hit his arm.

"It is!" He laughed a little and pushed me back.

"Ben could be the right person—"

But Will was already shaking his head. "He isn't. He isn't!" he insisted. "I know I've only had a boyfriend for like five days or whatever, but we've known plenty of other people in relationships. I know it shouldn't be this hard. Or this weird."

"But his dad just died—"

He shook his head again. "No, Z. There are no excuses for how he's been treating you. Can't you see that? The two of you are just wrong together."

Fire rose up in my belly. "Not everyone gets a Jonas, okay?" I spat. "Would I like a wonderful guy who was my friend for a long time and then suddenly falls in love with me? You bet! But look around! I'm seventeen years old and no one has ever wanted to *hold my hand*, much less *kiss* me. And Ben likes me, okay? I'm sorry it's not up to your pristine standards, but forgive me if I want to see what happens!"

"This isn't just about the kissing, okay?" he hissed. "And maybe keep your voice down?"

I shook my head and rolled my eyes.

"This," he continued, "is about his coaching, too. He's not being a good coach. You don't have to put up with that. You—"

"Yes, I do!" I couldn't take it anymore. I sprang to my feet, momentarily forgetting about my toes. I yelped in pain and flopped back down. I settled for folding my arms instead. "I am the only girl in fifteen *years* to make Varsity. This isn't just about me."

He cocked an eyebrow. "Who else is this about?"

"Women!" I exclaimed. Two guys in baseball caps walking down the path below the porch looked up. I forced a smile and waved. After a moment of hesitation, they waved back. I lowered my voice. "When I make a mistake, or have a bad scene, it's not just about me, Zelda, the individual doing that. These guys add it to evidence that girls aren't funny. It's *all* women."

Will scoffed.

My eyes pricked with tears again, and I hit Will's arm. "It's true!"

"You think you're a stand-in for *all women*? Come on, Z, you're putting a lot of pressure on yourself."

I clenched my jaw. "Do you know what High Ropes Jake said to me during rehearsal yesterday? 'You're pretty funny for a girl.'"

"That's one jerk. Or he was joking."

"When I messed up on auditions during 185, Brandon muttered, 'That's because girls aren't funny.'"

"*Two* jerks."

I whacked Will on the arm again. "Will! Don't make me feel like a crazy person! This is happening! Why haven't there been any girls on Varsity for fifteen *years*?"

"Well, maybe—"

"If you're thinking it's because no one has been good enough," I threatened, pointing a finger at him, "I seriously doubt that."

"Hardly any girls come here," he said, not meeting my eyes.

"Maybe because it's not a safe place to be a girl!" I hissed. Rehearsal was letting out and people started streaming out of the Main Lodge.

Suddenly, Will shook his head like he was waking up from a nap. "Z, *I'm* the one who said he's a bad coach. *You* were defending him. And now . . ." He shook his head again, slower this time. "What are we even arguing about?"

I opened my mouth, but no words came out.

"I don't think you can have it both ways," he said, cocking an eyebrow.

I leaned over to wipe that look off his face, but he dodged my hand.

"Look," I said, pressing on, "whatever. I have to be on Varsity. For Paloma and Emily and Hanna and Sirena. And whatever this thing with Ben is . . . that's what I have. I didn't come to you for a lecture, Will."

"Well, I just want—"

"Will? Are you ready for our hike?" It was Jonas's voice.

I stared at Will, daring him to finish his sentence. He stared back.

"Hey, guys," Jonas said, but he only looked at Will.

Will's eyes held mine for a split-second longer, then broke away to beam up at Jonas. "Hey. Are they calling it for the day?"

But Jonas had noticed my foot. "Zelda!"

"I tripped," I said, forcing a smile.

Jonas looked over his shoulder at the crowd. "Hanna! Paloma! Come here! Zelda hurt her foot!"

I groaned a little as their footsteps thundered across the porch.

"What happened?" Paloma asked, hands on her hips.

I shrugged. "I tripped."

Hanna raised a skeptical eyebrow. "On?"

Inwardly sighing, I forced another smile. "A tree root."

I picked at the paint chipping on the bench, but I could feel Hanna's gaze.

"You, Zelda-girl, are leaving out details."

I shook my head. "Nope. I just wasn't looking."

"Because you *were* looking at . . ."

"Can we not—here?" I begged. "Are you done for the day or what?"

Hanna smirked. "Done. Where are we going?"

Will looked like he had something else to say, but Jonas swept him away.

Hanna plopped down in Will's chair. "You were saying?

"I wasn't," I said. "Not here."

"To Gilda Radner!" Hanna announced.

Ten very slow, hobble-y minutes later, Paloma and Hanna and I retreated to the inner sanctum that was Gilda Radner.

Hanna dug into her bag and pulled out a package of Twizzlers. We climbed onto her bunk, side-by-side-by-side and leaned against the wall, legs out in front of us.

"By the way," Hanna said, ripping open the bag, "I stole these Twizzlers from some Varsity guy's backpack." She bit into one straight from the package.

"Hanna!" Paloma and I protested.

She smirked. "Also Jolly Ranchers. Candy stolen from jerks tastes extra delicious."

We shook our heads at her, but I accepted a Twizzler and secretly agreed.

The screen door banged open, revealing Sirena and Emily.

"We just ran into Jonas and Will," Emily panted.

Sirena crossed the cabin in a few short strides and plucked two Twizzlers from Hanna's bag, passing one off to Emily.

"Stolen Twizzlers, Sirena," Paloma warned her.

"From?" Sirena hesitated.

"That Varsity ass with the beady eyes."

She flipped her braids over her shoulder. "Well done."

Paloma huffed a little, but I noticed it didn't stop her from plucking her own Twizzler out of the bag.

Then the two of them settled themselves on the bunk across from us. Taking a big bite from their Twizzlers in unison, Sirena nodded. "I *knew* you weren't okay earlier. What happened?"

I swallowed. And then for the second time that day, I spilled.

"He wrote a *sketch* about you being a bad *kisser*?" A tear stole out of Emily's eye. Lip trembling, she swiped it away and leaned into Sirena. "That's . . . *so* mean." The others were slack-jawed with shock.

The shock on my behalf fueled my desire to continue to confess. When I got to the hike with the Boy Scouts, Paloma interrupted me. "Wait wait wait. Ben likes you. Do you like *him*?"

I hesitated. "Uh—wait a second until I get to the foot injury."

"Oh my god," Hanna grabbed my shoulders and turned me toward her. "Zelda-girl, there are three sculpted man-cubs who also like you. You have *four*—"

"The Boy Scouts don't *like* me," I argued, pulling out of her grasp. "We're friends."

Everyone exchanged a skeptical look.

"We have already agreed upon your assets," Sirena waved a hand like this was a done deal. "Zelda. You have four boys in pursuit of you."

I folded my arms. "Murph has a girlfriend—"

"*Three.* Still unreal."

"I really don't think—"

"Continue." Hanna interrupted me now, pulling out the bag of stolen Jolly Ranchers. "Please don't leave out any details. Was there Boy Scout kissing?"

My chest felt tight. "No, but—"

"But?!" That was everyone.

I told them about the fall and Ben and the Nurse's office.

"What?!" Paloma squawked. She scrambled off the bed. She looked ready to find him and punch him in the face. "*That* guy is a Class A asshole."

"But—" I accepted a handful of Jolly Ranchers from Hanna. "He did all the things someone does when they like you . . . right?"

"On the surface, maybe." Sirena looked to the others for backup.

"I said it before." Emily blinked away another tear. "He seems mean."

"He's not mean," I said.

"He wrote a *sketch* about you being a bad—" Paloma began, fists clenched.

"Yes, yes, I'm a terrible kisser—that's been well-established," I snapped.

Sirena cocked her head at me. "Okay, but how much kissing have you done in your life?"

I traced the lines of plaid on the sleeping bag I was sitting on. "Just . . . with . . . him."

No one said anything.

"Okay." Paloma rejoined me on the bed. "Indulge me for a second. Can you ride a bike?"

"Yes."

"Could you the first time you tried?"

I folded my arms. "No."

She poked me in the arm. "What did it take to learn?"

I rolled my eyes. "Practice."

"And who taught you?"

"My dad."

"And did he write a mocking sketch about how terrible you were at it the first time you tried?"

"Of course not," I mumbled, shifting on the bunk. Some Jolly Rancher wrappers drifted to the floor.

"Of *course* not," she repeated, punching the bed with a fist.

"Ben didn't know it was my first time," I said. "It's different."

Paloma growled. "I still disagree, but fine. What about when he yelled at you in front of the team at the high ropes course?"

"He was afraid. It came out as anger," I said.

"Or," she argued, attempting to tear up a Jolly Rancher wrapper, "it was all about power. You were talking that kid down—you were succeeding where he couldn't, and he turned the tables on you."

I shook my head. "That's not the whole situation."

"Okay." She leaned across me and dug her hand into the Jolly Rancher bag. "What about not checking to see if something was broken and just whisking you off to the nurse's office?"

"He was swept up in the moment!"

"Or he was jealous of the Boy Scouts!" Paloma said, angrily struggling to unwrap her Jolly Rancher until it flew out of her hands and skittered under the opposite bunk.

"He cares about me!" I exclaimed. Paloma was starting to climb under the bunk to retrieve the candy, but she managed to shoot me a disbelieving look first. "He does," I insisted. "He's different when it's just us alone together."

Paloma paused in her search under the bed. I felt everyone else's eyes on me.

"Is that what you want, Zelda-girl?" Hanna asked. She pushed my knee. "Someone who's only nice to you sometimes?"

I closed my eyes for a moment. They didn't understand. "He doesn't want people to think the only reason I'm on Varsity is because he likes me. He's protecting me."

Emily tilted her head. "Do you like him?"

"I—" My mind was buzzing with images of the past few days. "No one likes me like that. Ever. It's not really the flannel shirts. I'm too . . . something."

"Smart and independent and funnier than them?" Paloma bit out as she backed out from under the bunk.

I sighed and shook my head. In one hand I started arranging Jolly Ranchers in rainbow order. "All I know is no one has ever shown an interest in me until Ben. Maybe not everyone gets a perfect partner."

"*No* one gets a perfect partner," Paloma said. "But *everyone* gets to have a kind one. Look. Significant others are like airplane Wi-Fi."

I bit my lips and looked at Paloma expectantly.

"You don't *need* airplane Wi-Fi. You can read a book. Talk to people. Draw. But airplane Wi-Fi can be fun—you can watch a movie. Be on your phone. But if you're going to have Wi-Fi, it has to be consistent. Because if it's spotty, if it just stops and starts and freezes in the middle of binge-watching *Parks and Rec*, that's maddening. It's crazy-making. Better no airplane Wi-Fi than bad airplane Wi-Fi. Make sense?"

I quirked a half smile. "Paloma. How are you so freaking smart?"

Hanna threw a handful of Jolly Ranchers under the bed and raised her eyebrows at Paloma in a challenge. "Both of her parents are therapists."

"Both?" Emily, Sirena, and I demanded.

Paloma glared at Hanna then crawled back under the bed to retrieve the candy. "I lose my temper sometimes," she called out, "but basically I'm all kinds of adjusted."

We laughed.

But I had to make them understand. "Ben's not bad airplane Wi-Fi," I said.

Hanna shrugged. "Look. It's your life. You can date Ben, kiss as many consenting Boy Scouts as you want, or—I don't know—take a bikini-wearing ferret to the grocery store in December if it makes you happy. All we're saying, is you don't *seem* hap—"

"I'm fine," I insisted. "It's complicated, but it's not *bad*. Ben's not *bad*."

"Okay," Sirena said, but I could tell she didn't really believe me. She leaned forward. "Wait. So Varsity. It sucks. They're terrible. Having Ben as a coach is . . . complicated—at best."

I nodded.

"And you're staying on Varsity because . . . ," Sirena said, squinting at me.

I looked around at us. "Because of you. Us. Women."

"But you're miserable," Emily whimpered. "They're terrible to you."

I shook my head. "If I leave, they'll have won."

"If you stay," Sirena mused, "doesn't that excuse their behavior? Haven't they won again?"

I turned to Paloma, who had just climbed back on the bed. "You told me I had to do this for us. For women."

She looked at the ground, nodding. "I did. I did say that. Because . . . I thought it would be easier for you than for the rest of us."

I cocked my head. "Easier how?"

She glanced at the others. "The rest of us are just…carrying more. Sirena and I are people of color. Hanna's got albinism. Emily gets harassed for her size; she and Sirena are gay."

I chewed on my cheek. "That's true." I looked around at each of the Gildas. "But none of that should matter in improv."

Sirena gave me a tired half smile. "It shouldn't matter, Zelda, but it does."

Paloma bumped my shoulder with hers. "It *is* easier for you, probably, than it would be for the rest of us, but it's still freaking hard. I didn't fully realize how abusive they were being to you."

"It's not *abusive*," I protested.

She put a hand on one hip. "Two therapist parents. Trust me. I know abuse when I see it, and I also know you don't have to stay in an abusive situation to try to win a moral victory, Zelda."

I lifted the ice pack off my foot. My toes were numb. "I can do it. I have something to prove."

Sirena shook her head at me. "Just remember: you're not alone, Zelda."

"Neither are you," I said back to her.

"And neither are you," Sirena said, turning to Emily.

"And neither are you," Emily said to Hanna.

Hanna looked at Paloma. "You, on the other hand, are the only well-adjusted one here. So, you are totally alone."

The laughter soothed my lungs.

Hanna and Paloma went to the Lodge at dinner and sneaked back a whole tray of coffee cake, a bag of oranges, and a bowl of unshelled peanuts. A strange little meal, but no one was eager to face the world outside Gilda Radner for very long yet.

After dinner, we shoved the three bunk beds we were using into a triangle. We pulled the mattresses off the other five unused bunks and carpeted the floor with them.

"I love it." Emily sighed happily, helping lug the last mattress into place. "It's so cozy in here now."

"It's too bad we don't have like a thousand blankets," Sirena said, collapsing onto her back. "That would make Mattress Island even better."

"Wait," Hanna announced, holding up a hand. "*I* have something that'll make the *whole cabin* even better. Close your eyes. It's a surprise."

Paloma raised her eyebrows at Hanna. "The last time you told me to close my eyes for a surprise, I found all of the pepperoni had been stolen off my pizza."

"It *was* a surprise, though. Admit it," Hanna said, waving her away. "Close 'em! This surprise is not food-related."

Still favoring my foot, I plopped down next to Sirena and obeyed Hanna.

There was a click, and a pleasant beep. Then, "Whoooooooooo oooooooaaaaaaammmmm! Whuuuuuuuuuuuuuuuuuaaaaalllll!"

Our eyes all flew open.

"*Pacific Coast Whale Sounds!*" Emily and Sirena and I shouted, laughing.

"This is worse than the pepperoni surprise," Paloma moaned. She scrambled to her feet and launched herself at the Discman on the dresser to shut it down, but Hanna threw her body on top of it, shouting, "I love it now! It's the sound my soul makes!"

Sirena and Emily and I lay back on our elbows in the middle of Mattress Island, laughing, as Paloma finally got a hand between Hanna and the Discman and disconnected it from the speakers.

"What are you guys *doing*?" It was Will, outside the cabin's screen door.

Jonas pushed open the door, kicked his shoes off, and somersaulted onto Mattress Island. "Genius!" he shouted.

Will met my eye. His raised eyebrows asked if I was okay. I shrugged and tried to give him a reassuring smile. It had been nice to forget about Ben for a little while, but ultimately, I really wasn't sure *what* to think.

"We can't stay," Will said as Jonas leapt from mattress to mattress. "Because it's curfew soon and—Jonas? Did you just unironically say 'Weeee!'?"

CHAPTER NINETEEN

Jonas and Will left, and the rest of us stayed up late, all drunk on the slumber party atmosphere. Consequently, we slept through breakfast.

Luckily, we had coffee cake leftovers; so after throwing on some clothes, jamming my stocking cap over my frizzy curls, and promising myself to shower today and actually *do* something with my hair, we toasted with coffee cake and hauled off to rehearsal.

Before Sirena headed up the stairs with the others, she grabbed my sleeve. "Remember. You're not alone."

I nodded. "Thank you."

Xander and Brandon passed us on in the way in. "Hey," they said.

"See?" I smiled, whispering to Sirena. "They greeted me. It's going to be great."

She raised her eyebrows. "Glad to see your high expectations." She gave my arm a squeeze and took the stairs two at a time.

Ben was arranging rehearsal blocks on stage and didn't see me limp in. I tried to smile at everyone else as they entered, but no one made eye contact.

I attempted not to stare at Ben as he lifted one rehearsal block after another, his biceps flexing and straining against his UCB long-sleeve T-shirt.

He liked me. A really hot guy liked me. And I liked him. Right? He certainly made me feel things. Watching his body move on the stage and thinking about him touching me was making me feel warm all over.

Then he caught my eye. He pointed at his foot with a questioning look.

I gave him a small smile and a shrug. *It's okay.*

He held my gaze two seconds short of being downright seductive, then clapped his hands. "Party Quirks. Brandon, get the suggestions. Xander, Cade, Trey, Jake, and Ellie, you're up."

I frowned a little as I climbed on stage. He wasn't even going to mention what had happened yesterday? He'd told me they were writing apology notes. Where were they? And we were also leaping straight into a game structure without warming up? Were warm-ups suddenly on his long list of "crutches"?

"Brandon, start us off." Ben sat backward on a folding chair in the audience, and Brandon hopped forward and flashed me a friendly smile.

I looked behind me. I was definitely the only one there . . . *Okay.* Then again, maybe Ben *had* talked to everyone already and didn't want to beat a dead horse by bringing it up again.

Shake it off, I told myself. *It's fine. Trust yourself. Trust your partner. You can do this.*

Brandon held out his hands. "Okay. You know when you throw a party and people show up whose names you know you're supposed to remember but you can't quite do it? We are those people."

"Good explanation. It'll get a laugh, too." said Ben. "Keep going."

I glanced up and down the line. Everyone shared my determined look. I smiled and faced forward.

"We are going to go to—" Brandon looked down the row of players. "Xander's party. In a minute, I'll be looking for suggestions as to who we all are, and then Xander will try to guess our identities. So Xander doesn't hear the suggestions, can I get a volunteer to go with him into the hallway?"

Ben pretended to be an audience member. "Me! I'll go!"

"Settle down, man, I don't swing that way." Xander chuckled and jogged out of the room.

"Uh," I started, "that's not exactly awesome in terms of gay—"

Brandon kept going like he hadn't heard me. "See you soon, Xander!"

I looked at Ben to see if he was going to address Xander's homophobic joke, but he was focused on Brandon.

Brandon pointed at High Ropes Jake. "For Jake here, I need a historical figure."

"Abraham Lincoln," Ben called.

"And Abe has a secret."

"He's gay," Jake 2 hollered.

I rolled my eyes.

"Okay, for Trey, I need a movie star."

"Will Smith," Ben offered.

"Great. Will Smith has something he needs to give Abe Lincoln. What is it?"

"A punch in the face for not freeing the slaves earlier!" Jake 2 called. He turned to Donovan and clapped him on the back. "Right, my brother?"

My eyes grew huge. Anger flashed in Donovan's eyes, but it was gone so quickly, I thought I might have imagined it.

"Right," Donovan said. "Punch him hard, Trey."

Trey mock-punched High Ropes Jake in the stomach, and Jake played along.

"Guys," I said, meeting Donovan's eyes, "maybe we should stay away from—"

"It's just jokes, Ellie," Donovan said. "Jokes always offend someone or they're not jokes."

I didn't think that had to be true, but before I had a chance to respond, Ben inserted himself. "Let's all remember *I'm* giving the suggestions here," he said.

THAT was Ben's way of trying to right the ship?

"Sure, but that was a good suggestion," Brandon said. "I'll take it. Damn you, Lincoln."

Ben said nothing.

Donovan and Trey said nothing.

I said nothing.

But a new pit developed in my stomach. Had there been other crappy moments like Jake 2 calling Donovan "my brother," but I'd been too focused on myself to notice?

Brandon clamped a hand on Cade's shoulder. "Now for Ellie and Cade, I need two things that go together."

Ben paused a moment. "The president and the vice president."

I nodded. No prostitutes in sight.

"And they forgot something at Xander's house."

"The Constitution."

Lovely. Okay. Things were looking up.

"Now, when Xander gets close to guessing who's at his party, clap a little. When he gets closer, clap louder, and when he gets it, go crazy! Let's call Xander back in. One, two, three—"

We all hollered, "Xander!"

Xander trotted back in the room as we cleared to neutral.

"I told you, man, I've got a girlfriend," he joked as he mimed setting up the party.

I closed my eyes for a minute. These guys were trapped so hard in this tiny box of acceptable heterosexual male behavior. I tried to feel sorry for them instead of angry.

I pulled on Cade's arm and mimed knocking on the door while stomping my good foot to make the sound.

Xander mimed opening the door. "Welcome!"

"I apologize for all the security," I said, "but in this day and age, what can you do?"

"Right," Xander agreed, "Because you're the president's wife."

"Not quite," I said, trying to quell my irritability. "This—" I gestured to Cade.

"Oh, *you're* the president!" Xander said.

Ben applauded.

I really felt like I was taking the reins here. Wasn't it clear that between us, *I* was the one in a higher status position? But whatever. I could be the vice president. "Sure," I said. "And we—"

"Are you sure you should be out in public with him?" Xander hissed.

"Uh, we're in public together all the time," I said, my stomach dropping as I guessed where this was going.

"Really? The president is out with his mistress in public?"

"I'm not his mistress."

"Girlfriend?"

"No."

"Naughty daughter?"

"What? No."

"Sexy intern?"

"Buddy, I—"

"Sexy buddy? That sounds fun, having a sexy buddy."

"It is," Ben called, and everyone laughed.

My face went beet red. Was he talking about me? I stumbled out of character.

Cade spoke up. "We get that a lot, but she has a very important job to do for the American people."

"*Really* . . ." Xander smirked. "For *all* of us?" He took two steps toward me, and I flinched as he scooped me up in a fireman's carry over his shoulder. "I'll go next."

It was happening again. And Ben was doing nothing to stop it. I was numb as Xander marched with me over his shoulder and set me down off stage.

"Woo! Quick, but satisfying!" He mimed zipping up his pants. Bile rose up in my esophagus.

My jaw felt wired shut as I forced myself to descend the steps and sit on a chair in the audience. Leaving yesterday and standing up for myself had changed nothing. Ben and my connection in the nurse's office had changed nothing. This situation was never going to change unless Ben stood up—for women, for people of color, for LGBTQ_folks—but he wasn't going to.

I could guess why Donovan and Trey hadn't complained about weird racial comments. If they'd protested, they could be labeled as "difficult" or "angry" and could lose out on future opportunities. I could, too, and my exclusion would be justified around the accusation of being "too sensitive."

Like "sensitive" was an insult.

What was I supposed to do? Staying here was tantamount to condoning this scene—all the scenes. What Ben had shown me was it wasn't just sexist and mean-spirited suggestions I had to deal with, and it wasn't just sexist and mean-spirited teammates either—it was Ben. He was sexist. And mean-spirited. Or at the very least, he wasn't standing in the way of those things . . .

But he was under a lot of pressure from the Pauls. And his dad had just died . . . did that excuse any of this?

"Great work!" Ben called when the scene was over. "Xander, you're in line to host if we do this structure for the show."

Xander fist-bumped Brandon. "Thanks, Ben."

"Let's get set up for a Montage," Ben said.

I hated to stand up and face them again, but sitting felt like defeat.

I pushed myself to standing. My toes hurt a little as I climbed the steps to the stage where I stood next to High Ropes Jake.

"Those guys suck," he muttered to me.

I turned to him, shocked. "Yeah. They do."

He gave me a small smile and faced the stage again.

"Hey," I whispered.

He leaned in.

"Say something next time, okay? Stand up for me?"

But he stepped out to start the first scene.

The series of scenes in Montage was better than the last time; I wasn't a dead prostitute, but it didn't take much to improve upon that.

Montage is my favorite structure, but with these guys, every scene felt like I was target practice. I was exhausted when Ben called lunch. Gathering up my bag, I hobbled out onto the porch, away from the tables. I wasn't ready to tell my fellow Gildas they had been right about everything.

I stopped briefly at the orange ribbed water jug to refill my bottle, then I took the path away from the cabins into the aspens. It felt good to walk. At least that was forward progress of *some* kind. My toes ached a little, which slowed me down some.

That's probably how Ben caught up with me.

"Hey."

I stopped, not turning around. My body tensed as I felt his warmth a half second before he wrapped his arms around me.

"You," he started kissing my neck, "were wonderful." He lowered my bag to the ground and turned me around. "You"—he kissed my neck again. I shivered—"kept your emotions in check. Xander was being an asshole, but you didn't react. You're becoming a woman who owns her sexuality. You're becoming a professional."

I felt removed from his attentions like I was floating above my body. I watched as he backed me up against a tree.

"Well done, Ellie," he growled.

Now his mouth was on mine. I tried to pay attention to what his lips were doing. What his tongue was doing. I tried to mimic their movement. Kissing was supposed to be fun? I was supposed to want this?

Then his hand crept under my T-shirt and fluttered against the skin at my waist. Slowly, he took a step in closer to me and pressed his body against mine. He groaned.

He was back to kissing my neck and then his left hand moved north. His right hand moved up my back. My breathing grew shallow. I had a guess where he was going. Did I want that? Would anyone else ever want that of me? Was it okay to let him touch me just so I could feel what it felt like for someone to touch me there?

Before I had a chance to make a decision, the fingers of his right hand unclasped my bra and his left hand grabbed my boob.

The moment he made contact, I knew I didn't want it. I tried to step back, but I was still pushed up against the tree.

"Shhh," he whispered in my ear. "Relax, Ellie."

"Don't. Please, Ben. Just—" I tried to push him away with my hands, but he ground into me.

"It's okay," he murmured. "You're so sexy. I can't help myself."

"Ben—" I protested again, pushing at his chest, but he covered his mouth with mine.

"You're so beautiful," he murmured, "I think I'm falling in love with you."

I ceased my protests, stunned, but snapped to life when one hand started moving south.

A switch flipped in my head. A message flashed in my mind with lightning speed and clarity: Ben was not what love looked like. He was what danger looked like. And that's when Dad's voice shouted in my head, *Prime attack zones: spectacles and testicles!*

I jerked up my knee as hard as I could and rammed it into his crotch.

"Jesus!" he shouted. But it had the desired effect. Bent in half, clutching his groin, he backed up, and I skirted around him and grabbed my bag.

"Whoops! See you back in rehearsal!" I called.

And then, despite my aching toes, I ran like hell.

CHAPTER TWENTY

whatjusthappenedwhatjusthappenedwhatjusthappenedwhatjusthappened
whatjusthappenedwhatjusthappenedwhatjusthappened

CHAPTER TWENTY-ONE

Somehow, it was lunch and I was sitting with the Gildas. I hadn't told them what had happened yet. I couldn't find the words. Plus, how much of that had I been responsible for? I'd let him kiss me, after all. I hadn't protested right away when he'd touched me.

Ben appeared. "Come sit with us," he said coldly. "Team lunch."

I shuddered. I knew I was safe in public, but what was going to happen if he got me alone?

"She's eating with the Gildas." Sirena smiled, but it was forced.

Ben smirked. "I don't think so."

Hanna and Paloma clattered to their feet, but I did, too, holding up a hand. "I'll just go," I said, figuring the calmer I could keep him, the better off I'd be. I avoided their eyes as I found my bag, grabbed my tray, and followed him.

He pointed at the seat next to him. I sat.

He reached for the salt and whispered, "Your knee slipped."

I stared at my tray, not daring to speak.

"Right?" he said so quietly, I almost didn't hear him. "It was an accident."

Except it wasn't. I moved the turkey tetrazzini to the other side of the middle square of my divided tray.

"Because I know you would never *intentionally* do that."

Yet... I picked up one pea at a time and nestled them into the mountain of tetrazzini.

"Because if you *did* do that intentionally, and you *told* anyone, everyone would know you only got on Varsity because I thought you were hot."

"Think," I corrected him, eyes still on my peas. "They would *think* that's the reason."

"*Know.*"

My head jerked up.

"You think you're as talented as Brandon? Xander?" he smirked. "You're hot. And the Pauls told me to cast a girl because Nina Knightley's coming." He shrugged. "That's all."

That wasn't true. He was just saying that because he felt I'd rejected him. I'd heard those guys laugh at my sketch. I'd had a great audition. And Ben had remembered my application materials. I was talented. I'd earned my spot—I deserved to be on Varsity... Right?

My eyes returned to the tetrazzini.

"It was an accident," he murmured.

I poured milk onto Tetrazzini Mountain.

Say yes...

"It was an accident," I repeated, my voice flat.

CHAPTER TWENTY-TWO

"JV will be our audience this afternoon," Ben announced. "Let's get set up for 185."

One-liners. Great.

I felt like a zombie. Every time my mind flashed back to the memory of panic at his body pushing mine against the tree, I tried to replace it with a happy memory. Being in the car with my family. Performing on stage back home. Hiking with the Boy Scouts. But keeping my mind out of the woods with Ben was taking a lot of working memory.

High Ropes Jake called out, "Why doesn't Zelda control 185? She's got great timing."

Even in my haze, I could tell he was trying to help in some small way. I nodded, making eye contact with him.

"I'll control it," Ben said. "Ellie needs the practice."

Both JV teams chattered as they filed into the room. I tried to pretend I hadn't heard Ben. I tried to go back to only a few short hours ago when I was defending him.

"Okay. Start with teachers," Ben said.

I looked into the crowd to find my people. Will and Jonas and the Gildas smiled and clapped. But I felt like I was looking at them through a tunnel.

"185 teachers walk into a bar," Brandon started. "The bartender says, 'Sorry, we don't serve teachers here,' and the teachers say, 'Bartender, you fail!'"

Not a great joke.

Now it was Xander. "185 teachers walk into the bar. The bartender says, 'Sorry, we don't serve teachers here,' and the teachers say, 'We'll "chalk" that up to your bad mood!'"

I nodded slowly. Better.

I listened, but never jumped. I should have, but I couldn't bring myself to put one foot in front of the other, much less tell a joke.

After three rounds like this, Ben called, "Ellie. Step up."

The audience cheered.

Blankly, I stared at the crowd.

"Three in a row, Ellie," Ben commanded. "185 . . . prostitutes."

My stomach dropped.

"Come on, Ben." Dion and Roger were leaning against the wall of windows with their arms crossed. Dion rubbed the back of his neck. "Give her something else."

Now Ben crossed *his* arms, making his biceps bulge. Looking at them made me realize how strong he was. How lucky I'd been to have escaped relatively unscathed.

"People will suggest 'prostitute,'" Ben protested.

"Doesn't mean you have to take it," Roger argued.

"It's my rehearsal," Ben reminded them. When he looked away, Roger and Dion exchanged a glance and shrugged.

"185 prostitutes," Ben repeated, staring at me in the eye.

No one laughed.

Trembling a little, I stepped downstage. "185 prostitutes walk into a bar. The bartender says, 'Sorry, we don't serve prostitutes here,' and the prostitutes say..." I swallowed. *Be in the moment. You can do this. Just logic it out: How would a sex worker feel being denied a drink at a bar?* I swallowed again. "And the prostitutes say, 'Well, that seems discriminatory.'"

JV chuckled. So did High Ropes Jake.

"Stick to the format, Ellie." Ben widened his stance.

I set my jaw. "185 prostitutes walk into a bar. The bartender says, 'Sorry, we don't serve prostitutes here,' and the prostitutes say, 'First Planned Parenthood funding, now this?'"

JV laughed louder. Even Brandon and Xander smiled.

"The format, Ellie. This is a pun structure," Ben said.

"Hey, it's working for her. Who cares?" Hanna called out.

"*I* care, because it's the rules of the structure," Ben said. "Again."

I shifted on my feet. "185 prostitutes walk into a bar. The bartender says, 'Sorry, we don't serve prostitutes here,' and the prostitutes say, 'That's fine. I'm saving for law school anyway.'"

The room erupted, and Ben banged his fist on a table. The laughter evaporated. "Pun. Structure. Do you need instruction on what a pun is, Ellie?"

"Ben," it was Roger this time. "Lighten up, man. She did three, she used prostitute, what more do you want?"

"I *want* them to know what the *real world* is like!" he exploded.

No one said anything for a moment.

"The real world is the one we help create," Dion said softly. "Hey. You okay?"

I suddenly realized that last part was addressed to me. I nodded, even though I wasn't sure I *was* okay.

After a moment, Roger muttered, "We're going to head back upstairs."

Silently, JV filed out. I didn't try to meet anyone's eye.

When JV had gone, Ben climbed the steps onto the stage. Slowly, he passed behind each of us.

"Who is coaching this team?" His voice hung heavy in the room.

"You are," everyone mumbled but me.

"So, who is in charge?"

"You are."

"And when I give a note, what do you do with that note?"

"Follow it."

"Correct." Ben stopped right behind me. "You follow it. Understand, Ellie?"

I hesitated, my heart thumping in my throat.

Say yes . . .

I nodded.

He leaned in. I could feel his breath on my cheek.

"Prostitute. Again."

CHAPTER TWENTY-THREE

We rehearsed for the rest of the afternoon without a break.

"Team dinner," Ben said by way of dismissing us. "No exceptions." He stared at me.

I tried to gather my things and go help set up tables, but Ben held me back.

"I'll be there in a minute," Ben called to the others as they hopped off stage. I tried to catch High Ropes Jake's eye, but he was gone.

Ben placed a hand on my back and tried to lead me toward the stairs.

"Uh . . . where are we going?" I asked in a tight, thin voice, resisting the movement.

"Upstairs. For just a second."

Panic welled in my chest. "Uh . . . I'd rather—rather—"

"Ellie . . ." He smiled with his mouth, but it didn't reach his eyes. "I just want to have a conversation."

I scanned the room for a friendly face, but he leaned in. "You're making a scene. People will talk. Do you want them to talk?"

I bit my lip and followed Ben upstairs to an unused rehearsal room. Behind him, the door closed and so did my throat. Then he turned to me. "You must be . . . furious with me."

I shook my head and swallowed. Petrified was more like it.

"I scared you today. First in the woods, then on stage." He stepped close and took my hand. "I'm sorry, Ellie, I really am. It's just my feelings for you are so strong—I can't control myself." He smiled and tucked yet another curl behind my ear. "You . . . drive me crazy."

He was moving in for another kiss, and I did not want that. But I was worried about how he might use his physical strength to get what he wanted if I protested too much. I stepped back and held up my hands.

"It's fine," I said, forcing lightness into my voice. "Let's just go to dinner. I'm hungry."

He pouted. "Come on, Ellie." He reached for my hand again. "Forgive me. I shouldn't have . . ."

This I was interested in. "You shouldn't have what?"

He shrugged and smiled sadly. "Look: you can't imagine the kind of pressure I'm under from the Pauls. Money's really tight, and they're counting on alumni donations to get out of the red. This show has never been more important. Plus . . ." He looked at me like I was a puppy. "I can't help how strong my feelings are for you."

"Yeah. You said that. Can we go?" I tried to take my hand back. He held on.

"Give me a smile first." With his other hand, he stroked my cheek. I twitched. "See? You have strong feelings for me, too."

"Yup." That wasn't a lie. They were strong feelings of revulsion.

"Let's go," he said, tugging at me like *I* was the one who was reticent to leave. He pulled me to the door. As he opened it, we were greeted by the Gildas, running up the stairs. I thought I was going to cry from relief.

"Hey, girls," Ben said, shaking off my hand like it was diseased. "What's going on?"

"Well, we're kind of embarrassed." Emily wrung her hands. "You know how when girls live together, their . . . cycles align?"

I shot a look at Sirena, but she was focused on Emily.

"Well," Emily continued, "we all need . . . supplies. Like, now. None of us brought any because we didn't think we'd need them, but apparently altitude can also trigger this kind of thing . . ."

Ben folded his arms.

"So, can you please drive down the mountain and get us this stuff?"

Paloma handed him a twenty-five-item shopping list and a wad of cash.

"It's two hours down the mountain," Ben protested.

"Sorry." Emily winced.

"Doesn't the nurse's office have . . . stuff?" Ben asked, scanning the list.

Sirena shrugged. "Everything went bad because it's been so long since a girl needed supplies."

Now I stared at Sirena. Menstrual products didn't *expire*. They're absorbent—not medicinal.

But apparently along with Ben not knowing women's cycles don't align after being together less than a week, he also didn't know about nonexistent expiration dates. Still, he didn't agree to the errand yet.

"Roger and Dion would go, but they left for a nighttime hike," Emily continued. "And we're too embarrassed to ask the Pauls. And we don't know the other coaches."

"Would anyone like to drive with me?" Ben looked at me.

"...Is something you'd say if staff were allowed to transport campers in their personal vehicles," I blurted.

Ben bit his lip. We all smiled expectantly.

"Look, I'll see if anyone has a trip planned down the mountain after dinner." He turned to me. "Remember. We're eating as a team."

"See, I'm not sure I can wait," Emily said, her voice trembling.

Ben sighed. "What difference is an hour going to make?"

Tears welled up in Emily's eyes. "It's just...there's blood everywhere. It looks like someone's been murdered in our cabin." She grabbed Ben's arm. "Murdered, Ben!"

He wiggled out of her grip. "I'm going, I'm going." Locking eyes with me, he said, "I'll see you later."

"Thanks, Ben!" we all chorused.

We waited until we heard him descend the stairs and turn the corner. Then I hugged each Gilda in turn.

"You are all geniuses," I whispered. "And I will pay you back every penny."

Sirena shook her head and hip-checked Emily. "It was her idea."

"Brilliant job, Emily," I said. "And those tears at the end! What a finale!"

"Why, thank you!" She curtseyed. "I figured my constant crying had to be good for something."

I looked at each of them as they chuckled at Emily. I took a deep breath to tell them about Ben in the woods. But then Paloma cracked her knuckles and said, "Time to go tell the Pauls."

"Whoa whoa whoa," I put my hands up. "Tell the Pauls what? Ben was a jerk to me?"

"Uh," Paloma squinted at me like I was dumb. "That, and the other things. The things you told us. The nurse's office?"

If Paloma wanted me to talk to the Pauls now, there was no way she wouldn't march me in there herself if she knew about what Ben had done to me in the woods. But wasn't that partially my fault? I hadn't told him no right away. And how could I prove what he had done?

I decided to keep the woods encounter to myself.

"How is telling them going to make *me* look?" I said. "Sure, yes, it's been hard, but I can handle myself. Prime attack zones: spectacles and testicles."

Paloma rubbed my back. "You looked like you had PTSD or something coming out of that room with Ben. You can't spectacle/ testicle your way out of emotional trauma."

"I'm not getting emotionally traumatized," I insisted.

They frowned at me.

"I'm not!"

Paloma sighed. "Look. We saw what happened at rehearsal. That's abusive. And you're getting *used* to it!"

I shook my head. "It's never been that bad before."

"What makes you think it's going to be buckets of sunshine from here on out?" Hanna asked. She rapped her knuckles on my skull. "Wake up, Zelda-girl. That guy is an asshole."

"I'm not telling the Pauls," I said. "I mean, best-case scenario—they tell Ben to be nicer to me, and I look like a cry baby who can't handle playing with the big boys."

"Didn't you hear Dion and Roger today?" Sirena asked. "They thought he was out of line, too."

I shrugged. "Did *they* go talk to the Pauls afterward?"

Everyone looked at each other. "I don't *think* so," Sirena said.

"So? It was just a difference in philosophy. It's not going to stand up in court. You know, Paul court. We're not going."

After a moment, Emily asked in a small voice, "So all those tampons were for nothing?"

"You should see that list." Sirena smiled. "We asked for triple all-day protection extra-strength tampons with wings."

"Tampons don't have wings," I said.

"Ah, but, we figured Ben doesn't know that." Hanna slid an arm around me and led me down the steps where we ran into Will.

"Are you going to tell the Pauls?" he asked. The Gildas passed around us, giving us some privacy.

"You, too?" I shook my head. "I'm fine. I'll be fine."

He pulled on one of my curls—a habit from childhood that always delighted him and infuriated me. I batted his hand away.

"Okay. Still fighting," he said. "I'll take it . . . for now."

It was close to midnight when we were all in bed with the lights off. I had just closed my eyes when I flashed back to the feeling of Ben's cold fingers unclasping my bra. He did it with one hand like it was nothing. How many bras did you to have to unclasp before you could do it one-handed? How many girls had Ben told he was falling

in love with? How many *more* would he pursue after I was gone? If someone before me had said something to the Pauls, would I even *be* in this situation?

Maybe I'd tell the Pauls. After the show was over. And after Nina Knightley.

"Ellie . . . Ellie."

God, now I was hearing his voice, too.

"Ellie. I'm back. Open the door. I've got all the . . . girl supplies."

He was here. My bunk was right by the window, which we'd cracked open just a little for some fresh air. He could see me. I could hear him through the screen. We'd barricaded the door with the extra bunk beds after swearing up and down no one was going to have to pee in the middle of the night and then finding a bucket in the closet to use just in case.

So I was safe. As long as he thought I was asleep. And as long as he didn't have a razor blade to cut through the screen. He wouldn't go that far, would he?

Would he?

I heroically slowed my breathing and tried to look as unconscious as possible.

"Ellie . . . Ellie . . . I know you can hear me . . . Ellie . . . *Ellie.*"

Paloma moaned a little.

Ben dropped his voice to a whisper. "Ellie."

I probably looked more dead than unconscious, but I was terrified to move. Just when I was tempted to open my eyes and see if he'd left, I heard his voice one more time.

"Bitch."

My blood boiled as he thumped away.

CHAPTER TWENTY-FOUR

It took a long time to fall asleep, but when I woke the next morning, I was sure about two things: 1) Ben was never getting me alone again. And 2) If I was a bitch, I was going to be the funniest bitch that asshole had ever seen.

Ben kept trying to catch my eye at breakfast, but I stared at Hanna as she told an elaborate story about when she and Paloma tried to get into this secret restaurant back in Milwaukee called the Safe House.

"What kind of business model is that?" Hanna demanded. "You have to know a *password* to get inside? You're willfully *keeping out* customers?"

Paloma kicked me under the table. "Laugh, Zelda," she muttered, "you're having a great time."

"What?" I breathed.

"Ben is looking over here. You're having a great time. You don't need him."

Automatically, I turned my head to look at him, but she grabbed my hand and called out, "Hilarious, Hanna!"

Right. I forced a smile on my face and tried to join in the laughter.

"I'm just nervous," I muttered when the laughter ebbed. "If I know where he is, I feel better."

Paloma pursed her lips. "It doesn't have to be this way, Zelda."

I nodded. "I just have to hang in there for one more week," I said. "It's not like he's going to follow me back to Minnesota."

She tried to smile. So did I.

At rehearsal after breakfast, my eyes automatically swept the main room of the Lodge for Ben. Jake and High Ropes Jake were tying their shoelaces together on stage, and Trey and Donovan were throwing grapes into the air, trying to catch them in their mouths. But no Ben.

I exhaled.

"Get the girl supplies? I left them on the porch."

Whirling around, I pointed at Ben's chest and demanded, "Please don't sneak up on me."

He twisted his features into a "you're-crazy" face. "Okay, jumpy." Then he dropped his voice. "I came to your cabin when I got back. Thought you might like to go for a midnight hike."

I made a noncommittal noise and started digging through my bag to give me something to do and someplace to look that wasn't Ben's face.

He took a step and we were facing opposite directions, our shoulders touching. "Want me to come by tonight?" he muttered, pretending to watch the others.

It felt like cold water had washed over me. "The Pauls are strict about curfew, remember?" I said evenly. "Plus, I'm much funnier when I've slept." I selected a pen out of my bag like it was the prize I'd been searching for this whole time. "Hey, Jake!" I called and walked away, not waiting for Ben's answer.

Neither Jake discovered which one of them I was calling for, though, because Ben clapped his hands and said, "Edge of the stage, people!"

After we seated ourselves in clumps, he folded his arms. "We have one week until the performance. That's seven days before improv reps and an increasing number of high-profile alumni will be in the audience. Past Varsity performers have been recruited straight to the big leagues from here. And I know I don't have to tell you where alumni of those places go: *Saturday Night Live*, Hollywood, and television."

"Did they ever recruit *you*?" I asked. I was baiting him, but it came out before I could stop it.

"I was invited to audition for Second City mainstage, but I didn't want to move to Chicago," he said, meeting my eyes, daring me to ask why.

"Too bad," I said.

He shrugged. "Too cold for my taste."

"Yeah," Brandon said, "Ben likes it *hot*."

Whether the snickers that followed were in support of the innuendo or to make fun of Ben, I wasn't sure. Regardless, the tension broke.

"We're putting the cold open on its feet, and then Ellie will go off and revise." He nodded to me. I stared back. He pursed his lips and turned to everyone else. "Okay. I've cast 'Sleepwalking Bear.'"

I frowned. Back home, the convention is whoever writes the cold open sketch for the beginning of the show also casts it. But I knew what little good it would do to say anything, so I bit the inside of my cheek instead.

"Xander, Brandon, you're the hikers. Jake, Cade, and Donovan, you're the circus performers. Trey, you're the pilot, and other Jake, you're the bear."

He passed out scripts and the others got to their feet to start rehearsal.

Did I miss something? Had he called my name, and I didn't hear him?

"Uh, Ben?" I followed him as he climbed the steps up on stage. "Who am I?" I had been hoping to play the pilot, but I wasn't even one of the circus performers?

He didn't even turn around. "The writer."

"Right." I hurried to catch up and snagged his shirt.

He paused, turned around, and folded his arms. "Yes?"

"I know I'm the writer. But who am I in the sketch?"

"No one. Traditionally writers aren't in the sketches they—"

"That's not true," I interrupted. "Amy Poehler. Tina Fey. Kristen Wiig. People on *SNL* both write and perform all the time."

"Well Marcus didn't here, so we don't."

I put my hands on my hips. "If you're trying so hard to prepare us for the professional world, why have special rules here? Aren't special rules a crutch?" I was pushing it, but the moment he'd sidelined me in my own sketch, I'd stopped caring.

He met my eyes. "I will run my team the best way I see fit. And you will accept that."

We were getting too loud—the others had quieted to listen in.

"Have a seat, Ellie," he said. He handed me a script. We stared at each other.

Part of me wanted to walk out. But then I'd look like a bad sport. So I didn't get cast in my own opening sketch. At least it was my writing coming out of everyone's mouths. Surely that would count for something with the reps from the improv companies, right?

I tried to smile, but it came out like a grimace. "Will do, coach." I started to cross to my bag for my notebook, but Ben snapped his fingers. Automatically, I looked over my shoulder.

"Sit by me, Ellie," he demanded.

I seethed. "Just getting my notebook first," I snapped.

"Hallway. Now." He dropped his clipboard with a clatter and pointed.

The easiest thing to do was to follow him. But I couldn't be alone with him. I'd promised myself. "Whatever you want to say to me there, you can say to me here," I insisted, crossing my arms. I expected some sort of vocal reaction from the team, but they were still and silent.

Ben barked out a laugh. "Fine. You sit where I tell you. You revise what I tell you. You play structures the way I tell you. You are a player. I am your coach. You. Will. Listen."

He held my gaze until a vein in his forehead started to pulse. Then he pointed at a chair in the front row.

For a moment, I flashed back to the weight of his body against mine, pushing me into the tree. This was not like fighting with my brother. Ben could really hurt me. I glanced at the team. They all stared at the floor. No help there. Snappy comeback Zelda was not going to score any points here. In fact, she just seemed to set off Ben.

"May I get a pen?" I asked quietly, not meeting his gaze.

"Yes," he hissed. Then he barked, "From the top!"

I nearly opened my mouth to ask for a read-through of everyone in their parts before we tried to put it on its feet, but I clamped it shut. Ben had made it very clear what my role was. I sat.

An hour later, I had notes scribbled all over the pages of my script. The fight with Ben dissolved as I became an invisible scribe, and he commandeered the players on stage.

"Take five, everyone." He handed me a list of notes. "Ellie, go and revise and be back in an hour."

I grabbed my bag and skittered out of the rehearsal room before he had a chance to pull me aside. I ran out the door, not even stopping to fill up my water bottle. I had to get out of there and disappear so he couldn't find me.

Before I decided in my head, my feet were running toward the Boy Scout lunch hiking path. I'd write on the rock. Maybe I'd still be there as Jesse and Ricky and Murph passed on their way up or back. But even if they weren't, being there felt safe. And in order to focus on my revisions, I needed to not be afraid of Ben finding me.

My sprint had slowed to a jog before I realized how much better my toes felt. Lungs, too. I knew it took months to fully acclimate, but even being at altitude for nearly a week felt like I was walking around in a different body.

Before long, I arrived at the rock. I was negotiating with my bag to climb on top when a male voice called out my name. I froze. Then I heard it again.

"Zelda? Why are you hiding behind the—"

"Jesse!" The relief threatened to pour out of me as tears, but

I willed them back. I hopped off the rock and returned Jesse's welcomed hug.

"What are you doing here?" he asked, still hugging me. I sighed and let myself be held, holding on to him, too. The tears I had willed away from their ducts were clogging my throat instead.

Jesse pulled back to look at my face, and that's when I spotted an ax on the trail by his feet.

"Uh . . ." I began.

He followed my gaze and chuckled. "My turn to clean up a felled tree across the path a bit up ahead." He shrugged. "What. You don't carry axes around at improv camp?"

I smirked and stepped back, crossing my arms around my torso. "Maybe I should start."

He met my eyes. "What happened the other day? Your foot's okay? That guy . . . he's your . . ."

"Coach—just coach," I supplied before he had a chance to guess something more embarrassing. I shook my head. "I'm fine. It's fine."

He nodded slowly. "Okay . . . I thought about coming to check on you yesterday, but . . ." he shrugged. "He seemed . . . angry."

I rubbed my eyebrow and shook my head again, not trusting my voice.

". . . Okay," he said. Suddenly, the air felt awkward.

Be in the moment. I looked around. "Hey—where are Murph and Ricky?"

"We don't go *everywhere* together." He smiled.

The awkward air slunk away. It was easy again. "You should," I said. "You make a great team."

"I'm okay being alone sometimes," he said, looking somewhere in the vicinity of my elbow. "Murph is constantly talking about missing his girlfriend, and Ricky . . ."

"I like Ricky." I smiled.

"Yeah?"

I nodded. "I've never met anyone who loves rocks the way that guy does."

Jesse laughed half-heartedly. "Yeah. Rocks."

We were quiet for a moment.

Make active choices. "You want to go for a walk tonight?" I blurted. "Murph and Ricky, too? If they want?"

He met my eyes. "A walk?" He smiled.

"Or . . . whatever? You guys know this place better than I do."

"A walk sounds great. I'll ask them if they're not busy . . . They might be busy."

I nodded. "But you're not busy?"

"I'm not busy." He was still smiling.

"Good." Warmth spread from my stomach.

"Yeah?"

I nodded. "I'll meet you by our gate? After dinner? Say, seven o'clock?"

He paused, then reached down for the ax. "Zelda."

I tucked a curl behind my ear. "Jesse."

"Is everything okay?"

I opened my mouth, but, for once, thought about speaking before I spoke. What if I told Jesse about Ben? About how controlling he was? How scared I'd become? He'd probably tell me to tell the Pauls. But I wasn't going to do that. So what good was it going to do?

Better for him to just see me as funny, fun, carefree Zelda. Better to have one person here who didn't feel sorry for me. Plus, I suddenly realized, I didn't want him to think there was something going on between Ben and me.

Make statements and assumptions. "I . . . I've got this script to revise. I wrote the cold open. You're coming, right? Saturday night?"

"To the improv show? Yes. I don't know what a cold open is, but I'm glad you wrote it. I'm sure it'll be the . . . coldest, most open one there."

I laughed. "See you tonight."

He nodded slowly and grinned at me. "The gate. Seven o'clock."

Feeling lighter, I watched his progress through the trees.

CHAPTER TWENTY-FIVE

Two hours later, waiting for JV to settle in to watch a run-
through of my revised cold open, I was under strict instruction from
Ben to "just sit still" and let him "do all the talking." I alternately bit my
nails and sat on my hands.

"Okay, JV," Ben called in a commanding voice. "What you
are seeing is a revised version of a sketch we've been developing
this week."

I couldn't help it—I looked over my shoulder at the JV teams
and caught Will's eye.

"Didn't you write this?" he mouthed.

I nodded and shrugged.

He rolled his eyes and threw an arm around Jonas, whispering
something in his ear. Jonas nodded and gave me a thumbs-up.

I smiled and turned back to face the stage.

"Okay!" Ben started toward the seat next to mine. I tensed.
"Lights up!" he called.

Someone flipped off the house lights, leaving the seats dark but
the stage lit. I leaned in with my script to catch some of the light

so I could still see to write notes, but Ben pushed me back so I was sitting upright.

"I need the light—" I whispered, but he shushed me.

I started to vibrate with anger. How much was this guy going to try and control me? How much more could I put up with? What would happen if I really stood up to him?

Xander came on stage.

"Thank god for the Colorado woods," Xander said, miming setting down a heavy hiking backpack. "Rugged landscape, vistas for miles, and all the solitude a person could dream of."

Immediately, Brandon stumbled on stage, joining him. "Oh my god!" He grabbed Xander by the shoulders. "I'm so glad I found someone! I need to monologue all my feelings!"

The laughter began. And my anger dissipated.

As the scene progressed, it got sillier and more complicated, and by the time the sleepwalking bear showed up, I thought JV was going to lose their minds. At my new favorite part with the pilot, I glanced over to see Ben's reaction—out of habit, I guess—but his face was stone cold. He was clenching his jaw. His arms were folded across his chest.

I thought this sketch was good—maybe the best I'd ever written—but clearly it didn't meet his expectations.

"Scene!" Ben called.

JV broke into applause, and Will shouted, "Go, Zelda! That's my sister!" Laughter accompanied more whoops of appreciation. I turned and waved.

When the clapping died down, Ben stood and faced the audience. "Clearly there's still a lot of work that has to be done," he said.

I looked up at him skeptically.

"Really?" Roger asked, frowning. "That sketch looks show-ready to me. Who wrote it? And why isn't Zelda in it?"

"Yeah!" Hanna's voice called out. I stared at my hands.

"We really developed it as a team," Ben said.

My ears began to burn. I looked up on stage. Would any of them stand up for me? But once again, they were silent.

I would feel so stupid claiming writing credit. Plus, Ben had shown me what could happen when I disagreed with him.

"Thanks for coming." Ben forced a smile and waved like everyone had already made their intentions of leaving known.

"Didn't Zelda write it?" Will called out.

I couldn't help smiling into my lap.

"As I said, we developed it as a team," Ben insisted. "That's a wrap, everyone. Let's get the tables set up for dinner."

The guys on JV started to stand.

"Why wasn't Zelda in it?" Sirena demanded.

Emily joined in. "Yeah. Why isn't Zelda in it?"

"Not enough parts." Ben's forced smile moved into grimace territory.

Paloma stood up. "If you developed it as a team, why not develop enough parts for everyone? There could easily be another circus performer—"

Ben didn't even acknowledge them. He turned to his notes and wandered away like no one had spoken.

I slowly exhaled, staring at the floor. Wasn't this supposed to be the moment to celebrate my hard work? Why was Ben taking that away from me?

I felt someone standing over my shoulder.

Roger. He pushed his way between the seats and sat in Ben's vacated chair.

"Hey," he said.

"Hi." I turned to face him.

"Will says you wrote that sketch."

I nodded.

Roger's curly hair was like mine—boingy. The curls bounced as he shook his head.

"It's good. I hope Ben tells you that. Does he tell you that?"

I shrugged. "Yeah. Not in so many words, but . . ."

He rubbed his eyes with the heels of his hands. "Okay." He started to say something, then stopped himself. Then he stood up, took a deep breath, and sat back down. "Let me—or Dion—know if . . . if you need anything. Okay?"

I squinted. "Need anything?"

He glanced up at the stage, maybe looking for Ben. "Just. You know."

He squeezed my shoulder and called to his team. "Let's clear these chairs, JV!"

Will scurried over and hugged me. "*Say* something," he pleaded.

"To who?" I whispered. "And say what? It's not fair? I didn't get credit for something that was really everyone's idea in the first place?"

He grabbed my shoulders. "Please. Promise me you'll say something."

"Will—"

"Ellie?" Ben wandered back into the room and seemed surprised to see Will still there. "Aren't you two going to help set up for dinner?"

"Yes," I said, grabbing Will's arm. "Jonas and the Gildas will be waiting for us. That's okay, right, Ben? No team dinner tonight?"

"No team dinner," he said, slowly clicking his pen. "But we're running one-liners afterward. Seven o'clock. Rehearsal room B."

I furrowed my brow as a wave of disappointment crashed over me. "No—I can't. I have plans."

"With who?" Ben snapped.

I opened my mouth to answer, but decided I didn't owe him the truth. I shrugged and stammered. "Th-the Gildas."

"It's a required rehearsal," Ben insisted.

"But it's not on the original schedule," I protested. My heart rate was increasing as my irritation at his demands did.

"You're there, or you're off Varsity." His calm, snake-like voice was back. "And none of us wants that."

Then he was gone.

"I'm finding the Pauls," Will murmured. "This has gotten out of hand."

"Will! No!" I grabbed his shirt. "Please. Listen to me."

"No, I'm—" He pulled out of my grip.

"Then you're no better than he is!" I exclaimed.

Will looked like I'd slapped him. "How can you say that?"

"Let me make my own choices for my own life," I said. "Nina Knightley. Improv. Script writing. This is my life. If you tell the Pauls, I'm off Varsity."

"Or *he* is," Will retorted.

"Who will defend me?" I demanded. "The Varsity guys? No way. And the little that Roger and Dion and JV have seen? That's not egregious enough to get someone *removed*. And if Ben knows I complained, he'll sideline me. I'm already not in the cold open. I can't risk it. Let me handle this. My way."

"But he—" Will turned away. He was shaking. "He *controls* you. Can't you see that? You've got to quit Varsity."

I shrugged. "I'm not going to. There's too much at stake."

"Jesus, Zelda." His shoulders sagged. "Let's go eat. Maybe everyone else can convince you. Before your next *rehearsal* starts."

"Wait—I . . . I don't have plans with the Gildas tonight," I said. The disappointment crashed again.

"Okay." He caught my eye. "Who *do* you have plans with?"

I shrugged. "Some Boy Scouts."

His eyebrows shot up. "*Your* Boy Scouts? Those hiking Boy Scouts?"

I nodded and dug around in my bag for nothing.

"All *three* of those Boy Scouts?"

"Well, Jesse for sure, but probably Ricky and Murph, too. Jesse and I ran into each other when I was—"

"You ran *into* each other?"

"It's feeling like an echo chamber around here," I said.

"Good God, Z. How do you go from no guys liking you—"

"Thanks for that."

He ignored me. "To an older man—"

"Ben's only twenty," I protested.

"—And three all-American Boy Scouts all fighting for your attention?"

"Jesse and Murph and Ricky are my friends," I said firmly. "And Ben is . . ."

"Trouble," he finished. Then suddenly, he threw his arms around me. "I'm worried," he muttered into my hair.

I nodded and laid my head against his shoulder.

"Tell me what to do to help."

I smiled and pulled back. "Thank you. I'll handle Ben. I can think of something. But can you meet Jesse and the others? Tell them I'm at rehearsal? Seven p.m.—at the gate. Here. Let me write a note."

I grabbed a pen from my bag, a discarded cold open script from the stage, and scribbled on the back.

Hey, Jesse (and Ricky and Murph—if you could peel yourselves away from all of your rock collecting and orienteering)—

Last minute rehearsal, so I can't make our walk. Can we try again tomorrow? Same time. Same place. Same me. Same you. Just a different day.

The disappointment is all mine,

Zelda

P.S.—J—maybe leave the ax?

"The ax?"

I jumped. Will was reading over my shoulder.

"Hey!" I yelped.

"There are *two* inside jokes by my count." He smiled.

I folded the note and smiled a little, too. "So?"

"Are you afraid they're going to be mad?"

"Of course not. I hope he—they're disappointed. I sure am. But he won't be angry."

"They." He slid my note into his pocket.

"Huh?"

"*They* won't be angry. You said 'he.'" Will raised knowing eyebrows at me, which I ignored.

"Okay. *They* won't be angry."

"Is he—are *they* nice to you?" Will fiddled with the buttons on his shawl-collar cardigan—which, I noticed, he'd been wearing an awful lot since I pointed out that Jonas liked him in it.

"Yes."

"Do *they* insist you not eat with your friends?"

I lowered my eyes. "Will . . ."

"Do *they* try and control your behavior or belittle you or—"

"Will. I know Ben is not a good . . ."

"Person."

"I was going to say boyfriend candidate," I amended. "But I can handle him."

". . . Okay. But these Boy Scouts . . ."

"They are my friends," I insisted. My stomach growled. "Murph has a girlfriend, Ricky has . . . rocks, and Jesse isn't interested in me like that. Let's go eat."

"How do you know?" Will pressed.

"Because no one is," I said flatly. "It turns out the only person who has ever wanted to be with me only wanted it to feel powerful." My jazz hands tried to deflect some of the bitterness I felt.

"Z—"

"I'm tired of talking about this, Will. Let's eat."

CHAPTER TWENTY-SIX

About halfway through dinner, I tapped my fingers on the table. How was I going to avoid being in a room alone with Ben? Ben had said it was a required rehearsal, but I was pretty sure it was only required for me. Maybe if I got there before him . . .

After inhaling dinner, I slipped away and dashed back to Gilda Radner. My heart thumped as I pulled open the closet where we had found the backup toilet bucket and located what I had been hoping for: a tool box. I took a flathead screwdriver and a hammer and for just a second, felt the weight of them in my hands. I shuddered and tucked them into my bag. Then I ran back to the Lodge.

Most everyone was still eating, but as I climbed the top stair to the rehearsal rooms floor, Sirena was waiting for me.

"Zelda, don't go to this rehearsal."

"It's fine, Sirena," I said, panting. "I figured it all out." I fished out the screwdriver and hammer and held them up.

"You're going to *kill* him?"

"Jesus, no. I'm taking the doors off."

"What?"

I opened the door to the rehearsal room and jammed the tip of the screwdriver into the bolt securing the bottom hinge and whacked the back of the screwdriver with the hammer. Then I pushed down on the screwdriver and the bolt popped up. I pulled it out.

"If he can't close the door, maybe he won't . . . try anything."

Sirena's mouth dropped open.

"Help me with the one on top?" I asked.

"Wait. This is crazy."

"Yes, it is, but I'm doing it." I grabbed a rehearsal block, stood on it, and repeated the procedure. The bolt slid right out. "Steady the door?" I asked.

Sirena grabbed it as I hopped down.

"Okay, let's put it in Rehearsal Room C."

"He'll just put it back on."

"Ah, but he won't because it's going to be occupied."

"By who?"

"Yes, Ellie. By who?"

My heart dropped. I looked at my watch. 6:45. He was early.

"What are you doing, Ellie?" he asked, smiling sweetly. "Are you maintenance in addition to being the talent?"

I opened and closed my mouth. Sirena was still holding the door.

"Let me get that for you." He lifted the door out of Sirena's hands and set it back into its hinges. "And the bolts?"

I just stood there. He plucked them out of my fist and tapped them into place. He swung the door back and forth. "Good as new." Smiling at Sirena, he said, "Time for our rehearsal. See you later, Sally."

"Sirena," we corrected him.

"Let's go, Ellie." He opened the door wide for me to pass by him.

I locked eyes with Sirena.

"I . . . I'd like to stay with Zelda," she stammered.

He ignored her. "We'll start with Fun Fact." He passed into the rehearsal room and sat on a chair, notepad in hand. He faced the wall of mirrors, caught my eye, and clicked his pen. "Ready?"

Sirena folded her arms. "I'd like to stay," she repeated, louder.

"That's fine," Ben said smoothly.

Sirena and I exchanged a shocked look.

"But before we start, I have something I'd like to say to you, Ellie." He turned in his chair to face us.

Sirena took a protective step toward me.

"I'm sorry I yelled. You are perhaps the most talented female performer I've ever worked with, and it throws me off guard. You're going places, Ellie. I'm just worried about your soft heart. I want to prepare it—prepare you—for the world out there. You know how Olympic athletes train at high altitudes so running at sea level is easier?"

I shook my head—both because I didn't know that, but also because I couldn't make sense of what he was saying. I stepped closer to Sirena.

"Well, I'm hoping if you can handle the man-vibe here, everything out there will be easier. I'm sorry it's hard. But some day you'll thank me."

It was what I wanted to hear, right? That he was sorry? That I was talented? But he'd said it before. And things didn't get better—they got worse. And then cycled back to this apology part again. I felt trapped in an endless loop.

"I—" I began. I looked over to Sirena who shrugged a tiny shrug as if to say, "What are you going to do?"

I faced Ben. "Thank you. For apologizing...But look." I took a step forward. "If I'm so talented, don't you want to set me up for success when the improv reps are here? If I can't be in the cold open because I'm the writer, can't I at least get credit for the writing?"

In the mirror's reflection, I saw Sirena nod.

"About that." He shuffled through his notepad and pulled out the script. "I've made some changes. Thought we'd share writing credit."

I took the script from his outstretched hand and skimmed it.

"Where's the pilot?" I asked after a minute. I flipped the page over, read some more, then alarmed, asked, "Why did you change the end? These aren't—you changed parts that were working really well."

Ben shrugged. "I have more experience than you do." He smiled benignly.

"We were all in that room, Ben. We all heard that laughter. The pilot part is the best part. I—this isn't—"

Sirena's breathing grew louder.

"Look." He spread his legs wide and leaned his knees on his elbows. "All the best writers work in teams. Poehler and Fey, McKay and Ferrell, Nichols and May..."

I was getting tired of arguing with him all the time about our differences in improv philosophy. But all the fire was gone from this script—*my* script. "I liked it the other way," I finally said.

"And I like it this way. And I'm the coach." He shrugged. "Take it or leave it."

I looked over at Sirena's face, which had turned into a looming thunderstorm.

"Are you saying if I don't agree with your changes..."

"We'll cut this cold open and do the one I wrote instead. You'd be in it—you'd play Marcy. I wrote her for you anyway."

"The team hated that sketch."

"Not the version we revised after you left."

I wanted to scream. He had backed me into a corner—either I share writing credit for this terrible new script, or I humiliate myself in his porn-adjacent piece of crap.

Which improv rule was going to help me now?

"You know what?" I said, "I'm not feeling well." I picked up my bag. "Cramps. You do whatever you want." I turned on my heel, and Sirena put her arm around my shoulder.

"Asshole," she muttered.

"What was that?" Ben called lightly.

"I said you're an asshole." Sirena turned and faced him. "You're a jerk. Roger and Dion think so. Everyone on JV thinks so."

I pulled at Sirena's sleeve. "Come on. It's not worth it."

Ben smiled. "Sour grapes." He shrugged. "Not everyone can be on the top team. Or can coach it." He turned to me. "Take care of yourself. See you in the morning."

"Actually, it's a free morning, remember?" I said. "I'll see you in the afternoon."

Sirena and I flew out of the rehearsal room. Neither of us spoke until we hit the trail to the cabins.

"Thank you for being in there with me," I said.

Sirena nodded. "He's slippery, that one. Like—he says nice things, but you know he isn't nice. Like, you're the best 'female' performer he's seen? Why the qualifier?"

I shook my head. "Girls aren't that funny. Haven't you heard?" She snorted.

"I don't know what to do, Sirena," I said. Gilda Radner was just around the corner. All I wanted was to curl up and sleep.

"Maybe when this whole thing is done, you write a letter to the Pauls," she suggested.

"Yeah. Good idea. But now? The sketch?"

"I don't know."

We climbed the steps to our porch. I tugged at her elbow. "Thanks for . . ." I took a breath. "Thanks for knowing I needed you."

She bent down to hug me, chuckling. "Yeah . . . you're welcome. We're all here for you, you know. I know you're doing this partly for us. Even though *you don't have to.*" She pulled back and gave me a meaningful look.

I blew air between my lips. "It's a mess. Damned if I do, damned if I don't."

"Zelda!"

I turned at Will's voice.

"Hey!" I called out.

As he jogged up to the porch, the front door opened and Emily popped her head out. "Hi! Everyone else is going to the bonfire. Wanna come? I was just grabbing us hoodies."

"Yeah!" Sirena exclaimed. Will and I followed Sirena into the cabin and she took the hoodie from Emily's outstretched hand. Then she touched my shoulder. "You coming? We can talk about what you should do about the sketch."

"Absolutely," I said.

"Zelda and I will be right there," Will said, smiling.

Sirena and Emily wiggled into warmer clothes, then walked off together toward the fire.

"Did you talk to Jesse? And everyone?" I blurted as soon as they were out of earshot.

Will gave me a slow smile. "I did."

From behind his back, he produced a handful of wild flowers. "These are for you."

My eyes widened.

"And so is this." Between his pointer and middle fingers, he held a note folded in quarters.

He transferred the flowers to me—they were held together with a twist tie and a lavender ribbon those Boy Scouts had procured from god knows where. But when I reached for the note, Will jerked it away.

"Hey," I protested.

"Z. What does your stomach feel like?"

I frowned. "Like a stomach." I reached for the note again, and he pocketed it.

"Hey!"

He folded his arms. "Z. Listen carefully. I'm going to paint a picture for you."

I rolled my eyes.

"I'm standing at the gate—6:58, your Jesse—"

"He's not my Jesse—"

"*Your* Jesse arrives. Alone."

I examined the ceiling to avoid looking at Will's cocky grin. "I wonder why Murph and Ricky couldn't come."

Will shook his head and slowed the pace of his speech like he was speaking to a small child, poking my shoulder with each word. "He was wearing a shirt with *buttons*."

"Are you drunk?"

Will threw up his hands. "Z! This guy likes you!"

"No, he—"

"Zelda Bailey-Cho, I swear to god—"

"Look. I bet Ricky and Murph were busy. It was just a walk. And so what if his shirt had buttons? Lots of shirts have—"

"Okay. Once again from the top." He gripped both of my shoulders. "Z. I am a guy. I know guys. This guy's eyes, when I told him where you were, were *deflated*. A sports ball of some kind. With no air."

"Really?" I asked in a small voice.

He nodded, still clutching my shoulders. "I handed him your note and those eyes lit up like a Christmas tree in Times Square."

"There's already a lot of light in Times Square," I said, "so a Christmas tree wouldn't really—"

He threw up his hands. "In a dark field in southwestern Minnesota in the middle of nowhere so they had to bring in a generator, just for the lights on the tree. Okay? Lit. Up."

I pursed my lips to push down a smile.

"He read the note." Will paused for dramatic effect. "And he laughed."

"Yeah?"

Will nodded. "That guy's eyes when he laughs—"

"Right?" I blubbered. "His face just transforms into—"

Will's cocky grin was back. "He likes you. And I can tell—you like him, too."

I bit the inside of my cheek, not ready to give myself over to believing him. "So, your evidence, just to be clear, is eye deflation, eye brightening, laughing at my jokes, and shirt buttons?"

"And the way you pretend to wonder why Ricky and Murph weren't there! And flowers! And this note!" He fished in his back pocket for it but still held it out of reach. "But first—"

I rolled my eyes again.

"How does your stomach feel?"

I wanted to jump up and down and be excited—I really did. But— "It feels . . . worried."

"Worried?"

"Look. I'm here for improv. And Ben—"

"I hate that guy."

"I know. You'll hate him even more after I tell you what he did to my script."

Will just growled.

"Apparently, I have terrible instincts when it comes to guys."

"Z—"

"Ben is awful, but I liked him. I wanted him to touch me. To kiss me. Well, at first. Until I realized I was terrible at kissing—"

"I *told* you—"

"I know, I know. At the very least, jury's out. But what's not to say Jesse's terrible in some terrible way? Clearly, I can't trust my instincts. So, what *do* I trust?"

Will closed his eyes. He exhaled and opened them again, smiling. "Look. You knew Jonas liked me before I did. Those are instincts."

"So, I have them about other people but not for myself."

"Maybe it's easier to see these things for other people. While I couldn't see that Jonas liked me, I knew Ben was bad news. And I have good feelings about Jesse. Maybe this is what siblings are for. To clearly see the things the other person is too close to see."

I glanced at the flowers. I'd noticed the small, bright yellow ones, and the kind with the long, dark coral petals in the fields around camp. But somehow, they were even lovelier together.

"You have two jobs before you come to this bonfire," he said. "In this order: One, make a list of the ways Ben is an asshole. Two, read Jesse's note. That order. Promise me."

I nodded and lay the flowers on the dresser. He handed over the note.

I immediately unfolded it.

"Zelda!"

"I'm my own woman, and you can't tell me what to do!" I pushed him out of the cabin, swung the screen door closed, and locked it.

He laughed and yelled, "Please do the other thing!"

"I will if I feel like it!"

"Fine." Smirking, he shook his head and disappeared.

I threw my bag onto Mattress Island, kicked off my shoes, and somersaulted into a spread eagle. Then I rolled over on my stomach and smoothed out Jesse's note.

Hey, Zelda—

The disappointment is not all yours. Don't be selfish. Unfortunately, I'm not free tomorrow night because we have a very cult-y, all-camp ceremony. Will says you don't have a scheduled practice tomorrow morning, but that Ben has been playing pretty fast and loose with the calendar. If you find that you're free,

I'm on rock cairn duty, and I'd love to show you a new hike. I'll wait at our big rock around 11:30 for a little while and hope you can make it.

Don't worry about bringing food—I'll make us each a sandwich for lunch. If you can't come, I'll just eat your sandwich.

You know, I usually wish I'd brought a second sandwich, so maybe I'll just make myself two sandwiches—three sandwiches total. Unless you want two, too? Tell you what—I'll bring four sandwiches. Don't feel pressure to eat two, you can just eat—

(Your brother has just told me to knock it off with the sandwiches already. I am deferring to his better judgment.)

I'll also be at the gate Monday night at 7. We can try for that night walk again. Or you can send your brother with excuses. (Now he's telling me to wrap it up. He's very funny, btw. I can tell you're related.)

Reclaiming my half of the disappointment,

Jesse

I closed my eyes. How did my stomach feel? Like it wanted to flip over. Like it wanted to gush and analyze every word of this note. Like it wanted to beg Will for all the details—how long did it take him to write it? Did he chew on the back of the pen when he was thinking? Bite his lip?

Maybe I should run over to the Boy Scout camp and find Jesse now. Tell him I got out of rehearsal early.

Make active choices.

Running to Boy Scout camp at night, though. That was ridiculous. Wasn't it?

CHAPTER TWENTY-SEVEN

I scrambled to my feet and dug around in my bag for _The Scene_ _Must Win_, opening it at random. _Okay, Jane. Should I go and try to find Jesse?_

"It can be very tempting to reach for the cheap, base joke," the book declared. "Bodily functions can certainly be funny, but they rarely serve as solid foundation for a scene."

I frowned. That didn't really fit my situation. I closed my eyes. Maybe Jane couldn't be bothered with such trivialities as whether or not to visit a boy. I changed my question. _What should I do about the cold open situation?_ I flipped through the pages again.

"An improv team can be comprised of as few as three players and as many as—"

I exhaled sharply. _Come on, Jane. I need you._

"Zelda?"

My heart slammed against my chest. I bolted upright on Mattress Island and peeked over my shoulder. I exhaled. It was just Dion and Roger.

"Hi!" I said, clambering to my feet. "What are you guys doing here?'

I unlocked the door, and Roger and Dion stepped across the threshold, their tall forms filling the space.

"Hey," they said together. Roger swept off his stocking cap and pointed at Mattress Island. "That's cool. Looks like fun." He gave me a small smile. "The Gildas said you were here. Aren't you coming to the bonfire?"

Dion held up a bag of comically large marshmallows. "We're bringing back reinforcements."

I chuckled. *Was* I going to the bonfire? I touched Jesse's note in my back pocket. I wasn't sure I had it in me to go tearing off at night to a Boy Scout camp all by myself, especially when I'd never been there. But even if I didn't go to Boy Scout camp, I wasn't really in the mood for a bonfire where I'd have to face Ben again so quickly. "Um . . ."

"Come on," Dion said. He tossed the bag of marshmallows to me, and I caught it, surprising myself. "Paul DeLuca has a fire extinguisher under his arm, but he isn't standing close enough to the bonfire for P2's money."

Roger nodded. "Paul DeLuca refuses to relinquish the fire extinguisher and also refuses to stand any closer to the bonfire because it makes him 'too hot,' and Paul Paulsen is so agitated about the whole thing, I think he might turn in on himself and implode."

"Which would cause another fire," Dion added. He looked to Roger. "More room to roast marshmallows."

Roger grinned and nodded at me. "You don't want to miss that."

I chuckled.

"So, are you coming?" Dion asked. "Now that you're in charge of the marshmallows?"

I looked down at the clear plastic bag and squeezed it a little.

"Nobody from Varsity's there," Roger added quietly.

I jerked up my head and then coughed to cover it. "Oh, okay," I said, trying to make my voice sound as offhanded as possible. "Whatever. Uh, yeah. Bonfire sounds great. Let's go."

I grabbed a hoodie off my bunk and slipped into my Chacos by the door. Roger and Dion might have exchanged a glance somewhere in there, but I didn't look up to find out.

I threw open the screen door. "After you."

They preceded me out of the cabin. It was starting to get dark, but we could still see well enough to safely traverse down a set of log steps to a clearing at the bottom of the hill. There, by a wide stream, the bonfire was already blazing.

"You guys took the long way to get more marshmallows!" a deep voice called out. "Where have you been? My sugar high is crashing!"

I tossed the bag to the guy.

"Victory!" he shouted, thrusting the bag of giant marshmallows above his head.

Before he could open it, however, the kid who I'd seen playing Seeker in the Quidditch match leapt into the air and yoinked the bag out of his hands.

Deep-voice guy barreled after the Seeker into the woods with Paul Paulsen half shuffling/half chasing them, calling out, "Boys? Boys!"

Dion and Roger patted me on the back. "Have fun," Dion said. "Okay?"

I nodded, forced a smile, and they were absorbed into the crowd.

I knew I could go find the Gildas or Will and Jonas, but for once in my life, I was feeling quiet. I hung back in the shadows and watched the fire.

Dad loves this poem by Gary Soto called "Oranges." At one point, the poem says something like, "I peeled the orange, and it was so bright, it was like a fire in my hands." I thought about that moment in the poem, where the kid peels open an orange to share with the girl he's taken to the drug store to buy chocolate for. It's so sweet. *He's* so sweet.

Two boys, brows furrowed, sat on a log deep in conversation, their faces illuminated by the flickering bonfire. One of them gestured to the sky. The other shook his head. I tried to imagine what they were talking about. Time? Space exploration? God? The taller one leaned back and stretched out his hands to make a point, perhaps, but slid backward off the log onto his butt. His friend laughed and offered to pull him back up. But the tall one shook the help away and stayed down. He was laughing too hard.

Across the fire, Jonas jabbed two marshmallows onto one stick. I smiled, knowing who the second marshmallow was for. At first, he held his stick at the very edge of the bonfire. He grew impatient, occasionally touching the marshmallows, evidently finding them cold. He thrust his stick into the flames and both marshmallows caught fire. I laughed under my breath at the stream of swear words that came out of Jonas's mouth. He blew out the flames, but it was too late to save the marshmallows. They'd grown so hot, they liquified and plopped onto the dirt. Sighing, Jonas plucked two more marshmallows from a passing bag and tried again. This time, the marshmallows took only slightly longer to catch fire. Will appeared. He said something to Jonas who laughed and threw his stick and burning marshmallows into the bonfire. Then Jonas gazed at my brother who gazed back with so much tenderness, I felt like I was intruding and looked away. When I glanced back, they were gone.

Sirena's and Hanna's voices caught my attention next when they started singing a song about some girl named Cecilia who was breaking their hearts and shaking their confidence daily. I didn't recognize it, but a dozen other people did. Soon they all had their arms looped around each other's shoulders as they sang the song, even finding some harmony.

I loved nights like this. I loved the chasing and the bonfire-ing and the deep conversation-ing and the marshmallow-burning and the singing. But this whole week, I'd felt sidelined at camp from everything I loved. Especially improv.

Early on in my improv life, Mom asked me why I liked it so much when it seemed so scary. No script? No plot? Nothing preplanned?

"When I'm up there," I'd told her in the car, "everything falls away. I can't think about the past or the future. Just what is."

"Wow. That's really interesting," she'd said. "It sounds like you love improv because it forces you to be in the true present." She'd reached over and squeezed my knee. "And here's a little life secret: Living in the present? Not dwelling on the past or the future? That's where true happiness is."

But for a week about improv, where I should pretty much be in the true-happiness present all the time, this week hadn't been happy. There were moments, of course, with Will and Jonas and the Gildas.

With the Boy Scouts. But maybe the improv hadn't been happy because I couldn't ever let the past or the future fall away. I couldn't when I had to spend my energy protecting myself, worrying about what might happen. Dissecting what already had.

Somehow, Ben had stolen my present.

But what could I do? I couldn't *not* think about the past or worry about the future with Ben around.

I wrapped my arms around myself and stared at the fire.

Something popped in one of the logs and sparks shot up above the flames.

If Greek mythology was to be believed, humans had had fire since Prometheus stole it from the gods. Or maybe humans figured out how to harness it when lightning struck a tree.

When we get home, I decided, *Will and I should throw a backyard bonfire party for our friends.*

I coughed out a laugh. *When we get home . . .*

I looked around at the people, the trees, the marshmallows. RMTA wasn't forever. *Ben* wasn't forever. I studied the fire. Since the dawn of humanity, there had been countless bonfires before this one, and there would be countless afterward. Even in my lifetime, this night was just—a blip.

Hands on my hips, I blinked back some swirling feeling coming up from my chest, and I stared at the sky.

Stars were starting to peer through the twilight. I shook my head. They had been burning for millennium, too.

This camp, namely this *Ben*, was not the pinnacle of the universe. Not even close. I had worlds outside this place, outside him.

I exhaled sharply. I had to get out of his orbit.

I just wasn't sure how.

"You're crying," Paloma said, appearing by my side.

I reached up to touch my cheeks. They were wet.

I closed my eyes. "Paloma," I said, trying to keep my voice steady, "I'm supposed to be smart. How could I let it get this bad?"

In one second, Paloma had enveloped me in a hug.

"You *are* smart—you're just . . . a frog," Paloma muttered over my shoulder.

"What?" I pulled back.

She gave me a half smile. "You're like a live frog put in a pot of water. It slowly gets hotter and hotter until it starts to boil—how did it happen? But by then, it's too late. You're dead."

I took another step back. "What?"

Paloma reached in and wiped a tear from my cheek. "I don't mean *you're* dead, I—this metaphor's falling apart a little. I just mean it happens so slowly, you don't notice at first. You're not stupid."

I let out a shuddery breath.

"Only . . ." Paloma led me several steps farther away from the edge of the crowd. "How bad have things gotten with Ben?" she asked carefully.

"What do you mean?"

"Has he . . . hit you?"

I shook my head slowly. "No."

Paloma cocked her head. "But?"

"He . . . touched me. Waist up stuff. I—I thought I maybe wanted it at first?" My voice was thin.

She grew very quiet.

"But then?" Paloma prompted me.

I shrugged. "I didn't want it anymore. I asked him to stop. He told me to relax. I kneed him in the... testicle region..."

Paloma bit her lip. "Well done, you."

"He told me if I told anyone, they'd all know the only reason I got on Varsity was because he thought I was hot and they needed a girl. Which is ridiculous, now that I say it out loud... I know I should just quit, but I really want to do the show. This is the thing I'm good at. This show could really be the start of something for me. I just have to... tiptoe through a minefield to get there."

Paloma frowned.

"Will told me to make a list of all the ways Ben is terrible," I said.

"And then I think it's time to tell the Pauls," Paloma said gently.

"Paloma—"

"What Ben has done is immoral... and illegal. You're underage." Paloma rubbed her forehead. "You shouldn't have to go through all this to be in that show! You think the guys are worrying about this crap? Carrying around all this baggage? Tiptoeing through a minefield? No. They were at the bonfire. Having fun. When do you get to have fun, Zelda?"

Tears threatened to overflow the banks again. "What happens if everyone finds out about Ben and me? What if they all say I'm only on Varsity because of him?"

Paloma scoffed. "Everyone saw your audition, Zelda," she said, rubbing my arms. "Only idiots would think Ben chose you simply because you're a girl." She hugged me again. "It's time to jump out of the pot, Zelda. Make a break for it. You can't stay in this thing for womankind anymore. That way is death. Metaphoric death. Spiritual death. Choose life."

I closed my eyes and let the tears drip off my chin.

Paloma stroked my hair. "You look exhausted. My parents say sleep should be the entire bottom level of Maslow's hierarchy of needs."

I choked on a laugh.

"So sleep. This problem won't go away, but you'll feel better equipped to handle it. Plus, tomorrow is our free morning—we'll circle up and talk more then. Let me walk you back, okay?"

I *did* feel exhausted. There was no way I was going off in search of Jesse anymore.

"Hey," she said, raising her eyebrows. "You want me to put on *Pacific Coast Whale Sounds?*"

I smiled around my tears. "Not for ten million dollars."

Paloma laughed and we hugged, and I let myself be led back to the cabin to sleep as hard as I could for tomorrow. Because tomorrow was going to be a big day: for being a frog, for getting to the bottom of this thing with Jesse . . . if there even was a thing. But no matter what happened, tomorrow wasn't for Ellie.

It was for Zelda.

CHAPTER TWENTY-EIGHT

The next morning at breakfast in the Lodge, I reached for my juice and found Ben sitting across from me. I looked left and right— where had the Gildas and Will and Jonas gone? After I went to bed, Paloma had filled them all in on what had happened, so they knew I needed their protection.

Then I smelled it before I saw it—someone from the kitchen depositing a fresh tray of coffee cake onto the buffet line.

Animals.

"Hey," Ben said. "How are you feeling?"

I couldn't meet his eye. "Fine."

"Cramps feeling better?"

I shrugged.

"Not a morning person?"

I closed my eyes. "Nope."

"Hey," he whispered. "I miss you. Weren't we going to start those kissing lessons?"

I stood up so fast, I knocked over my chair with a bang.

A collective "whoa" gave way to silence. Neither Ben nor I moved. But as people realized it was only a chair, they slowly returned to their eating and chattering. However, the noise had also drawn the attention of my coffee cake glutton friends, and they rushed back to our table.

"Ready to go on that hike?" Paloma chirped, scooping up and righting my chair. Will looked ready to pound Ben. Jonas stepped in front of Will, a human barrier between my brother and his target.

"Yup. Let's go," I said and swept up my bag.

"I'll be around for ... extra rehearsal if you change your mind," Ben said. His voice sounded sincere, but I knew what he really meant. I spun away from Ben and strode out of the noise of breakfast into the hall by the stairs. The others followed, and Jonas closed the door behind us.

"I'm going to find the Pauls," I announced. Even with just those words, I felt a little freer.

Will put his arm around my shoulder. "Let's go," he said.

I shook him off. "Nope. Alone. I don't want a huge ..." I waved my hands around searching for the right word. "Ordeal. I'm just going to tell my story and ask for him to be removed. Maybe one of the Pauls can take over."

"Hold on!" Sirena caught my elbow. "Strength in numbers. Right?"

I met Sirena's unwavering brown eyes. Part of me wanted her steadiness with me as I faced the Pauls, but ... "I'm the one who's been in that room the whole time," I said, squeezing her arm back. "I appreciate your support, but I've got to do this on my own."

Sirena and Paloma exchanged skeptical glances. I pretended not to see them.

"Are you sure?" Emily asked, blinking quickly.

"The time for talk is over," Hanna said, smacking her fist into her open palm. "I say we take the industrial tubs of mayonnaise from the kitchen, sneak into the Varsity cabin, replace their shampoo—"

I cracked a smile and touched Hanna's shoulder. "I'm going," I said. "I'll find you after." I gave them a bracing nod, waited until they filed back into the dining area of the Lodge, and marched down the hall to the Pauls' office door.

I knocked. A deep voice called out, "Come in!"

Paul Paulsen was perched at an old metal desk that mirrored another—presumably Paul DeLuca's. P2's desk enjoyed a neat army of binders, a plastic Chicago Cubs tumbler doubling as a pencil cup, and an old laptop. It contrasted starkly with Paul DeLuca's desk, which was covered in stacks of files, well-thumbed books, and an array of used coffee mugs.

Paul Paulsen ran a hand over his balding head and gave me a knowing smile. "Hi. Ellie, right? What can I do for you?"

I looked around for Paul DeLuca, which was silly, considering how small the office was. Did I think he was hiding in a filing cabinet or something?

I had imagined this meeting with both of them there. *Should I come back?*

"Want a seat? Some water?" Paul Paulsen asked.

Suddenly, I was too nervous to say anything. What was I *doing*?

"Uh . . ." My tongue felt too big for my mouth. I sat in the proffered folding chair, but shook my head at the water.

"You know what we say here," he said, pouring water from a pitcher into a glass, "Pee clear!"

I forced a smile. "I remember." I took the water to appease him.

"Tell me, Ellie," Paul Paulsen said, sitting back in his chair, elbows on his knees. "What can I do for you?"

"Well." I coughed, then took a sip of the water. Paul smiled with his eyebrows as if to say, "See? Told you!"

I cleared my throat and straightened my spine. *I'm here*, I decided. *I might as well just get it over with.* "I'm here . . . I'm here to talk to you about . . . Ben."

Paul smiled kindly. "Ben said you might come by to talk about that."

My eyebrows shot up.

He leaned forward conspiratorially. "Do you have a little crush on Ben?"

I flew back in my chair, which squeaked. "What? No! I—well, I *did*, I think, but—"

"It's perfectly natural to develop crushes at your age." Now his smile seemed patronizing. "But we discourage that sort of thing between coaches and team members."

"I *know*," I spat, staring at my knees. "I—"

"And Ben told me he felt badly if he encouraged your little crush."

My eyes flew up. "My little—"

"But it must be so hard with all those hormones flying!" He gestured at my . . . my what? My body?

"I—"

"It's just not a good idea to . . . socialize . . . in that way."

Was this guy for real? I tried to breathe and flip through the talking points in my head. I glanced at the wall over P2's shoulder. A poster of much younger Pauls with their arms around a vibrant Jane Lloyd from what looked like the 1990s promised, "A Summer of Theatre in the Rocky Mountains!" Would things be different if Jane were here?

I shook my head.

"Look. Mr. Paulsen. It's not just Ben. It's also the team. It's a very misogynistic place to be and—"

"Great vocabulary! Look. Honey."

I frowned. "Zelda."

"Improv tends to attract more guys than girls. And while we're thrilled you're here, you have to learn to—"

"Play with the big boys." Fire was burning in my eyes.

"Exactly."

I gripped my chair and tried one last tack. "Sir, Ben has been emotionally abusive. And he's . . . touched me when I asked him to stop."

Paul waved a hand at me. "Ben also said you've been very sensitive and probably misinterpreted his coaching. And as far as touching you goes, that's just how theater people are! But . . ." His face grew serious. "You can always give him a little slap if he goes too far."

My mouth dropped open.

"Boys *will* be boys. We don't always know when to stop." He chuckled. "We rely on you girls to keep us in line! And look, since you came and confessed, you won't get in trouble for fraternizing with your coach." He gave me a wide smile. "So, you have a free morning! Are you going to go hiking?"

I nodded a little, flabbergasted at his response. *I* wouldn't get in trouble?

"Okay. Toddle-oo!"

I had been dismissed. That was it? I'd been holding in all of this hurt and these secrets . . . for *this*? Disbelieving, I slowly shouldered my bag and stood. I had one more question. "Mr. Paulsen," I said.

"Yes, sweetie?"

I huffed. "Zelda. How many women did you contact to be our counselor in Gilda Radner?"

"Oh—isn't it working out?"

I shook my head. "We're fine. But—do you think maybe the reason you couldn't get anyone to come up here is because word gets around?"

He frowned. "I'm afraid I don't understand."

I glared at him. "Clearly."

Before he could respond, I was gone.

Will was waiting in the hall.

"How'd it go?" he whispered.

"Come on," I hissed. "Let's get out of here."

We scurried down the hall, out onto the front porch, and got as far as the steps when we ran into Ben.

"I thought you were going hiking." Ben's voice was an accusation, but he plastered over his tone with a smile for Will.

"It's a free morning," I said, a pool of lead forming in my stomach.

"Talk to the Pauls?"

"No," I lied.

"That's good," he said, "because I hope by now, you know you can talk to me about anything."

I said nothing and ground my teeth.

Ben leaned over. "If you want those lessons later," he said into my ear, "I'll be along our path."

"*We* don't have a path," I said at full volume.

"I think you know exactly where I mean." He smiled, stepping back. "And I know you need those lessons."

Fury bubbled up in my chest. I wanted to pound him.

"Goodbye, Ben," Will said firmly. I stood my ground until Ben left.

"What is he talking about?" Will whispered as we hurried toward the cabins.

"Kissing lessons." I couldn't help it. Tears were everywhere these days.

Will wrapped his arm around my shoulder. This time, I leaned into it. "He is a *monster*," he hissed. "Don't listen to him. What did the Pauls say?"

I wiped some tears away with the back of my hand. "It was only Paul Paulsen. And Ben beat me to him. Warned him I'd be coming. P2 told me to toughen up. That boys will be boys."

Will stopped walking. "You know, I'm offended by that. Guys everywhere should be offended. 'Boys will be boys'? What—we're so out of control we can't be kind? Thoughtful? Human? 'Boys will be boys' aligns us with wild animals. I can think about what I say before I say it. I can anticipate how someone else might feel before I do something. I can *keep it in my pants*."

I smiled a little and squeezed him, pulling him forward again.

"I'm going to itemize a list of every crappy thing I've had to put up with. After this week is done, I'm going to send it to the Pauls and threaten to post it on social media if they hire Ben again next summer. You want decent human beings coming to your camp? You want your alumni to fund this place? Good luck after that."

Will stopped again and turned to me, frowning. "What if no one believes you? You could get your own reputation—as being someone who's . . ."

"Overly sensitive?"

He wrinkled his nose and nodded. "For starters. Do you want that?"

My conviction wavered for a second. But I shook my head. "If people think that, I don't want to work with them. It might make it harder, but these guys don't get to keep doing what they're doing to other women. You know, at first I said I was doing this to show people women belonged at the top. But now I'm doing this so when other women get to the top, they don't have to put up with this trash."

Will nodded. "Let's go make the list."

CHAPTER TWENTY-NINE

One hour and forty-five minutes later, my hands shook with rage as I folded the four-page, single-space, handwritten list of offenses committed by Ben and the team and tucked it into my backpack.

"How do you feel?" Will asked. He had found a Tootsie Pop in the dresser drawer meant for the counselor and was sucking away on it.

I shook my head at him, having used up all my words making that list. As I laced up my hiking boots, he bit through the last part of the candy into the Tootsie Roll center with a crack.

I shuddered.

"That bad?" His face twisted in concern.

I snorted, adding my water bottle and trail mix to the backpack. "Yes," I said, "but also that Tootsie Pop. It could be older than we are."

"I doubt it." He chewed thoughtfully. "But you're joking around. That's a good sign, right?"

I took a deep breath and closed my eyes, willing my hands to steady themselves. Finally, I admitted, "I don't know."

The floor squeaked, and I felt his arms go around me.

"Those guys suck," he growled. "You're doing the right thing. And it's done for now. Don't think about it. Just go have fun with Jesse."

"Thank you," I muttered, laying my head on his shoulder. "You're a good one."

"Yeah?"

"Yeah. You listen to me. You take me seriously. You love me."

He shrugged.

I pulled back and gave him a half smile. "And you gave up sneaking away in the woods with your gorgeous boyfriend to help out your dumb sister."

"You're not dumb."

"Yeah, I know." I punched his shoulder. "I just hope Jonas—"

The door banged open. "Hi!" Jonas and his grin bounded into the cabin. Then he noticed me. "Aren't you meeting that hot Boy Scout?"

I cocked my head at Will. "Jonas knows about Jesse? *And* what time I'm meeting him?"

Will had the decency to look chagrined.

"No secrets between boyfriends." Jonas laced his fingers with Will's.

"I'll keep that in mind with my future secrets." I smirked, slinging my backpack over my shoulders.

"And with your future boyfriends." Will smiled.

I rolled my eyes, but smiled a little, too.

I had not given myself a luxurious amount of time to get to the rock—our rock—according to Jesse's note—so even though I ran a lot of the way, it was 11:35 by the time I arrived.

Jesse wasn't there.

I clambered up onto the rock to try and see down the path, but like last time, the foliage was too thick. My stomach dropped. Had he already gone? Or was he not here yet? I filled my lungs with air. "Jesse!" I bellowed.

Some birds chirped and flew out of their tree. I had a quarter of a thought about birds and threats and instinct and togetherness, but the rest of my thoughts were focused on something else.

No Jesse.

Putting my hands on my hips and staring at my boots, I bit my lip. Had he been waiting so long he started without me, thinking I wasn't coming? Or did he change his mind and decide not to come at all and this was just the way it was going to be with me and boys forever? Disappointing?

I'm not Catholic, but I read somewhere nuns are, statistically speaking, really happy. And they live super long lives. With other women. Caring for one another, not worrying about boys—well, except for Jesus. But—

"Zelda?"

My heart leapt. Jesse's smiling face came clomping around the corner. "Sorry I'm late," he said, offering his hand to help me off the rock. I started to decline it, then thought, *You know, that's an awfully good excuse to touch him.* His grip was warm and sure around my hand, and I jumped to the ground.

"Hi," he said, still holding my hand.

"Hi." I returned his smile. After that leap, my heart was lodged somewhere in my throat. "I thought you'd left already," I said, swallowing around my heartbeats. "I'm glad you didn't."

"Me, too. I'm sorry I'm late. My campers, the Webelos—" He shook his head, cutting himself off. "It's not important. Well, it was important to them. But if you aren't ten years old, it's, like, super boring."

I laughed, watching worry lines appear and dance on his fore-head and nose. "It's okay. Let's go," I said.

Alert lines replaced the worry ones. "You don't have much time before you have to be back, I bet." His hand twitched in mine.

I shook my head and dropped his hand. "Rehearsal at one."

"Okay then." He cinched up the straps on his backpack and pointed us down the opposite path from the one we took during the lunchtime hike. "That's us. We're looking to make sure the rock cairns are in place and spaced close enough so people don't get ner-vous thinking they've lost the trail. You'll be useful because you've never been here. So, look for the cairns."

I raised my eyebrows at this all-business Jesse and tried to match his tone. "Rock cairns. Piles of rocks, right?"

He nodded. "Little stacks. They look human-made. If you start to feel like it's been too long since you've seen one, tell me, and we'll make more."

He peered over my shoulder and down the path, and my stom-ach dropped a little. Is that all I was? Useful because I hadn't been on this hike? I *knew* I was overthinking this whole Jesse-liking-me thing. Will was just trying to make me feel better after all the crap with Ben and the team.

Something must have shown on my face because Jesse touched my arm. "You okay?"

I looked up at Jesse. His deep brown eyes were pools of concern.

And then I decided. After all of the conversations with myself in my head surrounding Ben, the doubt, the interpreting, worrying about the past and the future—I didn't want to do that anymore. I wanted my present back. *Be in the moment*, Jane Lloyd would say.

Jane Lloyd would have also told me to *Say yes*, to Jesse's question, but that didn't feel like the right thing to do. Maybe *Say yes* was more complicated than I'd thought. Or *maybe* it was time I just focused on the first rule: *Trust yourself.*

I opened my mouth and blurted out, "I like holding your hand. Can I do that?"

His eyes lit up. "You can definitely do that. You have a hand preference?"

I grinned, all relief. "Let me look."

He made a production of presenting both hands to me, front and back. I examined them with mock solemnity.

"Left," I proclaimed.

He bowed a little and presented his left hand. I took it in my right.

"Ready?" he asked, his grip firm.

"Uh . . . one other thing." I couldn't meet his eye, but I had to know. "Did you ask me on this hike because you needed someone who hadn't been on it, and I was the only person you could think of, or—"

He tugged on my hand. I looked up at him.

"I asked you because . . ." With his free hand, he rubbed the back of his neck. "I wanted . . . to spend time with you. Just you. But I also know you like to be useful. And so . . ." he trailed off.

I dropped my head to hide the pleased grin blooming on my face. We'd only seen each other a few times, and yet, it already felt like he knew me.

"Is that okay?" he asked, his voice strained.

I met his eyes, still beaming. "More than okay."

"Okay." His smile was back. "Lead the way, new hiker."

We were quiet for a while. I concentrated on the feeling of holding his hand and of my hand being held by his. Apparently, he was doing the same thing.

"You have soft hands," he said. "Well, this one is anyway."

I laughed. "They both are," I assured him. Then I thought about Curley in *Of Mice and Men* and how he keeps one hand gloved with Vaseline to keep it soft for his wife, but as I have this tendency to make literary references no one gets, I swallowed it down. Then I shook my head. I didn't want to have to hide part of who I was, just to make sure someone liked me. Another thing I wasn't going to do anymore. So, I took a deep breath. "Have you read *Of Mice and Men*—"

"Oh yeah," he cut in. "Who is that guy. Curley? I always thought that was so gross. The glove thing, right?"

I stopped walking and nearly tackled him. "Yes!" I shouted, much too loud.

He laughed and wrinkled his forehead at me, probably a little confused at my reaction.

"I always thought it was gross, too," I amended in a more normal volume.

As we were stopped, I pulled his hand up and held it with both of mine so I could take a closer look. "Your hand, however, is *not* soft. Not super rough, but definitely not creepy-Curley-soft."

"It's summers here," he said, sliding his other thumb under his backpack strap. "My hands are much softer during the school year. All that paper-writin'."

"But here you get calluses from all that ax-swingin'," I joked.

He nodded, and his eyes crinkled when he grinned.

The way he was looking at me made it hard for me to breathe suddenly, so I returned his hand to my side and pulled him forward. A few steps later, I called out, "Rock cairn!" and pointed at a small stack of flat rocks.

For a quarter second, he looked like he had no idea what I was talking about, but he quickly recovered. "Good! Seem visible enough?"

I nodded.

"Great." He cleared his throat. "There should be another at the next crossroads."

I nodded again, my heart beating a bass drum in my chest.

"You know, I started to tell you this on our last hike, but the subject got changed," Jesse said. "Ricky and Murph and I are from Minnesota, too. A bunch of people from our troop come here every summer."

I whacked him in the chest with my free hand. "Shut up! Where in Minnesota?" I asked.

Laughing, he clutched his chest where I had whacked him. "St. Louis Park. It's west of—"

Now I pushed his shoulder. "I know where St. Louis Park is! How have we not talked about this yet? I live in South Minneapolis!"

"Really?"

"We're practically neighbors," I said, swinging our hands between us, "especially if one of us has a car."

"Do you?"

"Well, no."

He laughed. "Thank goodness I do then. I'd hate for us not to be neighbors."

I drew in a warm, buoyant breath. He had a car. We practically lived in the same town. I was trying hard not to look too far down the proverbial road, but . . .

"My sister drove it in high school," Jesse continued, "but she's going to college in New York, so she doesn't need it."

"Just an older sister?"

He nodded. "Micky. For Michaela. But don't ever call her that."

I smirked. Then I met his eye for a second. "Jesse and Micky. I like it."

"She's at art school. People say she's really good." He shrugged. "She's just my big sister who dyes her hair a different color every week and who always got paint everywhere growing up." He smiled again, and I broke apart a little inside.

I coughed, trying to pull it together. "Parents?"

He nodded again. "Two moms. Micky and I are both adopted."

"Oh!" I exclaimed. "I am, too, on one side. Will and I each have one bio parent and one adoptive parent."

Jesse nodded and then frowned. "How . . . how does that work?"

"My biological father died before I was born."

Jesse raised an eyebrow.

"*After* Mom got pregnant with me, *before* I was born," I clarified.

"Back firmly in the realm of science." He smiled.

The wind started to pick up, whooshing around in the treetops. "What about you?" I asked, "Know your biological parents?"

Jesse shook his head. "Naw. And not interested. Parents are the people who raise you. Not the people who give you chromosomes."

"Totally. Sometimes I wonder about my biological father, but I love my dad. I can't imagine a different one."

He made a sympathetic sound. "I feel that way now. But early on in high school, I suddenly got really sad about being adopted. Angry, for a while," Jesse confessed. "My moms are white and Micky is biracial—African American and white, but she can pass for white. Or sort of ethnically ambiguous." Jesse pulled a smooth, flat rock out of his pocket—probably one Ricky gave him—and moved it through his fingers. "It's not always easy being a brown-skinned guy in Minnesota. Or in the Boy Scouts. And no one in my family could really understand."

I nodded.

"But freshman year I had Mr. Grinage for English. He was the first black male teacher I'd ever had. He just—it was nice to have someone in my life who knew how it felt to face some of the same stuff I was facing. He helped me a lot. And our new Scout Master is black, and that's been . . . awesome." Jesse chuckled and repocketed the rock. "I can't believe I just told you all that. After my moms and Micky, you are the fourth."

My stomach felt warm. "Thanks for making me the fourth," I said.

He gave me a half smile. "You've got some kind of witchcraft in you, Zelda . . . what's your last name?"

"It's hyphenated—Mom and Dad's last names together: Bailey-Cho."

"Bailey-Cho," he repeated. "Zelda Bailey-Cho. I like it."

"So do I."

He smiled.

My heart leapt into my throat again. "And you?" I swallowed.

"Also hyphenated. Rose-Eerdmans."

"Jesse Rose-Eerdmans."

"Everyone thinks my middle name is Rose."

I giggled. "Poor middle school you . . ."

"Yeah. Micky always said it shouldn't matter that everyone thought I had a girl's name as my middle name as," he made finger quotes with one hand, "'Girls are awesome and things associated with them shouldn't be insulting to boys.'"

I laughed, already liking this Micky Rose-Eerdmans.

"But not all of the students at St. Louis Park Middle School had caught up with her progressive values, so I finally decided I had two choices: beat up everyone who laughed at me, or let it go."

"And you picked Elsa."

He chuckled. "I let it go . . . I like that you could already guess that."

We grinned at each other. But then he looked up over my shoulder, and his face fell.

I whirled around, sure it was Ben.

Relief flooded in. Just rocks and trees and the wind.

"I don't like the color of the sky," Jesse said.

I looked straight up. The heavens were suddenly a deep slate blue. "Where did that come from?"

"Storms come up fast in the mountains." He checked his watch. Then he peered at the sky again. "Trust me?"

My "yes" lodged in my throat. "That's a . . . bigger question than you probably mean it to be." I knew Jesse wasn't Ben, but— "It's just, Ben—"

Jesse's eyes were all concern. "Oh. I—we need to take cover. And there's a little alcove in some rocks, but it's off the path. That's all I mean. Will you follow me? You don't have to. We can run back. We might make it. Probably make it even. It's totally up to you."

I think it was because he offered me a choice. But that was the moment that I knew in my cells that being with Jesse felt totally different from being with Ben. *Trust your partner.* I was realizing I couldn't trust every partner in every situation. But it felt right to trust Jesse.

So, I did.

CHAPTER THIRTY

We skittered along a very narrow trail that Jesse told me was a deer path. After following it for only a minute or so, we emerged into a small clearing largely taken up by a porch-size rock as tall as me.

"Over here," Jesse said as the first drops of rain started to plop onto our backpacks. He offered me his hand, and I took it. We bushwhacked around to the far side of the rock, and it opened into a small cave with enough space for us to climb in with our packs out of the rain.

He pulled me in after him and slipped out of his backpack. I copied his movements and slid in next to him, and then seconds later, sheets of rain poured out of the sky like water from a pitcher. It took my breath away.

"Storms are nuts up here!" he yelled over the downpour, looping one arm around his knee.

"Seems like it!" I yelled back. I pulled both of my knees up to my chest.

Then lightning flashed across the sky and less than two seconds later, the thunder boomed. Instinctively, we leaned in to close the gap between us.

"How long do storms normally last up here?" I called over the cacophony.

His shoulder shrugged against mine. "Hard to say!"

But before I had a chance to consider our new position in this raging storm, Jesse turned to face me. "Will you tell me about Ben?" he shouted/asked.

I took in a deep breath.

He furrowed his brow. "Look—I . . . I like you."

My heart ping-ponged in my chest.

"But he's—here. I see it when you consider whether or not to say something to me. Whether and how to hold my hand. And before we ran here—I asked you to trust me, and you said his name. There's something about him in the way . . . I hope you don't think I'm being too forward." He offered me his hand. I took it in both of mine and laid it palm up. Slowly, I traced all the lines with my finger. His breath hitched.

I wanted and didn't want him to know. But I had told Jesse everything in my head so far today, and the hand-holding, the book jokes, even hesitating about trusting him—nothing had scared him away.

"He's a terrible person," I finally shouted.

Jesse nodded.

"And I'll tell you," I continued loudly, still tracing his palm, "but you have to promise me something."

He nodded again.

I took a breath and met his eyes. "Please don't stop looking at me the way you look at me."

He smiled a little. "And how's that?" he asked.

"Like . . . Like I'm not broken."

He face dropped. "Did he break you?"

I considered this. "I don't know. A bit. Not entirely. He—" I shook my head. "Promise me?"

He paused and adjusted his knees so he was facing me. "Can I first tell you why I like you?"

I smiled slowly. "Because I'm the only girl at Boy Scout camp?"

"No!" he groaned. "I was worried you'd think that. Do you think that?"

I shrugged and smiled. The wind changed direction and now it was blowing into the cave. We dropped hands and backed up as far as we could. The rain licked our boots.

"I started liking you when we ran into you hiking that first day," he confessed. Now that we were deeper in the cave, we didn't have to shout so loudly to be heard. "You're funny. I'm sure you get that all the time, but it's true." He huffed out a laugh. "And your funny isn't forced. I don't see the gears working—it just—flows out of you. It's not something you put *on*, it's something that you *are*."

I bit my lips and blinked back some surprising tears.

"And you're pretty. But you said that thing when we were talking about hypothermia. Why don't you just know this about yourself?"

I chuckled and shook my head, eyes back on the ground. "I look a lot like my mom, and I like that." I gestured to my hair, which was currently wound up in a bun under a scarf folded into a triangle. "We both have this insane mane of curls with a mind of their own."

He smiled and ran a hand over his close-cropped hair. "You should see the vertical feats my hair is capable of when I let it grow."

I grinned. "I like the way I look. But I don't turn a lot of heads."

"What is wrong with every guy you've ever met?"

Still smiling, I scooped up a pinecone from the cave floor and started picking it apart. "I don't know. Boys are friends with me. They like me."

"But they're blind and also stupid."

I laughed hard. "We've gone to school together since kindergarten. Some of us anyway. Maybe it's difficult to think someone's hot when you've seen them ugly cry at drop-off."

He smiled. "Maybe. Their loss."

I shivered.

He misinterpreted the cause of my shiver and reached over to rub my arm briskly a few times. "You're also really kind. Most people think Ricky's weird and just blow him off. But you listen to him. He likes you. He's kind of my canary in the coal mine. If he likes someone, I know they're good people."

"Ricky's easy to like."

"He is *not* easy to like!" Jesse laughed. "But it makes me really happy that you do."

We reached out for each other's hands.

"Those are my reasons," Jesse said, his voice sure. "Please note that 'You're the only girl I've talked to all summer' isn't on the list."

"But it's accurate," I protested.

He shrugged. "You were bound to stand out anyway, Zelda."

I peered at him, searching his eyes for the truth. He nodded.

Finally, I sighed, unzipped my backpack, and retrieved my

detailed list of Ben's crimes against humanity. "Maybe just read this. It explains everything."

Gingerly, Jesse took the pages, and he began to read.

I watched his eyes dart back and forth across the page and grow darker the more he read. Sometimes he'd mutter under his breath. Twice, he swore. Finally, he folded the pages with shaking hands and returned them, his jaw clenched. The thunder boomed again. Into the thunder, he yelled a very satisfying curse word. On the next crash, I joined him. We yelled and cursed again and again until I started giggling.

"Why are you laughing?" he asked, fists at his sides.

I picked up a fist and unfurled his fingers, one at a time. I placed the heels of our hands together, fingers touching.

"You have long fingers," he said. The rain was starting to let up.

"Or you have short ones." I smiled. "Or they're the right size to be fingers. Since we both have them."

He stared at our hands. Then his eyes snapped up to meet mine. "Look. I'm really mad at that guy."

I nodded.

"Cuz that guy is—he's really—" He sighed.

"I know." A corner of my mouth turned up.

"Why are you smiling?"

Why *was* I smiling? "Uh..." I laughed a little. "I think I'm just happy to be believed. You believe me."

His mouth dropped open. "I—" He shook his head, then looked

back at our hands. He dropped his fingers down, interlacing them with mine. "Everyone should believe you."

"Yeah, well." They didn't. But for the moment, it was enough that Jesse did.

After a long moment, he took a deep breath. "You've never had a boyfriend?" he asked. "Or girlfriend? I don't mean to assume."

I shook my head. "You?" I asked. "Anyone?"

"A couple girlfriends. Nothing long lasting. But Micky—it was very important to Micky that she teach me how to treat women. My moms, too, but for Micky it was like a crusade."

Giggling, I asked, "Then how are you single?"

He grinned. "No other girls have been interested in me. Maybe you're right about that whole kindergarten thing. Plus, I'm nice."

"And nice guys finish last?"

"I don't know. Maybe?"

"So," I teased, "when girls either dump or get dumped by everyone else, you'll be there with open arms?"

He squinted, considering this. "Understanding arms? 'Open arms' makes me sound like an opportunist."

I used the broken bits of the pinecone to scrape dirt out of the treads of my hiking boot. I wasn't quite ready to meet his eyes. "So, you don't think I'm stupid? Or naïve?"

He shook his head. "Funny. Pretty. Kind. Remember?"

I frowned. "So . . ." Was I really going to say *everything* that was on my mind?

You're trusting your partner, remember?

I let out a shaky breath. "Micky told you everything about . . ."

"Everything about everything. Yes."

"Did she..." I coughed. "Did she ever talk about people being bad kissers?"

He smiled softly. "Incompatible, yes. But kissing is communication. Expression. It's art. No one is inherently bad."

I frowned harder. "Please don't tell me art takes practice."

He smiled. "You don't want to practice?"

My brow furrowed. Now my whole face was a pinecone. "Not with him. And he kept..." I shook my head, unable to put words to what I wanted to say.

Jesse clenched his jaw again. "I really wanna punch that guy."

"Me, too."

We were quiet for a moment. The storm had now slowed to merely a steady rain. Jesse turned to me again. "Did kissing him feel good?"

I paused, considering this. "...Nnnno? It was mostly wet."

"When he kissed you," he chuckled, continuing, "what did those kisses say?"

I wrinkled my nose. "What did they *say*?"

"Yeah. If kissing is communication, it's saying something."

My expression must have done something strange because his face quirked up on one side. "Just...I'm sorry," he said and gestured to his torso. "This is what Micky made me into. If this isn't—"

I touched his arm. "No, it's...I've just...I've never talked about..." I swallowed and nodded. "Okay. What did the kisses say? They said...'I'm in charge.'"

His eyebrows lifted. "'I'm in *charge*'?"

I crumpled a little. "Is that not a thing they can say? I—I can come up with something else—"

"Oh whoa, sorry—" He held up his hands defensively. "I'm not criticizing *you*. I'm criticizing those *kisses*." He shrugged. "Sounds like he was the problem."

I bit the inside of my cheek. "I just felt so stupid."

"According to the Gospel of Micky, kissing is never supposed to do that."

The splatting of the rain gave us permission to be quiet for a while. It also gave me time to consider his words.

I sneaked a look at him out of the corner of my eye. There was tension in his jaw, and his eyes were closed. Emboldened, I turned my head more fully toward him.

"What . . . what would *your* kisses say?" I asked.

He smiled slowly, eyes still closed. "I like you. I have fun with you. Do you like me, too?" He opened his eyes.

"Do you want to kiss me?" I asked. I'm not sure even Jane Lloyd had this much *Trust your partner* in mind when she wrote that rule.

He coughed and rubbed the back of his neck. "You have no idea how much," he said, and my stomach flipped. "But I want you to really want to kiss me back. Correct me if I'm wrong, but it seems like if we kissed now, you'd be worried. And thinking about Ben."

I nodded slowly. "I think you're right."

"That's okay. You've been through a lot."

I twisted my hands together. "One last question. Purely academic. Do you know how to take a bra off with one hand?"

He spluttered. "Uh, we . . . that is, Micky did not teach me the finer points of—I mean, my god, a sister can only—"

"Good."

I leaned my head on his shoulder, and he wrapped an arm around me. He smelled like coconuts. And even though the rain was still coming down, and we didn't know when it would end, I felt safe.

CHAPTER THIRTY-ONE

We ate (all) of our sandwiches in the cave and talked and talked, holding hands. I knew Ben was going to be furious, but occasional thunder still crashed and lightning lit up the sky—and he himself had yelled about a storm's danger.

By the time the rain slowed to sprinkles, it was two o'clock. Jesse peered out of the cave and into the clouds. "Clear skies are coming," he observed, "I think we can emerge from hibernation."

We clambered out, slung our backpacks in place, and reached for each other's hands.

"So. Cult conversion tonight?" I asked as we scooted around the rock and up the deer path.

He stifled a laugh. "Yeah. Someone's getting their Eagle. I know you're joking, but I think if you saw that ceremony out of context, it wouldn't seem far off."

"Are you an Eagle Scout?"

He ducked under a wet, heavy tree branch. "Not yet. Hopefully by the spring of senior year. It's a lot of work. Only four percent of Boy Scouts ever become Eagle Scouts. And Eagles Scouts go on to—"

"You aren't trying to convert me, are you?" I smirked, pushing him a little.

Laughing, he shook his head. "Okay. Tonight's out . . . so when can I see you? How much longer are you here?"

I breathed in the post-rain ozone-y air. "Another week. And I don't know. A lot is going to depend on . . . you know." I bit my lip, a Ben-shaped pit returning to my stomach.

Jesse nodded. "Okay. Well . . . when we know more, we could leave each other notes. I could slide something under the door of your cabin if no one's there. And you could leave one . . ."

"Under the cushion of that chair on the Gilda porch. Or is there something by the gate?"

He smiled. "That chair is great . . . It'll be nice to text someday."

"But," I reminded him, "texting means we're not together in the mountains anymore."

"It also means you aren't on the worst-behaving improv team in the history of America anymore, either."

I chuckled. "True. Well, in the meantime, it's a good thing I love a chatty, handwritten note."

Smiling, he tugged on my hand.

We were quiet until we returned to the main path.

"What is he going to do when you come back late?" Jesse asked in a voice laced with worry.

I watched a far-off bird swoop down into the trees. "I don't know."

He pulled us to a stop. "Can I come with you? Act as your alibi?"

I grinned and faced him, taking both of his hands in mine. "What would you say?"

"Uh . . ." He put on a deep voice. "She wasn't skipping, Ben. We were stuck in a cave during the storm. I promise—I was with her the whole time."

I laughed and dropped my head. "That would make everything worse!"

Scoffing, he squeezed my hands. "Why wouldn't he believe *me*? I'm a Boy Scout, after all. The goody-two-shoes stereotype's gotta be good for something."

I looked up into his face, and his grin made my heart beat faster. "Oh, he'd totally believe you. That's the problem. He'd be furious that we were together during the storm. And even more furious if he knew that we're tog—" Suddenly, all my words were gone. And my breath. And my balance. Maybe this was a case for a little time delay on all that truth telling.

"Are you . . . are you . . . we're . . . together?" Jesse asked.

My cheeks burned, and I stared at the ground.

"Do you *want* to be together?" he asked quietly, taking a tiny step closer to me so our boots were touching toe to toe.

"Y-yes. Do *you*?" I sneaked a look up to read the expression on his face.

He smiled his Christmas tree smile. "Yes. But only if you—"

And then I kissed him. And his lips were soft, but sure. And it was slow and gentle. And then he broke away, our foreheads touching, and whispered, "Are you sure?"

And I took his face in my hands and nodded and we kissed and kissed, and I finally figured out what everyone had been talking about.

It took much longer to meander back to camp now that we ... had other things to keep us occupied.

It was nearly three o'clock before Jesse and I made it back to the parking area in front of the Lodge.

"Please let me come with you," he said again, his forehead worry lines back. "What is Ben going to do when he sees how late you are? What if you get kicked off Varsity?"

Even though I would have been worried about the same things a day earlier, today I felt totally free from Ben's orbit. "So, that's the thing. Maybe ... Maybe Ben isn't the improv gate-keeper. He thinks he is. He made me believe he was. But ... I don't know—what happens if I don't perform in the showcase? It's not like I can't audition or take classes at Second City or UCB or iO or someplace myself. Later. And maybe showing Ben he can't control every woman he sees is what I can do for women now." I shook my head. "Please kiss me. Then, somehow, I'll see you tomorrow."

I closed my eyes and slid my arms around Jesse's waist. He pulled me closer, and I kissed him, knowing it might be a while before that happened again, and thunder boomed in the background.

It wasn't until Jesse was ripped away from me that I realized that the thunder was actually footsteps.

And it wasn't until Ben bellowed, "WHORE!" that I realized those footsteps were Ben's.

But it took a cracking sound, blood pouring out of Jesse's nose, and Ben shaking out the hand that had punched Jesse to set off a bomb inside my body.

"How *dare* you!" I bellowed, rage vibrating my every cell. Ben charged at me, and I barreled toward the steps. All I could think was to distance Ben from Jesse and make it to the Pauls.

"How dare *I*?" He caught up with me in two strides and grabbed my arms. "How dare *you*?" He spun me to him. Fury contorted his face. "I let you onto Varsity and *this* is how you repay me?" His hands dug into my upper arms, and he shook my body. "By skipping rehearsal? By throwing a fit when I fixed your cold open?"

Then I saw faces in the screen door of the Lodge, but Ben's eyes were accusing daggers focused only on me. Desperately, I watched from my periphery as Cade and both of the Jakes crept silently onto the porch. I almost called out to them, but I clamped my mouth shut. The Pauls had to see this with their own eyes, or they wouldn't believe my word against Ben's. And I wasn't confident in Cade or the Jakes standing up for me . . . except for maybe High Ropes Jake. *Go get the Pauls, Go get the Pauls*, I begged him in my mind.

"The whole time, leading me on," Ben continued, spitting out his words like they were food that had turned. "The whole time, sleeping with *him*."

"Hey—I'm not *sleeping* with *anybody*," I insisted, another bomb going off inside me.

I tried to break out of his grasp, but he growled, "Shut up!" and shook me again.

Out of the corner of my eye, I watched High Ropes Jake turn tail and run inside. *Yes! Get the Pauls!*

"Ben, let her go." Jesse's voice sounded thick coming up from behind me.

I twisted around, but still gripping my arms, Ben kicked Jesse in the knee as he lurched toward us, which sent him stumbling back down into the gravel. Jesse's nose was bleeding so freely, the front of his shirt was a lake of blood.

"Jesse!" I hollered. I tried to go boneless, but the move just infuriated Ben more.

"Stand UP, bitch," he demanded, digging his fingers even deeper into my forearms. Whimpering from the pain, I listened.

Jake and Cade remained silent—why weren't they saying anything? How could they stand by and watch all this happen? But somehow, they also couldn't turn away—they were rooted in place like an I-don't-want-to-get-involved deer in the something-is-seriously-wrong headlights.

Jesse moaned and tried to get back up again.

"Does your little Boy Scout boyfriend know about us?" Ben taunted me. "Does he know you've been cheating on him with me?"

I opened my mouth to defend myself, but at that moment, the Pauls rushed out of the door, led by High Ropes Jake, just in time to hear Ben demand, "Does he know what a little slut you are?"

"Ben!" Paul DeLuca shouted.

Turning around in shock, Ben dropped my arms, so I grabbed his shoulder to force him back to face me, then spectacles-testicled him, and he collapsed to the ground.

CHAPTER THIRTY-TWO

Paul DeLuca stood over Paul Paulsen's shoulder in their office, reading my itemized list of Ben and Ben-sanctioned offenses. Paul DeLuca kept shaking his head. "Paul, she told you about Ben this morning, and you sent her back into the fray?"

He rubbed his hands over his head again and again. "I didn't realize—Ben told me she had a crush on him and—" He put his face in his hands. "We're done for."

"Y-You're *done* for?" I stammered. "How about 'I'm sorry?'"

"He's featured on our website! There's a whole page about him where he says we made him what he is today!" Paul Paulsen moaned. He opened up his laptop with one hand, furiously tapping a pencil on the desk with the other. "I'm going to take the website down. Right now."

I gaped at him.

Paul DeLuca slowly took the pencil out of Paul Paulsen's fingers. "P2," he said softly, "snap out of it. Listen to yourself."

"Who is going to want to come here after this gets out? How

will we get funding? Especially if she presses *charges*?" Paul Paulsen regarded me, worried. "*Are* you going to press charges? Will the *Boy Scout* press charges?" He reached over to select another pencil from his collection, but Paul DeLuca stilled his hand.

"I—" I looked around the office, like the answers would be on the walls or ceiling but found nothing. I swallowed. "We'll have to talk to our parents."

P2 sunk his face into his hands again. "Parents. Oh god."

Maybe I should have expected his reaction after the way he dismissed me this morning, but I couldn't help it—I was stunned.

Paul DeLuca gestured for me to stand up. "Paul and I need to discuss some things. Why don't you see how the Boy Scout is doing? He's in the nurse's office."

"Jesse. The Boy Scout's name is Jesse," I said. I tried to find something in Paul DeLuca's eyes—sympathy? Understanding? But the only feeling I could discern was worry. And it wasn't worry for me or for Jesse.

"Right, okay," Paul De Luca said, his back already toward me.

Frowning, I stepped into the hallway and closed the office door.

"What if it gets out that the Boy Scout is black?" The door barely muffled P2's panicked voice. "That will make us look even worse."

Fury gripped me, and I flung open the door.

"Free advice," I spat.

Startled, they stared at me.

"Maybe stop worrying about how you're going to defend yourselves, and start asking what you can do to help."

Without waiting for a response, I pulled the door closed and strode down the hall. My breath shook in and out as I walked.

But as gross as it had felt to overhear Paul Paulsen's comment about it being worse for them that Jesse was black, I knew it would have been even harder for Jesse to hear it.

This thing was layer after layer of suck.

I took a minute to calm down. But then I felt strange approaching the nurse's office again. Dad always says places hold memories, and this place only held a memory I wanted to forget.

After knocking twice, I tentatively pushed open the door and peeked inside.

Jesse was perched on a stool facing a sturdy white woman in her fifties who was shaking her head as she washed her hands in the sink. Jesse's face had been cleaned up, but his shirt was still bloody.

"Hey," I whispered, "can I come in?"

"Yeah!" Jesse's eyes did that Christmas-tree-in-a-dark-empty-field thing and he started to smile, but flinched.

"Oh no," I said, taking a step inside. "It hurts to smile?"

He nodded.

"I bet laughing is worse. If I can't make you laugh, then I'm only down to two things you like about me. Is that enough to sustain us?"

Trying very hard to push the laughter down, he gestured for me to join him.

"You must be Zelda," the nurse said as she dried her hands. "You're a brave one—coming to a place like this? Putting up with all this crap?" She stepped over to Jesse and ever-so-gently prodded his nose with her fingertip. "We'll just have to see—broken noses have minds of their own."

Jesse nodded.

"Okay now, Jess. I've got a clean T-shirt in my bag. Why don't you step out and change, and I'll check out Zelda here."

"Where is *he*?" Jesse turned to me and squeezed my hand.

"In a rehearsal room upstairs. Roger and Dion took him after . . . he could walk."

Jesse nodded. "Have the police been contacted?"

"Yes," the nurse said. "The Pauls called me, and then I called the police. But you know how it goes—it'll be at least two hours before someone can get up the mountain from town."

I furrowed my brow. "Called you? From where? You aren't our nurse?"

"She's *our* nurse." Jesse flinched again. I knew he wanted to smile.

"That's right. I've known Jess since he was what . . . twelve? I'm Karen."

"Hi." I was a little taken aback. "We don't have our own nurse?"

Did Ben know that? Had he taken me to the nurse's office *knowing* the nurse would never come? I shivered in revulsion.

Karen raised her eyebrows and lowered her voice in a confidential tone. "No one will take the job," she muttered.

My jaw dropped.

"So," she continued, "I'm covering. The Pauls assured me they'd have someone by the first Tuesday. But, here we are in week two . . ." She shook her head. "Jess, hon, go change." She patted Jesse's shoulder.

He slid off the stool and squeezed my hands again. "I'll be right back," he promised, taking the BSA T-shirt Karen handed him.

I nodded, my heart somersaulting.

Karen waited until the door clicked shut before turning to me. "Okay, hon." She took out a notepad. "Tell me everything."

I told my story again from the top. And by the time I was done, I'd half filled the wastebasket with tissue.

She sighed, dated her notes, then flipped the cover shut. "I wish they'd listened to you the first time."

"Me, too," I said, letting out a shaky breath. "Jesse's nose wouldn't have been broken."

"Sure. Among some other things . . . But adults don't always think teenagers know what they're talking about. And men . . ." She rolled her eyes. "Are you going to press charges?"

"I don't know. The Pauls asked that, but I need to talk to my parents."

She nodded. "Have you called them?"

"They're hiking in the mountains for two weeks—no cell service. It's not the kind of voicemail you want to leave, you know? If Ben's gone, I can hang out for a few more days."

Karen tucked her notebook back into her bag. "That makes sense . . . Okay. Let's look at those bruises."

I frowned and followed her gaze to my upper arms—bright blue circles had formed where Ben's fingertips had gripped me.

Tears dripped off my nose as she clucked and murmured sympathetically. Then she asked me to hold out my arms, and she photographed them.

After she took the last photo, Karen asked, "You okay?"

I pursed my lips and nodded.

She pulled up a stool, a sad smile on her face. "Listen, hon. I'm just going to say this once, and then you do whatever you're going to do—it's your life. But . . ." She put a hand on my back. "I see the way you look at Jess. The way he looks at you. But are you sure this is what you want, right on the heels of this thing with Ben?"

I took a breath.

She held up her hands. "It's really none of my business, but I'm just telling you. It might be good for you to be alone for a little bit first."

Frowning, I considered this. "I . . . I can see your point. But—I've *been* alone. I *know* how to be alone. I—I want to be with Jesse."

Karen nodded and put her hand on my back again. "I know you do. I knew you would. But I also want you to know it's okay to ask Jesse for some time."

"Okay . . ."

There was a tap on the door, and Jesse's voice called out, "Can I come back in?"

I quickly dried my eyes with my shirt. "Yes!" I cried, a little over-enthusiastically. Karen chuckled and shook her head.

Except for the swollen nose, Jesse was back to looking like himself. I expected him to come over next to me, but he said, "There are some people here to see you . . ." He opened the door all the way, and Will's and Jonas's and the Gildas' concerned faces filled the frame.

"Okay." Karen stood between Jesse and me and the others in the doorway and shooed them away. "That's too many people for this tiny office. Let's go into the main hall. I'll stand sentry there."

As I passed through the door, Will grabbed me and locked me in a hug. His arms felt like home, and I fell apart again. Neither of us said anything for a long while.

By the time the pair of police officers arrived, dinner was starting. I insisted the Gildas and Will and Jonas go eat, and the police interviewed me in the Pauls' office. The Pauls and Jesse waited in the hallway—P2 looked ready to pass out the whole time.

After I spoke to the officers, it was Jesse's turn. I regarded Paul Paulsen, still in the hall. "You know why girls don't come back now, right? You can see that?"

He fixed his gaze at a spot near his elbow. "Ben is—he's passionate. Talented. He's . . . he's just very intense."

I stared at him. "Dion. Roger. Also talented. Also passionate. But not inappropriate and not violent. How can you defend Ben?"

Paul DeLuca put his hands on Paul Paulsen's shoulders. "Best not to engage right now, P2. We have a lot of things to chat about."

Paul Paulsen just stared at the floor, looking pale.

Paul DeLuca turned to me, shifting a little, not meeting my eyes. "I have some bad news, I'm afraid, Zelda."

I raised an eyebrow. "Worse than, 'You have an abusive coach but no one cares and, whoops, now he broke your friend's nose'?"

He grimaced. He clasped and unclasped his hands. "Maybe. We have a very strict policy about physical fighting. Remember the first night? We talked about it before dinner. If you get involved in a fight . . . you can't perform."

My jaw dropped. "Even if I was *defending* myself?"

Paul DeLuca shook his head and weakly lifted his shoulders. "Paul and I had arrived on the scene. You struck him after that."

I gestured to Paul Paulsen. "You told me if Ben went too far to give him a little slap!"

If it was possible to grow even paler, he did. "Well . . . that was more of a figure of speech. Plus, what you did wasn't little."

"This place." I shook my head. "This is insane."

Paul DeLuca frowned. "We have a zero-tolerance policy for physical aggression."

"Incredible. Okay. You know what? That's fine. I have six days left here. I'm just going to hike. Maybe play with JV. I really don't need those Varsity guys anyway." Even if I couldn't play, I could at least meet Nina Knightley.

Paul DeLuca coughed uncomfortably. "Uh, see, you misunderstand me—it's not just that you can't perform. You can't *stay*. We have to ask you to leave."

Suddenly, I was cold all over. "*What? I* have to *leave?* Why am I being punished for defending myself—especially when you guys wouldn't?"

"You're making her leave?"

I whirled around. From the direction of dinner, Karen approached our trio with two sandwiches in hand and passed me one of them. "Eat." She smiled at me, then turned sternly back to the Pauls. "Where's the sense in that?"

"Karen—" Paul DeLuca began, but she cut him off.

"You've got a camper who came to you for help, and you blew her off, and now you're making her pay for your mistake?"

Hopeful, I took a step closer to her.

"Karen—" Paul DeLuca tried again but she cut him off once more.

"Guys, I like you. You know I do. But when Jane died, you lost your—"

"Those are the rules!" Paul Paulsen shouted. "She has to leave!"

I felt like I had been slapped.

No one said anything. Finally, I opened my mouth. "My parents are hiking in the mountains for two weeks. They're unreachable."

Paul Paulsen exhaled sharply through his nose. "You signed a form. Your *parents* signed a form. You're expected to have contingency plans in place."

"Can she stay with us?" Karen asked. I looked up at her face, her set jaw. "I can take her in my cabin back at Scout camp."

"I ... I'm not sure ..." P2 rubbed his eyes with the heels of his hands.

"I'll decide for you, then," I said, suddenly desperate to get out of there. "Happy to take you up on your offer, Karen. I'll go pack. Meet you in front in a half an hour."

"But—" Paul DeLuca protested.

"Tell Jesse where I've gone?" I asked Karen. She nodded.

Leaving her to sort out the details, I marched down the hall with my sandwich in hand, out of the Lodge, and off in the direction of the cabins.

I hesitated as I neared Gilda Radner. Crossing its threshold for the first time, I had been so excited. Crossing it for the last time ... well, so much had changed.

Suddenly, footsteps pounded in the dirt behind me. And even though I *knew* the police had Ben in custody, my heart pounded, too, sure it was him. I spun around.

Paloma and Emily were running toward me.

"Zelda!" Emily panted, her voice thick with tears. "They're making you leave?"

I gave her a hug and a tight smile. "So it seems."

"That's terrible," she said, swiping at her eyes.

"It's okay." I squeezed her arm.

Paloma thumbed behind her, catching her breath. "The Pauls are *not* very popular over there right now."

I felt a tiny bit happier hearing it, but sighed. "Was any of this worth it?"

Paloma put her arm around my waist and we trudged into the cabin together, Emily right behind us. "Was what worth it?"

"I made Varsity. I wrote a hilarious sketch. I tried to show those guys I belonged there. But now I'm getting kicked off Varsity—kicked out of *camp*. I didn't show anyone anything."

"You got Ben removed," Emily said as the three of us sank onto Mattress Island.

"I did that, I guess," I conceded. "But in the process, I also got *myself* removed."

Emily furrowed her brow and chewed on her lip. "I always thought when you try to make things right, you just point out the bad thing, and it gets fixed. Like, you see a turd in the pool and you shout, 'Lifeguard! Get the turd out!'"

I smirked. "But really," I said, unlacing my boots, "you're *swimming* in the turd water when you notice the turd. And when you point it out, no one wants to touch it. And in order to fix it, not only do you have to get everyone out and drain the water, people are mad because no one gets to swim and you get blamed for noticing the turd in the first place when it's the person who *put* the turd there that *should* be blamed!"

Paloma pushed down a smile. "Pointing out turds is never going to make you popular, that's for sure. But you don't strike me as some-one who wants to swim in turd water."

"No. I don't want it for anybody else, either." I sighed and flopped onto my back on Mattress Island. "So, now I'm a Boy Scout for six days."

She leaned over me and smiled. "Yeah, about that. Can we talk about Hottie McBoy Scout, please?"

I chuckled and sat back up. "He's . . . he's *nice* to me."

"*Good*," Paloma and Emily said at the same time.

"But does it feel weird? Being with him? After . . ." Emily trailed off.

"After Ben?" I asked. "I know. But you know what's different? I'm not worried about how Jesse's going to react to every little thing I do or say. And I can tell him the truth about how I'm feeling and what I want."

"That's good." Paloma nodded. "What about the physical stuff?" She kicked me a little.

I opened my mouth, blushed, and shook my head.

"Oh, we are so getting more out of you than *that*." Emily got on her knees and grinned. "Have you kissed?"

I nodded.

"And . . ."

"And . . . it shouldn't even be the same word for what Ben and I did—what . . . Ben . . . did to my face. With his lips."

They chuckled.

"It's really . . . I like it. I like it with Jesse."

"Good. Did you do anything *else*?" Emily waggled her eyebrows at me.

"When did *you* get so nosy?" I asked, pushing her off her perch.

"Deflection." Paloma pointed at me. "And she's not being nosy, she's just making sure you're okay . . . Are you okay?"

I nodded little nods. "I . . . think so. I will be? We haven't . . . *done* anything other than kiss and hold hands, but I *really* like him."

"Even so, it's okay to need some time," Paloma said.

"That's what Karen, the nurse, said." I took a deep breath. "I'm a *little* worried that if he . . . touches me . . ." I closed my eyes, trying to find the right words. "Where *Ben* touched me . . . it'll be . . . it'll make me think of Ben?" I scrunched up my face. "I don't want to think of Ben. I just want to—I want that for me. For Jesse and me. I don't want Ben in the room." I opened my eyes. Paloma and Emily were nodding.

Paloma tilted her head. "When Jesse kisses you, do you think about Ben?"

"Nnnnn . . . ooo. Mostly no. He's kissed me like five hundred more times than Ben ever did."

Emily grinned, and Paloma chuckled. "Okay. So, Jesse's kissed you more. And what else is different?"

"Heeeee genuinely likes me. . . . He's not trying to manipulate me."

"Right. So, you trust his lips."

I smiled. "Yes."

"And what about when you hold his hand? Do you think of Ben?"

"No. Not at all."

"So, you trust his hands?"

I saw where this was going.

"And you've been marching around in the woods with him. To places you've never been before. Right?"

I nodded.

"So, you trust his brain? And his decision-making abilities?"

"You're good." I smiled.

"And you trust you," Paloma continued.

My smile faded.

"Zelda..." Paloma and Emily reached for my hands. "Don't let Ben take that from you," Paloma urged me. "You're smart. You didn't know how assholes like him operated. Now you do. And you know how to recognize their crap."

I took a deep breath and slowly let it out.

"Look," Paloma said, "you don't have to touch Jesse or be touched anywhere you don't want to be. All I'm saying is this thing with Jesse is totally different. And that makes what you do together different. When you're ready."

I knew by now she was another partner I could trust.

Emily shook her head at Paloma. "Can I take you with me for always? Maybe shrink you down and put you in my pocket?"

I giggled. "You'll have to fight me for her."

CHAPTER THIRTY-THREE

As I packed my things, the rest of the Gildas piled into the cabin along with Will and Jonas. No one could believe how unfair my punishment was, but I just kept thinking about the swimming pool metaphor. I had done the right thing, but the right thing had also given me a stomachache.

"So you can't even *watch* the final show?" Will asked.

"Once I'm off camp land, I'm not allowed back."

"Unbelievable."

"Tell me about it." I zipped up my suitcase. "Try to get Nina Knightley's autograph for me, okay?" Will bit his lip and nodded. "Thanks," I said. I stood and turned to face everyone. "Time for me to go."

A knock came at the door, and I jumped, sure it was Ben. Jesse poked his head in, and I wondered how long the ghost of Ben's abuse would ruin normal moments like that for me.

"Ready, scout?" Jesse was still trying not to smile, but his eyes gave him away.

"There's one person who's glad she's going," Will said.

"I just want Zelda to be happy," Jesse countered. "Getting kicked out of improv camp doesn't make her happy."

"But . . ." Will pressed.

"But if she can't have improv camp, I'm happy to try and make her happy a different way."

Will coughed and folded his arms.

"Like by hiking!" Jesse protested.

"Forgive him," I said, whacking Will's shoulder. "We're protective of each other, but after this whole thing, Will might be on overdrive."

"You guys should come over," Jesse sugggested. "Meet Murph and Ricky. We can hang out. Get to know each other better."

Will gave Jesse a half smile. "Yeah . . . Okay. Let's do that."

We all marched back out to the field in front of the Main Lodge where we were met by Karen, the Pauls, and one of the police offi-cers. The second officer was loading an exhausted-looking, hand-cuffed Ben into the police SUV. Instinctively, I stepped back into the circle of Gildas.

"Zelda," the officer said, approaching me, "I know you need to talk to your parents when they return, but do you want to press charges against Ben?" She had serious, but kind eyes. "You can always drop the charges after you speak with your parents."

Squinting, I asked, "Why are you loading him into the car if I might not press charges?"

She nodded at Jesse. "Ben broke Jesse's nose. That's third-degree assault—a felony. What I need to know is if you also want to press charges."

Biting my lip, I shifted from one foot to the other. "What happens if I don't?"

"We process him for the assault...but nothing goes on his record for what he did to you."

I shuddered. "And if I do?"

"Then it's added to the list of charges. The nose-breaking third-degree assault charge is a felony, but with no priors, it'll probably get knocked down to a misdemeanor. Even with the fifth-degree sexual assault in the woods, it'll all probably end up as community service. Maybe a fine."

But a sexual assault charge wouldn't look good on a background check, right? And if he got convicted, who would hire him to teach anymore? And if the story got out, he might not have a future at any reputable improv company, either. I shuddered again. "I don't want to be in charge of someone's future like that."

She nodded. "Sounds like he didn't mind being in charge of yours. But it's your choice."

"Detective?"

We turned at the sound of Paul DeLuca's voice. He waved her over. She glanced at me. "I'll be right back."

I watched her stride over to the Pauls, but their voices were too low to overhear. She flipped open her notebook, jotted something down, nodded, and strode back over to me.

"Mr. DeLuca and Mr. Paulsen would like me to tell you that they would be happy to let you stay at camp if you don't press charges against Ben."

I couldn't help it—I whipped my head around to look at them.

They were staring at me. Nausea roiled around in my stomach. I jerked my head back and studied my dusty, Chaco-ed feet.

I could stay at camp! I could maybe even perform. It was what I wanted, right?

But if I stayed and performed, it was at the cost of saying what Ben had done and said was acceptable behavior.

I thought about startling at the sound of the door. Of the mental anguish at rehearsal. Fear for Ben's next move. Even the worries I had about Jesse's intentions. It had only been a week, and Ben had done all that.

"No," I said finally, biting my thumbnail. "I don't want to stay. I want to press charges. I just . . . I worry Ben isn't sorry. That the Pauls aren't sorry. Like, no one will learn a lesson if Ben just walks free. I want the Pauls to take camper concerns seriously. And I don't want Ben to do this to other people. I don't want Ben to go to *jail*. I just want him to notice. I want him to get help. I don't want what he did to be a normal thing."

She handed me her card. "Call me here when your parents come. We'll work it all out."

I ran my fingers over the embossed police seal. "Detective Kristi Margolis."

Detective Margolis smiled and led me a few steps away. "You going to be okay? Because I can take you into protective custody if you don't feel safe at the Boy Scout camp."

"The Boy Scout camp is perfect," I said. "They're great guys."

She smiled. "Great guys are out there. Glad you found some. Talk soon."

She shook my hand and exchanged a few words with the Pauls that resulted in Paul Paulsen aggressively rubbing the heels of his hands into his eyes yet again. Then the detective joined her partner in the SUV. I wasn't going to watch as they drove away, but at the sound of a thud, my head jerked up reflexively. It was Ben. As the SUV passed us, Ben's face twisted in pain, and when he caught my eye, he yelled, "Ellllllllllllllieeeeeeeeee!"

I broke eye contact immediately, but even as the ranks closed in to protect me, it felt like cold water had been dumped on my head. Then I frowned. I didn't want my last act with Ben to be hiding from him. I stepped between Paloma and Hanna, filled my lungs with air, and shouted as the SUV drove off, "My *name* is *Zelda*!"

Dust from the gravel road filled the air, and soon, the SUV disappeared.

I let out a huge breath, then turned to the Gildas and hugged each one of them. Then I hugged Jonas. Then Will held me close. Then I shouldered my backpack, and Jesse and I reached for each other's hands.

I faced the Pauls. They looked at me expectantly.

"I wish it hadn't turned out this way," Paul DeLuca said. "If you just hadn't turned violent there at the end."

"Yeah. *That's* the regrettable part in all this," I said.

"Wait!" We all turned and watched someone tumble down the front steps of the Lodge.

"High Ropes Jake!" I yelled and waved.

"Oh yeah. That guy," Jesse muttered as Jake caught up.

"Where are you going?" he gasped.

"I'm gone," I said, trying hard to keep bitterness out of my voice. "Because I hit Ben. Zero tolerance policy."

"What?"

"I'll just be across the road—I'm a Boy Scout now."

He tugged at his ears. "Look, I—I'm sorry. For not defending you. I saw what was happening and I—I didn't do anything."

"You're right. You didn't."

We stared at each other for a moment.

"Well?" he asked.

"Well what?" I frowned.

"You say, 'It's okay, Jake.' You forgive me."

I looked over my shoulder at the Gildas, whose disbelieving faces mirrored mine.

"No, I don't. I asked you to help me. Multiple times. But you were afraid for yourself. That's fine, but I don't have to be okay with that. I needed you, and you didn't stand up."

He furrowed his brow. "I said I was sorry."

"And I'm saying, I'm not ready to accept your apology. So take that sorry and do better next time."

He folded his arms. "I ran and got the Pauls."

We were seriously arguing about this?

"Thank you for that. I don't know what you want from me, Jake." I held up my hands. "Go forth and be good onto others, child."

He huffed. "You're being kind of bitchy, Ellie."

The Gildas stepped forward.

"Zelda. It's Zelda. Look. You were brave when you ran and got the Pauls. But I needed you to be brave a lot earlier, okay? Maybe next time you will be."

He rolled his eyes and half stomped away.

"That guy was rude," Emily muttered.

Paul Paulsen shook his head. "This was a lot easier when just boys came here."

I spluttered. "I bet it wasn't. But you've never had anyone willing to stand up before." I gave the Pauls a wan smile. "Time to motor."

I turned to the Gildas. I was trying to come up with something to say that encompassed my gratitude for everything they'd done, but instead, Emily exclaimed, "Oh my gosh! I almost forgot!" and pulled a CD case out of her bag.

I gasped, flipping it over. "You're not *giving* me *Pacific Coast Whale Sounds.*"

"It's a loan." She smiled. "Until we see each other again."

I blinked hard to keep the tears back.

So did she. "Turns out," she said, her voice watery, "we were our own Oprah."

I nodded and took her hand.

Jesse lifted my suitcase, and I tightened the straps of my backpack. "Ready?" he asked.

I clutched *Pacific Coast Whale Sounds.* I didn't have a CD player, but it didn't matter. In the CD, there was strength, and hilarity, and love. I found Jesse's warm, brown eyes. In them, lived patience, and kindness, and hope. "I'm ready," I said.

It was a five-minute walk all the way down the dirt road to the gate, and Karen and Jesse and I were quiet the whole time. They seemed to sense I needed it.

But when we crossed into Boy Scout territory, a pile of ten-year-olds surrounded us.

"Jesse! Jesse! Jesse! What happened to your nose?"

"Hey, Webelos. I broke it . . . Fighting a dragon. I want you to meet Zelda. She's staying with Karen for the rest of the week."

"Ooh!" one cooed. "Is she your *girl*friend?"

He met my eyes. I smiled. "Yes, she is," I said, "and I'm a dragon slayer, too."

Now they only had eyes for me. "There aren't really dragons," a particularly serious one protested.

"Well, I guess I can't teach you if you don't believe in them." I waggled my eyebrows at them.

They shifted, seeming unsure.

"I can also teach you improv," I said, "how about that?"

"Ooh! My brother does improv!" one yelled. "It's funny!"

"It doesn't *have* to be funny," I said, "but it can be. If you learn the skills, it makes you a better listener, a better friend, more quick-witted, and more courageous."

One kid squinted. "How about we learn dragon slaying instead?"

Jesse laughed, then winced, touching his nose. "You need the courage for the dragon slaying. Let's let Zelda settle in. But then maybe some improv tomorrow?"

They scampered off, and we turned toward Karen's cabin.

"This might be really fun, actually," I told Jesse. "Shaping the future. Encouraging boys to be like you."

Jesse's eyes closed briefly. "That is the nicest thing anyone has ever said to me."

I smiled slowly. "It's true."

"Okay, you two. Some ground rules." I'd forgotten Karen was there. "No being in a cabin just the two of you. No kissing in front of the Boy Scouts. No—"

"Uh, Karen?" Jesse interrupted.

"Yes?"

"It's me. You've known me since I was twelve."

"But—"

"I promise. We will be totally above board."

She pursed her lips. "*No* Boy Scout camp babies."

My face turned red. "No one wants *anything* to do with that."

Jesse and Karen raised their eyebrows at me.

I tripped on my feet. "Well, you know, the babies part. The other part." I shook my head and buried it in my hands. "Ughhh."

Karen patted my shoulder. "Best to stop talking, hon."

"Yes, ma'am."

When we arrived at her cabin, a version of Gilda Radner with several small rooms, she said, "Go get settled, Zelda. I'll be in the infirmary. Right here. Clanging around. Popping in at any time. Also calling your moms about this whole broken nose situation, Jess."

Jesse winced. "Clang around for a while first, okay? I should be the one to call."

Karen nodded once and opened the door to my room—a set of bunk beds and a dresser with a mirror above it on the wall. Jesse and I stepped in and she made a big production of leaving the door open.

"Welcome home," he said. I kissed him.

"Clanging around!" Karen called.

CHAPTER THIRTY-FOUR

"Are you *sure* you're okay if Ricky and I go to the show?"
Murph asked, tugging at his baseball cap.

I nodded, kneeling to double knot my hiking boots. "Absolutely. I need a firsthand report on how it all goes down. And tell me if they do my cold open. It's about a pilot and circus performers and a sleepwalking bear."

"Okay. Consider us your eyes." Murph grinned.

"And ears." Ricky nodded stoically.

"Especially ears," I said, lightly punching Ricky in the shoulder. He pretended to be hurt, and Murph and I laughed.

"Okay! Ready to go?" Jesse trotted up to meet us.

"Wait a minute," Murph said, putting his hands on his hips and looking back and forth between Jesse and me. "Hiking boots? Backpacks? *Headlamps? Now* I see why you're okay with us going to the show," Murph said. His eyes narrowed "You two are going on a sexy two-person night hike!"

"Not *that* sexy," Karen called. "Everyone in this camp will be back in two hours, and I expect *you* will be, too." She squinted one eye and

and curled her pointer finger to beckon Jesse closer. I couldn't hear her talking, but a stern-looking monologue and several severe hand gestures later, Jesse rubbed the back of his neck and jogged over to me, chagrined.

"What was that all about?" I asked as everyone waved goodbye and headed off toward the improv show.

He sighed and reshouldered his backpack. "It's embarrassing."

"It's okay. You can tell me things. I'm your fourth person, remember?"

"I've told you plenty of things now even my moms and Micky don't know."

"Okay then." I clicked on my headlamp, adjusted it in place, then smiled. "Tell me this thing."

He rubbed the back of his neck again. "She said that there are . . . c-condoms in the infirmary but she doesn't want to encourage us to do anything, and that humans are never as fertile again as they are as teenagers, and so if we insist on gambling with our futures, we should at least use protection, but I didn't hear it from her. Then she said there are—" He buried his head in his hands. "I can't—"

I laughed and took his arm. "*Please* tell me."

He sighed. "She said there are at least five hundred other things two human bodies can do to each other that aren't sex and maybe starting there would be a good idea."

I laughed, but then I flashed back to Ben pinning me against the tree, and my face fell.

Jesse reached over and squeezed my hand, which was grasping his arm. "Tell me."

I tried not to look at the trees. Tried not to remember the trapped feeling and the panic. I closed my eyes and exhaled. "Um. I want to tell you. I *will* tell you. I just—I need a minute. I think . . . I think forward motion will help."

Arms linked, we hiked in silence for a while. I focused on the nighttime sounds of the mountain—crickets, the wind in the leaves, the occasional owl hoots.

"Where are we going?" he finally asked.

I straightened up. "It's a short hike, really, but steep. Lots of switchbacks. It'll get us up high fast. I found it a couple days ago when you were all merit-badging the afternoon away."

He laughed. "Amazing."

Soon we were both huffing and puffing, and I dropped his arm to use both of mine to propel me forward. My legs started vibrating. Panting, Jesse suggested a break. He leaned against a tree, and I gulped down water from my Nalgene and tried to steady my breathing. "When Ben touched me—"

I felt Jesse's body tense.

"He touched me places no one has touched me before. And when you said that thing Karen said about the five hundred things people can do to each other that aren't sex . . . I thought about *him*. But I don't want that to be the thing I think about. I want to think about happy things. I want to think about *you*."

Jesse was quiet. "I want you to think about me, too. How are we—you? We? Going to do that?"

I clipped my water back onto my backpack. "Not exactly sure . . ." I glanced at his face—his deep brown eyes caught mine, but then he bit his lip, worried. My core felt warm. Suddenly, I felt steady. Grounded. "But I think tonight's the night to find out. You ready?"

"Uh, yeah." He stumbled, then regained his footing.

The rest of the hike was quiet with both of us lost in our own thoughts.

As we approached a bend in the trees, I stopped him. "It looks different in the dark, but I think this is it. You've seriously never been up here before?"

He shook his head.

"Okay. Turn off your headlamp. And take my hand..."

We turned the corner and stepped out onto a large, flat overhang of rock. When I had been there a couple days before, I could see for miles, but at night, we were treated to a bright, full moon, and more stars than I'd ever seen in my whole life.

"Oh," Jesse breathed, and my lungs expanded as big as the sky. He squeezed my hand. "Thank you for bringing me here," he whispered.

The air was cool, and I welcomed his warm lips on my cheek. "I'm glad I finally got to show you something you hadn't seen before," I murmured.

He smiled. "You want to sit?"

I unzipped my backpack and pulled out a soft, thick wool blanket I'd found in Karen's cabin. "How's this?"

We took off our boots and settled ourselves side by side on the blanket, stretching out our legs. Jesse opened his backpack and plucked out a little chocolate and more water. I happily accepted the chocolate and kissed each of his eyelids. "You know, I've been thinking about that section of the woods that was burned down by the fire."

"Yeah?" Eyes still closed, he smiled and took a bite of chocolate. "I sort of feel like that."

Blinking, Jesse considered this. "Ben burned you down?"

I nodded. "But I'm growing back. Differently."

Scooting closer to me, he smiled slowly. "Do you remember what I said about that section of the woods?"

I nodded again, the corners of my mouth tugging upward. "It's your favorite."

He reached out and boinged one of my curls. "That it is."

I laughed and batted his hand away. "That's your one free boing," I said, pointing a finger at him. "There are consequences from here on out."

Chuckling, he leaned in and kissed a spot under my ear. "Like what?" he whispered.

I breathed in his warm smell of coconuts and pine and sweat and earth. Bravery surged through me. "For starters," I said, plucking at his collar, "this shirt's gotta go."

Expectant eyes met mine. "You sure?"

"Don't get any big ideas," I said, suddenly not sure what I was agreeing to. "No one's having your babies any time soon, Mr. Rose-Eerdmans."

He dropped his head, laughing. "I happily agree to your terms, Ms. Bailey-Cho." He sat up straight and removed his shirt in that mysterious way boys do by grabbing the back of the collar and pulling it forward. My marvel at that universality was short-lived, however, because it was replaced by his lean, firm chest and arms.

I exhaled a shuddery breath. Then I sat up a little straighter and eyed his bare chest. I'd touched him through his shirt and even under his shirt, but he'd never taken his shirt off for me like this. It felt . . . different. Exposed.

He grinned. "If this is my punishment for boinging your curls, you can expect a lot of boinging from here on out."

I laughed. "I believe we have moved on to the exorcism portion of the evening," I said in a lofty voice, trying to hide my nervousness.

Nodding, he cupped my cheek, and I tilted my head into his hand. "I'm all in," he said in a low, quiet voice.

A while later, Jesse touched his forehead to mine. "You are awesome. So awesome, I think I need some water. And to recite the state capitals in alphabetical order."

He rolled over to his backpack and pulled out his Nalgene.

I gaped at him. "State capitals? W-Why?"

He shot me a half smile. "Let's just say my body *really* likes you touching me." He took a big glug of water. "And I need to calm it down a little. Plus, I think you'll find my state capital knowledge is *pretty* impressive." He cleared his throat and folded his arms over his chest. "Albany, Annapolis, Atlanta, Augusta—"

I realized what he was doing and laughed. "Did you know," I said, sitting up, "that when I learned about sex, I figured penises were straight like sticks all the time? I didn't ask anyone, but I felt really sorry for boys. It sounded extremely uncomfortable."

Jesse burst out laughing.

"Better?" I asked, smiling.

"No!" he exclaimed. "I told you—I love that you're funny. It does not make . . . things calm down."

"It's always seemed to have worked before."

Jesse shook his head, then leaned in slowly and kissed my neck. I sighed.

"We've established this. Those guys are idiots," he whispered, his breath tickling my skin.

I smiled and tilted my neck. "I like that."

He kissed my neck again. "What else do you like?" he asked.

I tugged on the hem of my T-shirt. "Let's find out."

CHAPTER THIRTY-FIVE

An hour later, hand in hand, I realized that we were about to emerge from the woods. Anticipating that tomorrow a million people would be around to pick up and be picked up from camp and we wouldn't have any alone time, I dropped my pack, flicked off my headlamp, and pulled Jesse to me. After he dropped his pack and headlamp, too, I kissed him, trying to memorize the way his body felt pressed against mine.

"I'm so glad I met you," I said, my arms still wrapped around his neck.

"I'm the luckiest Boy Scout of all time," he marveled, keeping me close. "Who meets any girl at Boy Scout camp, much less the best girl?"

"There should be a merit badge for that."

Jesse laughed and kissed me again.

"And hey—in three weeks when Boy Scout camp is over, and you're back in Minnesota, I want to meet Micky. And your moms."

He nodded and smiled. "Three weeks is going to feel like a lifetime," he said.

"Three lifetimes," I agreed. "One for each week."

He picked up his backpack, stared at it, then dropped it, and kissed me again. Laughing, I kissed him back, taking his hand and guiding it under my shirt, but Jesse pulled away. "Karen—"

I chuckled. "No one'll be here for at least twenty more minutes," I murmured.

"No—Karen! There! Now!"

My head whipped around to follow where he was pointing. Karen, plus the Gildas, were marching with purpose toward the nurse's cabin.

"Hey!" I called out, waving an arm over my head. "How was the show?"

At the sound of my voice, their heads snapped my way, and like a flock of birds with a shared instinctual brain, the Gildas flew toward us. Karen waved, but kept marching toward her cabin.

"Zelda!" Hanna called, "Go get changed! You need to look like a Boy Scout!"

I frowned and asked Jesse, "What is she talking about?"

"No idea."

The Gildas arrived in a clump, breathing heavily, all talking on top of each other.

I held up a hand. "What is going on?"

Everyone turned to Paloma.

"Okay," she said, "We don't have much time. Karen is finding a shirt and shorts and a Boy Scout baseball cap for you. She has extras in her cabin. That's the first thing—run there! Go! We'll explain the rest on the way back to camp!"

"But—"

Paloma put her hands on my shoulders. "Zelda. Do you trust us?"

"Of course."

"Then change! It's important!"

Three minutes later, I emerged from Karen's cabin in my own hiking boots, a pair of ill-fitting olive shorts, and a button-up BSA khaki uniform shirt with patches sewn on the sleeve. I'd stuffed my hair into a messy bun and tucked it all under the baseball cap she'd given me. My pleas for Karen to explain had been met with tight lips and head shakes.

"My job was to get you the clothes," was all she'd allow. "The Gildas would *kill* me if I told you the rest."

"Okay," I said, letting the screen door slam behind me. "I'm a Boy Scout. Now what?"

"I'm ready!" Jesse called, jogging up to meet us on Karen's porch. He'd changed into an outfit that looked just like mine, only he also had a scarf cinched around his neck with a medal slider.

I grinned at him. "You're very cute."

He waggled his eyebrows at me. "So are—"

"We don't have time for this!" Emily yelled, flapping her hands up and down.

"Come on—let's go!" Sirena called. She and Emily grabbed my hands, and the pile of us hurried down the road.

I twisted around. "Are you coming, Karen?"

"You go on!" Karen called. "I'm not going to run, but I'll get there as fast as I can!"

"Okay!" Instinctively, I turned to Paloma and pleaded as we ran, "*Please* tell me what's happening!"

"Okay," she huffed, "Varsity did not do your cold open."

"Oh." It wasn't surprising news, but a wave of disappointment still washed over me.

"But hold on," Paloma continued, "High Ropes Jake walked up to Nina Knightley before the show and handed her a copy of your script. He told her the whole story about Ben and you and you getting kicked off the team for hitting Ben and—"

"How do you know this?" I interrupted.

"Nina told us," Hanna exclaimed, punching the sky.

"*What?*" I spat.

"Hold on, Hanna," Paloma said, whacking Hanna's shoulder. "I'm not there yet! So, Nina Knightley goes up to the Pauls with the script and points and gestures and I don't know what really happened because we were so far away, but they looked all flabbergasted and they made calm-down hands and she pointed some more and then Dion and Roger came up, and I think they must have confirmed High Ropes Jake's story because she huffed and came over to *us* and asked us if we knew you."

My knees nearly gave out.

"And we did!" Emily squealed.

I barked out a laugh. "Yes. Okay. Okay. Okay?"

"And then she said, 'Can you get her over here after the show?' and Karen showed up out of thin air and said she had an idea."

Karen to the rescue. Again. "So that's why I'm dressed as a Boy Scout."

"Exactly. Because," Paloma paused for effect, "we're sneaking you in to meet Nina Knightley."

The temperature in the Main Lodge was twenty degrees hotter than the air on the porch, and the difference made it feel like we walked through a wall made of warm air. With the Gildas and Jesse as cover, I kept my eyes on my boots and tried to move as masculinely as possible . . . whatever that was supposed to look like.

Laughter swelled in the audience, and I sneaked a look up. Darkness enveloped the crowd, but the stage lights shone bright on the players. My heart lurched, and I focused on my boots again. After this was all over, despite what had happened—or now, because of it—I was going to meet Nina Knightley. I had to remember that was way more important than any one improv show.

We slid into the back row and I looked around, trying to spot her. There was a row of men I didn't recognize off to the side—probably the guys from Second City and iO and UCB—but Sirena touched my arm before I could find Nina.

"Don't draw attention to yourself," she hissed.

I glued my eyes to the floor.

"Thank you so much for coming and for being such a great crowd!" Brandon called out over the applause. "We've got some talent scouts and big-name alumni in the audience tonight, and it was an extra pleasure to perform for you!"

I closed my eyes, steadying myself for meeting my hero. What would I even say to her? Sirena elbowed me. I opened my eyes, and she nodded at the stage.

Paul DeLuca and Paul Paulsen were clapping and pointing at the Varsity team, who took an additional bow. Then the team jogged off, waving at the crowd. The Pauls took center stage.

"Well, well, well," Paul DeLuca bellowed, a microphone in hand, "it's hard to believe another fortnight of improv at RMTA is coming to a close. And what a performance! Give it up one more time for Varsity!" He clapped his hands against the microphone, which produced a low thudding sound. The applause peaked and died down. "Now, none of this would be possible without all of you coming back year after year, so give yourselves a round of applause, too!"

I exchanged sidelong glances with the Gildas. Less enthusiastic applause accompanied this microphone thudding. I rolled my eyes and resumed looking at the floor.

"RMTA is a great place with great, talented people," Paul DeLuca continued.

I clenched my jaw.

"And we can't wait to see you again next summer. We—"

"Paul, do you mind if I say a few words?"

I wasn't looking at the speaker, but I'd know that voice anywhere. The room erupted into applause and cheering, and my head snapped up. There she was: Nina Knightley. Looking . . . like a regular person. I mean, she wore *nice* jeans, but they were still just jeans. And she'd paired them with what looked like a vintage RMTA T-shirt. Her long black hair was swept up on top of her head, held in place with two pencils. She could have been me.

"You know, I've missed this place," Nina Knightley said, taking the microphone from Paul DeLuca. The crowd clapped and cheered. She crossed downstage, closer to the audience. "I came here four summers in a row and stayed in Gilda Radner each time."

The Gildas whooped, and I couldn't help but join in.

"And I only made Varsity my last year, but I'll never forget that show. It felt . . . electric. I was invincible. Because I had a great coach, and I had the best teammates, and we all set each other up for success. Jane and the Pauls had a magical thing going on here. But we lost Jane the year after I left. I still feel the loss of her positivity and wisdom in my life. But I especially feel it coming back here tonight."

The Pauls exchanged a glance, and Paul Paulsen shifted from one foot to the other.

"When Jane was here," Nina continued, "things weren't perfect. But if someone had made me a dead prostitute in a scene against my will, that sort of thing would have been *shut down*. We're improvisers, not lemmings. 'Yes, and' has its limits. And it's up to the adults to show young performers where those limits are."

My heart started thudding in my chest.

"So, in honor of Jane, I'd like to be indulged. Pauls, if you would be so kind."

They opened their mouths, but she cut them off. "I'd like this year's Gildas to join me on stage."

Polite applause filled the space, and we looked at one another in astonishment. But then I remembered I wasn't supposed to be there, so I leaned forward and put my elbows on my knees. "Go," I hissed, mostly out of self-preservation. What if I was found out before I got a chance to meet her? "Get up there."

The Gildas hesitated for one more moment, then followed each other up on stage to join Nina Knightley. Jesse slid over and put his arm around me.

"Hey," I whispered. "I'm a boy, remember?"

"So?"

I grinned into my hands.

I sneaked a look up on stage and watched Nina count the Gildas. "One more . . ." she muttered. "Where's Zelda?"

Now my eyes were dinner plates. What was she doing? I wasn't supposed to be here. Didn't she understand that?

"Now, Nina," Paul DeLuca said, panic in his eyes, "I'm afraid she's not here." He turned to the crowd. "But let's have a round of applause for all of our hardworking girls!"

The look Nina flashed Paul had enough venom to kill a mountain lion. He recoiled a step, and she turned to smile at the crowd. "You know, these days, all I get to do is promote the camp and donate an awful lot of money to it." At the not-so-subtle threat to their already tenuous funding and good name, the Pauls backed off stage. Nina smiled. "But I really miss playing here. Gildas, would you like to join me in a Montage?"

The crowd burst into applause and the Gildas grinned, immediately clearing to neutral.

My heart lurched. What I would have given to be up there . . .

"To start us off, I need a suggestion for the animal that should have been sleepwalking in the cold open you didn't see."

There was a split second of confused audience silence. Then I couldn't help myself. "A bear!"

Nina sent a slow smile in my direction. "Care to join us on stage?"

More than anything, I wanted to get up there, but what was going to happen if the Pauls found out I'd been sneaked back in?

"What do you need, an engraved invitation?" It was Karen. I

whipped my head around. "She's just threatened a huge line of their funding. She can do anything she wants. And she wants *you*. Go!"

I got to my feet. Jesse squeezed my hand and grinned. "Knock 'em dead!"

The applause grew as I leapt onto the stage.

"Hi, Zelda," Nina said, smiling at me.

The audience gasped. I laughed and chucked my hat into the crowd. "Hi, Nina Knightley."

"...I'm just saying, we don't actually fly the plane anymore—the computers do it for us now," I said. "If anyone knew how easy it was, they'd slash our enormous salaries! Or worse—we'd lose our jobs and be replaced with a bunch of fourth graders!" I pretended to smoke a cigar. It was even hotter on stage than it had been in the crowd, but I hardly noticed the sweat trickling down my back.

"Still," Nina demurred, brushing "ash" off her shoulder, "I think things have gotten a little extravagant around here, Captain. Not to mention cocky. Smoking in the cockpit? That's against FAA regulations. And really. In an emergency, how would we be able to fly from this hot tub?"

The crowd laughed.

I groaned and mimed flicking water at her. "I suppose next you'll be trying to get me to get rid of Ivan."

Hanna jumped out, bouncing a small "ball." "Are you ready for your midflight tennis lesson, Captain?"

I held for the laughter. "After the bubbles run out, Ivan. In the meantime, can you have Francois whip up that caviar pâté omelet I love so much?

Another round of laughter.

Nina frowned. "Captain, this is getting out of control. When we land, I'm going to have to report you."

I waggled my eyebrows at her. "What if I get you your own Ivan?"

"Captain—"

"Personal barista?"

"I don't—"

"Fleece jammies."

"It's just—"

"A kitten? You want a brand-new kitten every day of the week?"

Nina folded her arms. "What I'd like is a little respect for our passengers."

"Fine." I shrugged. "They can have kittens, too."

The lights blacked out, and the crowd erupted.

Both the stage and house lights came on together and I scanned the crowd for Will as Nina and Sirena grabbed my hands for our curtain call. We bowed, the applause feeling like it would never end.

But someone turned music on over the PA system and the crowd eventually calmed down.

"Holy freaking ever-changing teen slang, Batman." Nina grinned and gave me a high five. "You were on *fire*."

I laughed. "You—I can't believe you did this for me. For us. Thank you." I turned to the Gildas as they gathered around Nina. "Thank *you*." We all put our arms around each other, our heads touching.

"There's a lot of crap out there," Nina said, her arms around my and Sirena's shoulders in the huddle, "and I've seen my fair share of it. But the way you get through it is together. Find your people. And then keep helping people up. It's the only way. Got it?"

We nodded.

"Now, go to college and stuff," she continued. "Learn and write and read everything you can. But when you're ready for the next step in this business, let me know. I can't get you work, but I can get you seen. Contact my agent. She'll know to pass you on to me if you use the code word—" She looked at the ceiling. "Coffee cake. Do they still make that amazing coffee cake here?"

"Yes!" Sirena said as we all laughed. "It is the only amazing food here."

"Or maybe it isn't," Hanna mused. "Maybe just compared to the turkey tetrazzini . . ."

We laughed again, Nina leaned back, and we all dropped our arms. She turned to me. "It sucks *so hard* what happened to you. I'm sorry."

I nodded.

"But you're going to be okay?"

I teared up a little but nodded again.

She squeezed my shoulder and shook her head. "That kid with the ears. Thank that kid with the ears."

"Jake," I smiled. "He's come a long way."

Then, as the throngs of people started to flood around Nina, she pulled me in for a hug. "Nice to meet you, Zelda."

I grinned into her shoulder. "Nice to meet you, too, Nina Knightley."

CHAPTER THIRTY-SIX

The next morning, after one last night as a Boy Scout, I found myself back at RMTA to collect Will and Jonas. Sirena climbed the steps to the Main Lodge's porch, where I was waiting with the rest of the Gildas, and she took Emily's hand. "I got us settled in the van—as far away as possible from Erick and Ty, the snoring lawnmower parade."

"Wait!" I exclaimed as Emily kissed her cheek to thank her. "That reminds me." I unzipped my backpack and pulled out five, flat, square-shaped presents wrapped in newspaper.

"That's not—" Hanna gasped.

"Guess who had a desktop computer, a stack of blank CDs, and something called a 'CD burner' in his office?"

Emily tore off the newspaper. "There are *five copies* of *Pacific Coast Whale Sounds* now?" she squealed.

"Thanks to Greg, the Scout Master who is not interested in advancing his office technology, yes. Five copies. One for each of us."

Emily and Sirena hugged me tight, but Paloma shot me a look.

"You know what you just did, putting this CD into Hanna's hands," she said.

I wrinkled my nose. "Created a monster?"

"Not quite," Hanna corrected me. She cupped her hands around her mouth. "Youuuu created a mooooooooooonsterrrrrrr!"

We giggled, but I couldn't totally give myself over to the moment. I kept eyeing the screen door.

"Hey, Z," Will called from the gravel lot in front of the Main Lodge. "You want me to put your backpack in the car?"

"Not yet," I called back to him. "But thank you!"

"Okay. By the way, I put my suitcase and your suitcase and Jonas's suitcase on your seat, so you're going to have to ride in the trunk."

I smirked over my shoulder at him. But then, passing between a couple of parked, fifteen-passenger vans, I spotted my Boy Scouts. "Hey!" I called, taking the steps down two at a time to meet them. Murph and Ricky jogged up behind Jesse who wrapped me up in his arms. "I thought you wouldn't be able to get away this morning!"

Jesse pulled back from our hug and grinned. I wanted to kiss him, and I could tell he wanted to kiss me, but there were a million people around. Instead, he raised his eyebrows and boinged one of my curls. My stomach flipped over, remembering what had happened the last time he did that, but I batted his hand away and pointed at him, mouthing, "You're dead to me."

He laughed and thumbed in Ricky and Murph's direction. "We struck a deal with the Webelos," he said.

Murph nodded. "Let's just say us coming here involved a lot of contraband candy."

"Thanks, guys." I released Jesse long enough to hug Murph and give Ricky a high five. "I'm excited to see you both back in Minnesota."

Ricky nodded, reached out, and palmed me one last, smooth rock. I flipped it over in my hand. Ricky had penned, "Climb on." I met his eyes, speechless, and nodded. He nodded back and slipped behind Murph.

I cleared my throat, realizing that the Gildas had left the porch and joined our little group at the foot of the stairs, and so now my moment with Ricky had an audience. I turned to my Boy Scouts. "I'd really like you to meet our parents," I said, my hand in Jesse's. "But they're inside talking to the Pauls."

Jonas and Will jogged over to join us. "Uh, 'talking' is probably not the word you're looking for," Will said, one eyebrow raised.

This morning had been a bit of a whirlwind. Mom and Dad had arrived at RMTA to find only one of their children. Will had done his best to explain, but before he got terribly far, Mom had stormed inside to find the Pauls, and Dad had leapt back in the Subaru to pick me up at Boy Scout camp. Dad let me tell my whole story without saying a word. Then he'd made me promise fifteen times that I was okay before he drove us back to RMTA to get Will, Jonas, and Mom.

After the night I'd had with Nina and the Gildas, I really was feeling okay. But it was going to take a while to get my parents there with me.

"Milwaukee folks!" a voice I didn't recognize called out. "We're outta here!"

"That's us. Okay, Gildas," Paloma said, hands on her hips. "Flights are weirdly cheaper to Denver from Milwaukee and Minneapolis than they are in any other configuration, and plus, of the three cities, Denver has the superior March climate, so spring break in Denver?"

Nodding, I dropped Jesse's hand, and all the Gildas stepped in, our heads together and arms around each other's shoulders like we'd stood with Nina the night before.

"But I don't want to wait that long to see you," I said, impending tears thickening my throat.

"Fall break?" Paloma asked.

Sirena was the first to cry. "I'm sorry," she gasped, seemingly surprised by the tears on her cheeks. "I'm supposed to be the steady one."

"All crying means," Emily said, tears rolling down her own face, "is that you're feeling something, remember?"

Sirena dropped her head and nodded. We clutched each other.

"As soon as we get a signal, I'll start a group text," Paloma offered, sniffling. "It'll be like we're all still together."

"I call naming the group text," Hanna said, shooting a hand into the sky.

"Oh god, Hanna," Paloma moaned.

"It's going to be called 'The Destroyers.'"

Paloma dropped her arms, and we all stood up, smirking and wiping away tears. "It's going to be called the Gildas," Paloma insisted. "That's who we are, Hanna."

Hanna slung her backpack over her shoulder, firmly ignoring Paloma. "The Estrogen Avengers. The Coffee Cake Coterie. THE GUILD OF GILDAS!"

"Unnecessary!" Paloma exclaimed, throwing up her hands.

"I'm glad we all came here," I said quietly.

The Gildas stilled.

"Yeah?" Sirena asked. "Despite what happened with Ben?"

I bit my lip and nodded.

"Because you got to meet Nina Knightley?" Paloma asked, smiling.

"Because you met Jesse?" Hanna smirked.

"No," I said. "Yes!" I amended over my shoulder. Jesse grinned back.

"Because of *Pacific Coast Whale Sounds*," I said.

Emily gasped.

"Emily!" I laughed. "Because of us. The five of us. I'm glad because of us."

The Gildas became a pile of arms and teary faces, not for the first time.

And not for the last time, either.

ACKNOWLEDGMENTS

Firstly, thank you to my sisters and to our parents who have always encouraged our creativity. (Including, but not limited to, the time we made a murder mystery movie in honor of the Greek musician with long, flowing locks we'd seen on PBS and called our film *Yanni Cuts His Hair.*)

Deb Peterson was my singular high school theater director and acting teacher. Much thanks to her and to the people on my high school team for launching my love for improv.

Karen Estrada, Mike Holmes, Dan Jessup, Kurt Meyers, Roger Payton, and Adam Prugh taught me that improv with people who love and respect each other is a form of magic here on earth.

As I transitioned into teaching and writing, Jennifer Dodgson at the Literary LOFT took me seriously as a writer long before I did.

I estimate that I have had more than four thousand teenagers in my classes over the past thirteen years. Their curiosity, kindness, and hope has made coming to school less like work and more like joy. Thank you to every single one of you.

Terri Evans, my former school librarian, brought many authors into our building and showed me they were simply people—not magical unicorns.

Gene Luen Yang was our first visiting author. When Gene found out I was the creative writing teacher, he asked me if I did any writing myself.

I stumbled around, admitting that I'd always *wanted* to write a book. "You should," he told me.

The thing that pushed me over the edge to actually put pen to paper was E. Lockhart speaking at Teen Lit Con. "When I was writing *We Were Liars*," she said, "I'd tell myself, 'Today, all I need to do is get the kids on the boat.' And I'd write a bunch of words—some of them decent, a lot of them terrible—but I'd get the kids on the boat." I'd heard many writers talk about crappy first drafts. But something about Emily's image spoke to me.

Thank you to the Creative Writing and Literature for Educators MA program at Fairleigh Dickinson University, especially fellow students Lori-Ann Desimone, Mickey Diamond, and Kate Overgaard, and professors Renee Ashley and Kathleen Graber.

I was on airport duty to pick up Nina LaCour for an author visit to our school, and Nina said I would recognize her due to her bright blue pants. I pulled up to the curb, and indeed, there she was—bright blue amongst the sea of gray and black. A decade later, Nina has continued to be that beacon for me through writing and agenting and selling. I am lucky to call her my friend.

I'm so grateful to David West. Our ten Julys together teaching improv at MITY were an absolute joy. To all of our students—and now Karen and my students!—thank you for sharing some of my best times with improv.

My principal, Mike George, and the CPHS English department have cheered me on from go. Thanks to them and to Steve Slavik at the district for their rock-solid support.

Special thanks to my loyal, fierce best friends: Dr. Kaia Simon, who shares my roots; Chris Baker-Raivo, who shares my brain; and Karen Estrada, who shares my heart.

I finished the first version of this book ten feet away from Dr. Ellen Margolis on our two-woman writers' retreat in Door County, Wisconsin. She has been a mentor to me as an actor, teacher, writer, mother, and badass.

Thank you to my sagacious agent, Sara Crowe, who passed on the first book I tried to write, then snatched me up six days after I sent her this one.

Thank you forever to Kristi Romo, my critique partner. She is a phenomenal reader, questioner, and feedback-giver, and this book wouldn't exist without her.

Beta readers Chris Baker-Raivo, Karen Estrada, Terri Evans, Jann Garofano, Joe Gaskill, Allison Hackenmiller, Belinda Huang, Dan Kronzer, Ricky Kubicek, Micky Kurtzman, Nina LaCour, Kelsey Lauer, Dr. Ellen Margolis, Maame Opare-Addo, Erin Payton, Kristi Romo, Heather Sieve, Katie Widestrom-Landgraf, Bethany Watson, Riley Wheaton, Annika Williamson, Kevin Yang, and Meng Yang offered me such thoughtful feedback. Many of these folks also shared their personal experiences as people of color, identifying as LGBTQ, living with albinism, and surviving abuse. Also, essential insights on improv comedy, the Boy Scouts, and medicine. *Unscripted* has stronger legs and more nuanced details thanks to all of you.

My school nurse, Sheila Davies, and my school police liaison officer, Detective Andy Dickman, were endlessly patient with my endless questions.

Allison Hackenmiller, my superlative school librarian, supports me in a thousand different ways.

Daniel and warren Mosier have given me years of wonderful friendship and excellent beta reader manuscript prices at Cornerstone Copy Center in Burnsville, Minnesota.

I'm so thankful for my creative writing students who listened to and gave me feedback on early chapters of this book.

Thank you to my godsend editor, Maggie Lehrman. When she signed off her very first email to me "Zip, zap, zop, Maggie," I knew Sara Crowe had found someone special. With her own background in improv, Maggie understood what I was trying to do and say. Because of her, this book is better in every way.

Thanks also to Emily Daluga and the entire team at Amulet for taking such good care of Zelda and me.

My daughters, Eliza and Eleanor, can often play with each other for hours without me needing to intervene. This, probably above everything else, was the reason I could string time together to write. Monkeys, you're in the house right now as I type this, making a pizza hat for Daddy. (God, I hope it's not real pizza.) I love being your mom.

Lastly, Danny. Seriously. When I said to him, "I think it's time to write my book," there were a million reasons not to do it. But Dan isn't the kind of person who focuses on reasons for not doing something. He's the kind of person who says, "Sure. How can I help?" I will never stop thanking him for loving me.

ABOUT THE AUTHOR

Nicole Kronzer is a former professional actor and improviser who now teaches English and creative writing. She loves to knit and run (usually not at the same time) and has named all the plants in her classroom. She lives with her family in Minneapolis, Minnesota. Visit her online at nicolekronzer.com.